What in the hell *had he been thinking?*

After fourteen years of avoiding even the remote possibility of entanglements that might put his daughter in a vulnerable position, he'd willingly brought a beautiful woman into his house, into all their lives, even if only for business reasons. She was here, and the memory of her, he knew, would linger even when she'd left.

His daughter liked her. His grandmother liked her.

He even liked her, maybe a little too much.

He avoided entanglements, sure, but he'd never claimed to be celibate, and right now his libido was in rage mode. Damn. What *had* he been thinking, indeed?

Dear Reader,

Well, June may be the traditional month for weddings, but we here at Silhouette find June is busting out all over—with babies! We begin with Christine Rimmer's *Fifty Ways To Say I'm Pregnant*. When bound-for-the-big-city Starr Bravo shares a night of passion with the rancher she's always loved, she finds herself in the family way. But how to tell him? *Fifty Ways* is a continuation of Christine's Bravo Family saga, so look for the BRAVO FAMILY TIES flash. And for those of you who remember Christine's JONES GANG series, you'll be delighted with the cameo appearance of an old friend....

Next, Joan Elliott Pickart continues her miniseries THE BABY BET: MacALLISTER'S GIFTS with *Accidental Family,* the story of a day-care center worker and a single dad with amnesia who find themselves falling for each other as she cares for their children together. And there's another CAVANAUGH JUSTICE offering in Special Edition from Marie Ferrarella: in *Cavanaugh's Woman,* an actress researching a film role needs a top cop— and Shaw Cavanaugh fits the bill nicely. *Hot August Nights* by Christine Flynn continues THE KENDRICKS OF CAMELOT miniseries, in which the reserved, poised Kendrick daughter finds her one-night stand with the town playboy coming back to haunt her in a big way. Janis Reams Hudson begins MEN OF CHEROKEE ROSE with *The Daddy Survey,* in which two little girls go all out to get their mother a new husband. And don't miss *One Perfect Man,* in which almost-new author Lynda Sandoval tells the story of a career-minded events planner who has never had time for romance until she gets roped into planning a party for the daughter of a devastatingly handsome single father. So enjoy the rising temperatures, all six of these wonderful romances...and don't forget to come back next month for six more, in Silhouette Special Edition.

Happy Reading!

Gail Chasan
Senior Editor

Please address questions and book requests to:
Silhouette Reader Service
U.S.: 3010 Walden Ave., P.O. Box 1325, Buffalo, NY 14269
Canadian: P.O. Box 609, Fort Erie, Ont. L2A 5X3

One
Perfect Man

LYNDA SANDOVAL

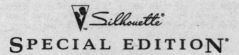

SPECIAL EDITION

Published by Silhouette Books

America's Publisher of Contemporary Romance

For two of my biggest supporters, my uncles Arsenio Sandoval and Ray Sandoval.
Thanks for making me feel like what I do is important.

Big thanks to the following people for the help and support they gave me while I wrote this
book: Amy Sandrin, Terri Clark and LaRita Heet, my venerable writing pals and critiquers.
Patricia McLinn—for keeping me honest, Nicole Burnham—for the chats and confidences,
Karen Templeton, for the nod! (You rule.) Gail Chasan, my editor. I'm so thrilled to be
"one of yours." Jenny Bent, my agent, friend and wise adviser. A million times, thanks (dude).
My mom, Neva Sandoval. My biggest fan! I love you. And to Trent, for all the ongoing
support, and my best dog-pal, Smidgey, with much love. I *swear* I'll change out of my
fleece footie pajamas more often as I write the next book. <g>

 SILHOUETTE BOOKS

ISBN 0-373-24620-X

ONE PERFECT MAN

Copyright © 2004 by Lynda Sandoval

Visit Silhouette Books at www.eHarlequin.com

Printed in U.S.A.

Books by Lynda Sandoval

Silhouette Special Edition

And Then There Were Three #1611
One Perfect Man #1620

LYNDA SANDOVAL

is a former police officer who exchanged the excitement of that career for blissfully isolated days creating stories she hopes readers will love. Though she's also worked as a youth mental health and runaway crisis counselor, a television extra, a trade-show art salesperson, a European tour guide and a bookkeeper for an exotic bird and reptile company—among other weird jobs—Lynda's favorite career, by far, is writing books. In addition to romance, Lynda writes women's fiction and young-adult novels, and in her spare time, she loves to travel, quilt, bid on eBay, hike, read and spend time with her dog. Lynda also works part-time as an emergency fire/medical dispatcher for the fire department. Readers are invited to visit Lynda on the Web at www.LyndaLynda.com, or to send mail with a SASE for reply to P.O. Box 1018, Conifer, CO 80433-1018.

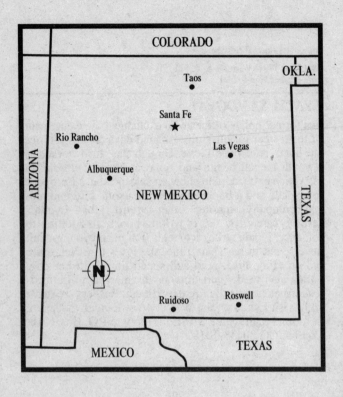

Chapter One

*There are two lasting bequests we can give our children:
One is roots. The other is wings.*

— Hodding Carter, Jr.

Erica Gonçalves clutched her cell phone between ear and shoulder—no small feat considering the contraption was about the size of her palm and flat as a compact. The side of her head felt superglued to her shoulder, and the opposite side of her neck had stretched to the point where she'd likely need alternating heat and ice tomorrow just to function. She paid only scant attention to her mother's voice on the other end of the line as she moved around the soon-to-be-full hotel meeting room with purposeful strides, assuring every minute detail had been attended to before everyone arrived.

Nothing annoyed her more than a poorly planned meeting, and seeing as how this was her dog-and-pony show, she wouldn't stand for anything less than efficient structure, smooth flow and a high degree of productivity. Time was money, after all, and she never seemed to have enough of either. If she did, she'd be running her own event-planning company instead of working for someone else. Not that she didn't love her job. She did. But as far as she was concerned, the more freedom and control she had in all aspects of her life, the better.

"Have you heard a word I've said, *m'ija?*"

Oops. "Yes, Mama," she fibbed. "I'm sorry. I'm doing a million things at once."

"You should slow down, honey. Take a breath."

"No time." She flicked her wrist over and checked the sleek black face of the Saint Honoré watch she'd splurged on during her last vacation—a solo trip to Paris last summer. Had it really been almost a year since she'd had a break? "My meeting starts in—ugh! Too soon. I need to go over the agenda one more time." A subtle hint. She waited. Unfortunately Mama didn't pick up on it. Erica stifled a sigh. "What was it you were saying?"

"Just wondering why that boss of yours always makes you travel alone. A woman alone. It makes no sense to me."

Erica couldn't manage to stifle the sigh a second time, not when faced with this dead horse of a topic her mother insisted upon beating. How many times could they go around about this? "He doesn't make me travel, Mama. I've told you before. I enjoy this part of my career. I like the freedom."

"Freedom." Erica heard the inelegant snort across the line, a sure sign her mother was going to launch into the familiar refrain. "Don't get used to that so-called freedom, baby—"

Erica began to mouth the words along with her mother, words to a speech she'd heard hundreds of times. She even pantomimed the finger wag she was sure her mother had going on the other end of the line.

"Once you marry and have children, your place is at home with them, not—"

"—gallivanting around the globe," Erica finished, her tone droll. The sixty-some-odd-mile drive from Santa Fe to Las Vegas, New Mexico didn't count as globe-trotting in most people's books, but Susana Gonçalves's book told another story altogether. If she could keep her children within the city limits of Santa Fe until she ascended to the pearly gates, her life would be considered a success.

"Exactly," the older woman said. "A husband and children will nip all this travel in the bud, so no sense getting accustomed to it. That's all."

Annoyance pricked at the calm reserve Erica tried so hard to cultivate prior to meeting with colleagues. She took a moment to line up the dry-erase markers in front of the whiteboard and straighten the projector screen. And breathe.

"Did you hear me?"

"Oh yeah, I heard you." The cell phone slipped from its precarious shoulder clutch, but Erica caught it in midair and held it back to her ear. "Which is exactly why a husband and children aren't in my future, Mother, a fact you well know."

"Oh, honey, you talk, but—"

"Are you listening to me?" Erica pronounced each word with crisp, controlled clarity. "Do you ever hear what I'm saying?"

"I just don't want you to give up hope."

A fireball of frustration ignited in Erica's chest. Hot blood pounded in her ears. "Hope! Hope?" She smacked her palm to her forehead, all attempts to stay calm and cool rendered instantly futile. "Listen to yourself, Mama. Why does it always come back to this? What you fail to acknowledge is that some women have no desire to fulfill the roles of wife and mother, and your daughter is one of those women."

"But, it's important, honey, and I worry—"

"Why is it so damn important? I take perfectly good care

of myself. You always seem to 'worry' just when I need to be focused before an important presentation or meeting.'' She lowered her voice to a rasp, glancing at the door to make sure no one had showed up early to catch her in mid-rant. She had a business reputation to uphold, after all. ''If I didn't know you better, I'd almost think you were trying to sabotage my career.''

''Don't be silly. You *do* know me better.''

True. But, still. Erica closed her eyes and counted to ten in English, then in Spanish. ''Mama, listen to me. Six very important words. I don't *want* marriage and family. I have no desire to *raise* human beings, and there's nothing wrong with admitting that. I can't even keep plants alive. Not to mention—do you remember what happened to my hamster, Morton?''

''Hamsters don't live forever. You were only twelve.''

''Old enough to know better.''

''Hmph.''

Erica sighed. ''I am simply not suited to your role. You need to accept the facts.''

''You can learn.''

''Sure, if I wanted to. The point is, I don't want to.'' She clenched her fist against her chest with fervor, though her mother couldn't see her. ''I love my career and my inde-pendence, and I love to travel. Alone. I want my life exactly the way it is. Why can't you respect that?''

Susana uttered an unhappy sound. ''Was it so bad, Erica? Growing up with a full-time mother in the home? So bad that the very thought of walking in your mother's footsteps makes you speak to her with such disrespect?''

''I'm—'' Erica bit her lip as defeat weighed heavily on her shoulders. She furrowed her fingers slowly through her hair and willed the bite from her tone. ''I don't mean to disrespect you, Mama. You know that. And, of course I don't regret growing up in a traditional family. I loved hav-ing you there.'' She struggled for words. How could she explain? "But living that way, putting the family first, was *your choice,* right?"

"Of course."

As much as Erica doubted the veracity of her mother's answer, she nevertheless went with it. "Well, all I'm asking for is my choice, as well. I *am* walking in your footsteps, Mama," Erica said, feeling like a liar. In truth, her mother gave up too much of herself for the life she led. Erica was trying to *avoid* her mother's footsteps—at least those she took after marriage. "Can't you see?" She paused, hoping this time it would sink in. "I'm trying to live the life of my choosing. That's all. Just like you did. My choice is simply different from yours."

"Don't you want love, *m'ija?*"

Erica eased out a breath. Sure, it would be great to have the love of a lifetime yadda, yadda, yadda. Who wouldn't want that? Unfortunately, that type of love was an empty Hollywood concept. Real love came with strings and ties and required sacrifices she wasn't willing to make. Real love grabbed you and took up camp in your world, like an occupying force. Real love twisted your life around and left you with the one thing she absolutely refused to have: regrets.

So, she wouldn't experience marital love in her life, but that didn't matter to her. She'd find companionship and sex along the way, with men who wouldn't compromise her goals, men with their own goals, and she'd have her independence. Not a whole lot sounded better than that.

"I love my career," she said, finally, knowing she could never adequately explain it to her mother. "That's enough."

Silence hung between them like a tug-of-war rope. Erica was tired of all the yanking and balancing. "But I really have to go. The artisans will be here soon and I want to be composed."

"You're always composed, little one. Too composed for

your own good.'' Mama laughed, but sounded tired. ''You're a regular Mona Lisa, don't you know that?''

''Ha.'' A grudging smile twitched Erica's mouth.

''I didn't mean to upset you, *m'ija.*''

''You didn't,'' Erica lied, to keep the peace. ''Look, I'll call you tonight. Okay?'' She really did love her mother.

''Okay. Is your hotel room safe?''

Erica rolled her eyes. No, she didn't know any better, so she'd taken a room in the local crack house. ''Of course, Mama. It's a small town, remember? Only sixty miles from home. I'm fine. The hotel is beautiful. Nothing to worry about.''

''So you claim. The optimism of youth.'' Another unsettled sigh came through the line. ''Well, then, I guess there's nothing else for me to say.''

''Okay, then.'' Erica rolled her hand. *Get to the goodbye. C'mon, Mama, please.*

''Good luck with your meeting. Be careful, and use the dead bolt and the chain when you're in the room.''

''Always do,'' Erica sang, in an overly patient voice.

''And keep your eyes out for available men,'' Susana said in a rush. ''Be open-minded. That's all I'm saying. Life is all about options, baby.''

''Mama!''

''*Bueno,* bye.''

The abrupt disconnection clicked in Erica's ear, and she pulled the phone away and stared at it a moment, incredulous, before shaking her head and snapping the flip-front down. Her mother would never stop trying to marry her off, no matter how many times Erica tried to explain her dreams and goals. A pity her mother expended so much energy on a lost cause.

It wasn't that Erica didn't like men. She did. She just didn't want to be subservient to one, as her mother had been to her father. Susana Gonçalves might claim she'd been fulfilled by feeding children, washing clothes and putting everyone else's needs before her own all these years, but she had been a promising folk guitarist in her youth, on the fast track to giving Joan Baez a little healthy competition.

Then she'd met Erica's father, and the rest was history. Moises Gonçalves had been raised a kind but strictly traditional man, and into the attic went his wife's guitar. No time for "frivolity" with babies on the way and a husband to tend, Erica supposed. What a shame.

Call her a skeptic, but Erica refused to believe her mother didn't have regrets about leaving that musical dream behind. As for herself, she didn't plan to have a single regret. No way would she give up her identity, her life, her goals and dreams for a band around her finger and the "opportunity" to serve a man all her life. No way in hell. Nothing Mama could say or do would ever change her mind.

"So, what I'm looking for are some really innovative ideas of how you'd like to represent your town in your particular medium," she told the gathered artisans, her voice composed, her look professional, her manner that of complete control. "The sky's the limit here, folks. I want to push the envelope and really get New Mexico into the news. This is the first Cultural Arts Festival of this type for our state. Let's make history." She smiled with confidence. "Ideas?"

The event planner sent down by some large company in Santa Fe crossed her arms and leaned one toned but still shapely hip against the edge of the front table. Her head tilted slightly forward and to the side, sending the razor-perfect ends of her straight black hair brushing across her shoulder to dance against her cheek like a sheet of satin.

Tomás Garza sat back in his chair and studied her. Erica Gonçalves. He hated to admit it, but she couldn't be more perfect if he'd conjured her up from his most fervent, most hidden fantasies. Organized, take-charge, encouraging and yet still approachable.

Hope wouldn't feel threatened—an important consideration.

His jaw tightened, but he pushed aside his inner resistance and refocused on the lady at the front of the room, trying to read her, to soak her in. He needed to get a handle on her before he approached with his proposition. With only five months left, he couldn't afford any more false starts or setbacks.

He listened while the sculptor representing Albuquerque suggested a Michelangelo-size idea to represent his city—a mixed-media sculpture that would suspend from the rafters of the event hall. A false sky, if you would, filled with faux hot-air balloons to represent the renowned Balloon Fiesta held in Albuquerque each October. An excited murmur rippled through the room as the artist and the planner discussed logistics for a work of this scope. Soon, others began offering their ideas, all praised and efficiently cataloged by Ms. Gonçalves with quick taps of her fingers on the laptop keyboard.

The tone of the meeting was electric, a creative thunderstorm, led by a woman who knew just what to say and do to make things happen. Tomás felt supercharged, both by the atmosphere and the fact that he may have just stumbled on a solution to his dilemma in the form of a petite, fast-track business dynamo named Erica.

The city representatives—specially selected artists, all of them—kept the flow of ideas rushing forth until only a few towns remained—his included. Without warning, the lady he'd been studying turned her dark-eyed gaze on him.

He straightened in his chair—a holdover habit from his less-than-stellar high school days, he supposed, when hearing his name meant he'd been busted for screwing around.

"Mr. Garza? Do you have any ideas for how to incorporate Las Vegas into your piece?" She smiled.

He relaxed his expression, but a flare of inexplicable self-preservation ignited inside him. Lifting one ankle to rest atop the opposite knee and smoothing his palms together, he took his time working his idea into words. Luckily, he had given this some thought, and he considered himself reasonably articulate, even paying only half attention. "Yes. I'd like to craft piñatas to replicate some of our city's historic buildings, for an interesting twist. An amalgam of Mexican craft work with New Mexican culture. And definitely representative of Vegas."

Her gaze brightened, and Tomás caught several appreciative nods from the other artists around the room in his peripheral vision. That pleased him. Some artists dismissed piñata making—his family's artistic heritage—as a child's craft rather than the endangered art it truly was. He worked hard to overcome the misconception, creating piñatas people wanted to display as well as those for children to break open at birthday parties. The reaction from his peers gathered here today seemed encouraging. He looked to the lady and raised one eyebrow in question.

"Fabulous," Ms. Gonçalves said. The distant look in her eyes told him that sharp mind of hers was already three steps ahead in the planning. "Really different."

"Gracias." He warmed beneath her praise.

"How many houses were you thinking of incorporating?"

"One to represent each of our historic districts. Seven total. They'll need to be big to capture detail. I don't want to overdo it."

"No, that's perfect. You're right."

"Great."

"Perhaps we can suspend them low over a map or photo of the town," she said, swirling her hands out in front of her as though she had the full picture in her mind, "approximately near the locations of the districts they represent."

He shrugged. "Works for me."

A raised hand caught their attention, and they both turned

toward a dazzling, dark-haired muralist from Angel Fire who sat near the far wall.

"I have a cartographer friend who'd jump on this project if the budget allows enough to pay him," offered Monét Montoya, bangle bracelets tinkling as she gestured. "He's worth it. His maps aren't just maps, they're art."

Erica nodded. "Great. Get with me after the meeting and I'll take down his information." Almost as an afterthought, she added, "If that's all right with you, Mr. Garza? It is your project, after all."

He appreciated the consideration. "Fine."

"Good, then." She typed the idea into her laptop with finality, and moments later it appeared on the projector screen:

Las Vegas: Display of seven piñatas in the form of historic buildings suspended above an art map of the city.

"Thank you, Mr. Garza." Erica smiled at him, and his stomach tightened with a distant emotion he vaguely recognized as lust. His wariness increased. Granted, she was hot. Any red-blooded man could see that. But he had no intention of bringing a strange woman into his life—or his daughter's life—lust or no. As Bob Marley so wisely crooned, "no woman, no cry." He and Hope had learned their lesson on that account long ago.

"My pleasure." He managed to smile with his mouth, but his eyes failed to cooperate. Not wanting to appear surly, he softened what he was sure had been a cold expression with a wink. To his surprise, her eyes widened slowly before she averted her gaze and cleared her throat. Interesting. When she raised her face to the crowd, Tomás noticed a flush to her chest in the V of her blouse, which belied the calm, cool exterior. He looked away, denying his own awareness. Awareness that had no place in this meeting room, or in his life.

"Okay, let's move on."

Please do, he thought, with palpable relief.

He watched Erica toss her hair and focus on another lucky artisan in the room. Grateful that her disconcerting attention had shifted elsewhere, Tomás tuned out a bit while the rest of the towns weighed in. He sat back to ruminate further about the best way to approach Erica Gonçalves with his proposition.

The job probably wasn't as prestigious as her regular gigs, but he needed her, much as he hated to admit it. She could pull this off without a hitch, and he…well, he wasn't so sure he could pull it off at all on his own.

The very thought of not being capable, of knowing he needed to seek help, brought self-disgust bubbling up in his throat. He and Hope had never needed *help* from anyone before. He hated admitting that he didn't have every aspect of his busy life under control. Lately though, where his little girl was concerned, he didn't seem to have a damn thing under control, and he'd do just about anything to make it better.

Part of it was her age, he knew. Kids went wacky during the middle-school years. Part of it was hormones, something he didn't want to think about in relation to his baby girl. He needed to accept the fact that Hope wasn't a baby anymore, however, and that sometimes young ladies acted…mysterious. Detached. More confusing the closer they came to womanhood—the nature of the beast. He pictured her and smiled with equal parts love, fatherly concern and sympathy, remembering age fourteen only too well. It wasn't so many years since he'd been there, considering he'd been little more than a child himself when Hope had come along.

But he wasn't the child anymore, he was the parent, and it was his responsibility to fix things, to make life perfect for his daughter. All that mattered was her happiness, and, much as he hated to admit it, the lady standing at the front of the small conference room could be the answer to his prayers. He wouldn't allow stubborn pride to keep him from reaching out to her. No. He'd buck up and solicit her help, no matter how galling it was to admit his parental short-comings. He'd do anything for Hope, even go into debt, even swallow his own foolish pride.

Calmer, more determined, he took in a breath and tracked Ms. Gonçalves's smooth, efficient movements with his eyes, feeling better by the moment. If anyone could pull this off, she could. Everything would work out, and his daughter would magically revert back into the adoring, open, happy girl she had once been.

Pride swallowed. Help accepted.

Problem solved. Balance restored.

Hope and Daddy against the world once again.

Chapter Two

The meeting had gone well. Erica smiled to herself as she organized her notes. Creating a statewide cultural arts festival out of thin air and big dreams was a monstrous undertaking, but luckily the artisans she'd brought on board were not only talented but creative and enthusiastic, as well. The firm had a full team of event planners working on the festival, but the art included was the most important part, and Erica was in charge of finding appropriate artisans. She felt good about it.

If the sculptor from Albuquerque could pull off his idea, if he got the scale right—and certainly he would—the whole festival would feel as if it were taking place outside, beneath New Mexico's blue skies and a rainbow of hot-air balloons. The undertaking was so huge, so fresh, it bordered on arrogant. She loved it. They'd make history...not to mention national news, which suited her five-year plan perfectly. She'd take all the help she could get making a name for herself in this competitive business. That out-of-the-box creativity was exactly what Erica had hoped for when she called this final planning meeting. Now that all the decisions had been made, they could all focus on pulling this beast together.

A knock sounded on the conference-room door, yanking Erica out of her thoughts. She glanced up and frowned, then checked her watch as she crossed the room, certain that she had another half hour at least before she needed to vacate the meeting space.

At the door, she hesitated, her mother's grave warnings bubbling up from somewhere in her subconscious. She smiled at the absurdity, but nonetheless asked, "Who is it?" before opening the door. She hoped the effort would win her a few respect-your-mother points in heaven.

"Tomás Garza," came the deep but gentle voice from the other side of the door.

The *piñatero?* Her heart revved, remembering her surprise when she first saw him at the meeting. When she'd sent a letter requesting his participation in the festival, she had expected him to be an old, paunchy man. How wrong her preconceived notions had been.

He was a quiet, watchful man, but certainly not old. And not even close to paunchy. She'd guess him to be in his early thirties, with long dark hair he wore pulled back into an utilitarian ponytail. It managed to look ultramasculine and enticingly rebellious at the same time.

She'd found him attractive, sure. But he'd stuck in her mind mostly because he'd been so...still. Utterly still, like an animal. Alert, aware, taking it all in, and ready to bolt at any moment. She found it disconcerting. Maybe she was crazy, but she'd gotten the feeling that Tomás had watched her every move during the meeting. His body motionless, deceptively casual. Those unusual brown eyes tracking her like prey.

She shivered, then pushed the ridiculous emotions aside and pulled open the door. "Mr. Garza," she said, by way of a greeting. "Did you forget something?" His eyes glowed almost, and she suddenly realized they reminded her of those polished tiger's eye stones sold in a lot of the tourist shops.

"Please call me Tomás."

"Tomás, then." She splayed a hand on her chest. "And I'm Erica."

He nodded. "I didn't forget anything. I wondered if you might have a few minutes to talk."

"I have a little less than thirty minutes before the hotel kicks me out of the room, but come on in." She stepped back, motioning for him to enter. "Is this about the festival?"

He smoothed his palms together, a vaguely hungry look in his eyes. "Actually, I came to speak to you about a different matter. A more…personal matter."

Personal? All of a sudden, Erica recalled the wink he'd so casually tossed her during the meeting. At the time, she prayed no one else had seen it. Now, she stiffened, imagining just what this personal matter of his involved. Why did this crap seem to happen to her on almost every job? She dressed professionally, didn't exude flirtatious vibes, as far as she knew. She simply wanted to be taken seriously in her career, not treated like fresh meat everywhere she went. Was that too much to ask? She hated to admit to herself how disappointed she was to learn that the quiet *piñatero* was just another in a long line of men who viewed the work arena as one big singles bar.

Her chin lifted. "Mr. Garza—"

He cocked his head, friendly curiosity in his eyes. "I thought we'd moved on to first names?"

She sighed. "Tomás, then. Before you say anything further, I'd like to make it perfectly clear that I don't date business associates. Ever."

His eyes widened, then crinkled with amusement. "You think I'm hitting on you?" He paused a moment, then added, mostly to himself, "Of course you do. Why wouldn't you, the way I phrased it." His apologetic gaze met hers. "Ah...I'm almost flattered, Erica. But it's not that kind of personal matter." He held up his hands, palms forward, in a gesture of surrender. "I would never be so presumptuous. Sorry if I gave you that impression."

Oh, God. Mortification oozed from her brain through her body like hot lava, miring her in its fiery thickness. The words were out there. She couldn't snatch them back. She had to simply save face as best she could. "I, uh, owe you an apology, then. Clearly. It's just that sometimes—"

"Don't worry," he said, holding up a hand. "I understand. I'm sure men come on to you all the time."

"Not...all the time." Ugh, she could perish.

"Well." His eyes smiled, but his mouth managed to remain serious and sincere. "Rest assured, me hitting on you is one thing you'll never have to worry about, Erica. Promise."

Never? Realization cut through her mind, and with it came a deeper gouge of humiliation. God, it just kept getting better, didn't it? Why hadn't she paid closer attention? She'd been too damn busy noticing how unexpectedly young and attractive the *piñatero* was to realize—

How uncharacteristically narrow-minded of her.

She worked with people in the arts community all the time, she should know better than to assume. Clearly, Tomás Garza was gay, and here she'd accused him of—oh, Lord. She really did want to shrivel up and die. She knew no other way to recover from this social gaffe other than just...sucking it up and admitting she'd acted like an ass.

"I've come to request your help. Or your services, to be more specific," Tomás continued, clearly not as bothered by what had transpired as she. "A business proposition."

"Ah. Business." She pushed out a humorless, self-deprecating laugh, wishing she'd fall through the floor, the earth, and all the way to China. "Okay. Well, give me a

minute to regain my composure. I'm thoroughly embarrassed.'' She twisted her mouth to the side and met his gaze
directly. ''Please accept my apology for the unfair assumption, Tomás. You must think I'm terribly arrogant.''

''Absolutely not.'' Tomás laughed, but the sound was
kind. He didn't seem the type to derive pleasure from other
people's humiliation. ''I think you're a woman who probably puts up with men's unwanted attentions all the time. I
understand.''

Her humiliation waned, thanks to his kindness. ''Still, to
automatically assume...well. I just hope this won't affect
our working relationship. Believe me—'' she laid a palm
on his forearm, then lowered her tone to an intimate level
hoping he'd recognize her sincerity ''—I work with a lot of
gay men, and consider many of them my closest friends.
This is completely not an issue for me.''

Startled confusion clouded his eyes for a moment, then
he smiled widely. She hadn't noticed that dimple before.

Don't notice it now, dummy. He plays for the other team!

''Look, ah...don't worry about it.'' Laughter laced his
words. ''I should've made myself more clear. *Obviously.*
But, what's done is done.'' He clapped his palms together.
''What do you say we start over from scratch?''

''Sounds like a fabulous idea.'' She gestured behind her,
relieved to have made it through the flaming hoop relatively
unscathed. ''I hope you don't mind if I pack up while we
talk.''

''Not at all. In fact, I'll help.''

''Thanks.'' He set about stacking chairs while Erica disconnected her computer and placed the components in the
leather carrying case. ''Tell me more about this proposition.''

He glanced up, then held her gaze. ''I'd like to hire you
for a special project. I need your expertise.''

Erica cocked her head to the side. ''What's up?''

"My daughter, Hope—she's fourteen. Fifteen in—" he checked his watch "—just about six months."

Daughter? Erica blinked, trying to grasp this newest bit of information and assimilate it into Tomás's swiftly metamorphosing profile in her brain. From paunchy old man to sexy young man to gay man to father of a teenager—all in the span of a couple minutes. How much was one woman expected to take?

"I'd like to celebrate it during the summer, though, which means I have about five months to plan one heck of an extravaganza to celebrate her *quince años*," he went on. "One perfect night for a very special girl turning fifteen. It's been a dream of mine ever since she was born to make it extra special for her. There's only one problem."

She forced her vocal cords to form words. "W-what's that?"

"I have no clue how to plan a *quinceañera*, and my little bundle of teenage hormones isn't giving me much direction." His mouth took on a rueful quirk.

Erica stared at him for a moment while her mind tried to catch up. She ran both hands through her hair. She needed more information, needed to pull herself together, needed…a drink.

"Well? What do you say?"

He wanted an answer now? She laughed, a small nervous sound. "Hold on. To be frank, I'm still trying to get over my shock that you have a daughter. And one that old. Fifteen?"

"Almost."

She shook her head, marveling. "And here I thought you were about my age."

His body stilled. He stood motionless before her, looking as he had during the meeting…wary, watchful. "I'm thirty-one," he said, the words devoid of emotion.

"Ah. So you are about my age. Three years older, in any

case." Erica did the math. Interesting. "Your daughter was—"

"Not a mistake," he said, his warning tone putting her on instant alert. His tiger's-eye gaze hardened.

She blinked in surprise. "No, I…I wasn't going to—I didn't mean it that way." Although she couldn't imagine a seventeen-year-old boy *planning* to father a child. What else could it have been but a mistake?

Almost as if he'd read her thoughts, he added, "I had her too young. True. That's my fault, not hers."

"Of course not. I never…" She stepped closer, hating this awkward turn in what should've been an innocuous business conversation. She'd felt off-kilter since the moment he walked in, and things kept spiraling ever downward. She used to think her communication skills were a strong asset. Ha. "If I've offended you, I'm sorry."

He studied her a moment, then his shoulders loosened. It seemed it was his turn to experience some embarrassment. "No. My fault. I'm…a little defensive where Hope is concerned. Undeservedly so in this instance, I fear. I'm sorry."

Erica shook her head and released a little huff. "We seem to be apologizing a lot here."

"Yes."

"Let's just stop then. Clearly neither of us intends to offend the other."

"Agreed."

"So, Hope." Erica brushed her hair off her shoulder and went back to packing up her materials. "That's her name?"

"Yes. Hope Genavieve Garza."

"Lovely."

He grinned. "Thank you. Picked it myself."

She returned his smile, but knew she needed to get the conversation back to its core. "About Hope's *quinceañera*." She sighed, reluctant to take the job, but equally hesitant to turn him down flat. He seemed like such a nice man, a concerned father. She admired him for that. "I don't accept that kind of assignment, I'm afraid. Weddings, sure. Parties, meetings, festivals. But *quinceañeras* involve all kinds of traditions I know nothing about.'' She shrugged. ''My family has been in this part of the country for generations. We don't celebrate any Mexican holidays or traditions.''

''My grandmother can help you. She lives with us.''

''Maybe she should be the one to plan it.''

He shook his head. ''She's in her late seventies, Erica, and she has multiple sclerosis. With the fatigue and pain, it's all she can do to make it through some days.''

Erica didn't know what to say, so she simply nodded. Tomás Garza certainly had a full plate. She studied him, chewing on her bottom lip. Something told her to tread lightly with her next question. She knew it would come off sounding like one of those lame, thinly veiled come-ons if she wasn't careful. ''Doesn't Hope's mother want to plan the event?''

A tension-buzzed pause stretched between them. ''No.'' Something in his shuttered expression warned her not to probe any deeper. Erica sighed. ''Listen, I appreciate the offer. But I am up to my ears with the festival, not to mention several weddings over the next few months. Plus…the truth is, I've never planned a children's event.''

Undeterred. ''Doesn't mean you couldn't.''

''No, but—''

''Besides, she's a young woman, not a child anymore, much to my chagrin.'' Tomás cringed and raised his eyes heavenward.

Erica laughed softly at his morose tone. ''I'm sure she's an amazing young lady. That doesn't change the fact that I don't plan young people's events, or that I'm overbooked.''

He moved closer, body taut, gaze intent. ''I've seen you in action, Erica. Busy or not, I know you could pull this off, or I wouldn't have asked.'' He paused, watching her.

She pressed her lips together, saying nothing.

"I can pay you."

Doubtful. "I'm expensive, Tomás." She cocked her head apologetically. "Far too pricey for a girl's party, anyway."

"Try me. Name your price."

Aha, so this was her out. The man was an artist, a single parent who also cared for an elderly grandmother with health concerns. Once she quoted him her exorbitant fee schedule, he'd swiftly realize she wasn't worth it, and she'd be off the hook. Calculating her usual charges for planning a large wedding, and throwing in a mental surcharge because she'd be forced to work with teenagers, she arrived at a sum.

Erica crossed her arms and leveled him with a cool, all-business stare. "I would have to work Hope in between my other responsibilities. Evenings, weekends. Sporadically. You might even have to bring her to Santa Fe a few times."

"No problem."

"Five thousand dollars." She let that sink in. "Plus all expenses, including my travel."

He blinked once but didn't balk. She watched his Adam's apple rise and fall slowly. "Done."

She frowned, arms dropping to her sides. "Excuse me?"

"I said, that's fine. Five thou plus expenses. You're hired." He offered his hand for her to shake.

Instead, she clasped her own together and implored him to be reasonable. "Tomás, do you realize how much this party is going to end up costing you? For one evening's entertainment? What about…her college tuition? What about—?"

"Let me worry about that."

She felt trapped, panicked by the thought of what she might have gotten herself into. She couldn't afford to take on another responsibility, and she didn't want to spend the next four months dealing with adolescent angst. Her heart raced as she struggled to come up with alternatives.

"But...you don't need someone with my qualifications to plan this. This is a family event."

"So's a wedding. You plan those."

"B-but...I'm a stranger."

"An event planner," he corrected. "Which is why I've come to you."

"What about asking family? An aunt, or—?"

"No aunts."

"Or...or a friend, or—"

"Erica—" he took her hand between both of his "—all I have wanted for the past fourteen years is to make my daughter feel special. Cherished. Can you understand that?"

"Sure, but—"

"I want memories of this night to resonate in her soul for the rest of her life." His eyes searched her face. "You're a professional. From you, I'll get perfection. As close as possible, at least."

She couldn't argue that. In fact, he'd managed to shoot down her arguments almost quicker than she could launch them. She bit her bottom lip.

"I said I'd pay your five-thousand-dollar fee. What's the problem?"

Cornered. Erica hung her head and thought about it logically. What *was* the problem? She'd gambled naming that fee, and he'd called her bluff. The only stand-up response was to accept the assignment, especially considering the man hadn't a single qualm about paying. Five thousand dollars would be a great boost to her savings. She'd be several steps closer to striking out on her own. How hard could it be, after all, to plan a *quinceañera?* She peered at the man standing before her, so still, anticipating agreement, she could tell. She had to give him credit for sticking to his goals.

What the hell, it was his money, and if he wanted to hand it over, she should be willing to take it. She could easily earn five thousand dollars planning a wedding, so she shouldn't suffer a moment of guilt for demanding the same for this job. A *quinceañera* was nearly as elaborate, and her time was at a premium. Feeling better about it, she took his hand. "Okay, Tomás. You've got yourself a deal."

He released a breath and clasped her hand between his. "Thank you. So much. You won't regret this, Erica."

She laughed. "Remind me of that when I'm going nuts trying to plan this festival, all the weddings, and Hope's party."

"Can I..." he swallowed "...do you need the money up front?"

"No. I generally take payment the night of the event." She didn't miss his look of relief. The guilt tried to resurface, but she pushed it away. The man had agreed to pay. "I'll need your approval for expenses, though. Those I'll bill as they occur."

"No problem. And listen." His tone lowered to a gentle, almost conspiratorial purr. "Go wild. If I have to assume a little debt for this thing, I'm okay with that. Just make it—"

"Perfect?"

He smiled. "Too much to ask?"

"Well, it's a tall order." She wish he'd keep those off-limits dimples to himself. Gay man or not, they made her stomach flop. "But I'll do my best for your daughter, Tomás."

"That's all I've ever tried to do. I wouldn't ask more from you," he said, his words soft and...slightly troubled?

They spent the next few moments exchanging phone and fax numbers, addresses and e-mail information—conduits to modern business function.

Feeling calmer, or at least more resigned, Erica extracted her PalmPilot from her briefcase. "I'd like to meet Hope as soon as possible." She consulted her planning calendar. "I'll be heading to Santa Fe tomorrow morning, but I'll be back next week. Monday. I've actually rented a place here just until the festival is over."

"You'll be spending that much time here?"

"I'll be back and forth, but I do want to keep a close eye on the site." She shrugged. "Short-term rental was cheaper than a hotel, and more convenient."

"Well, that's great. It will be nice having you close."

Her stomach tightened, and she chose to ignore the comment. "What works for you, dinnerwise?"

He seemed to take her lead, turning all business. "Monday?"

She shook her head. "Actually, that's my moving day, so probably not. Tuesday?"

"Hope has a softball game that evening. Wednesday?" he offered. "Dinner. At our house, so Ruby can meet you, too."

Erica glanced up sharply. "Ruby?"

"My grandmother." He grinned. "She says it makes her feel younger to be called by her first name, so we humor her."

"Sounds like my kind of woman." Erica looked forward to meeting her. "Wednesday looks clear." She glanced at the business card he'd given her, which listed an address in Rociada, AKA out in the boonies.

He seemed to read her mind. Again. "If you'd like, I can pick you up."

Not good. She always preferred to have her own transportation at hand, her own escape hatch, if you will. "Thanks, but I'll drive. Just give me good, clear directions."

"No problem. Six too early? We're more than happy to work our dinner hour around you."

She smiled genuinely at his consideration, thinking how nice it would be to know someone in town. And now that she knew his preferences, it would be easier to kick this unexpected and futile attraction she felt. "Six it is. Thank you."

"*Bueno.* Come hungry. I'm a whiz in the kitchen."

"You've got a deal."

Tomás headed for the door but stopped with his hand on the knob. He turned. "Erica? There is, ah, one other thing you should probably know."

Uh-oh. His words put her on instant alert. "Yes?"

His mouth spread into a slow smile, almost as though he knew the effect it had on her stomach, almost as though he liked knowing it. "You misunderstood me earlier," he drawled, a mischievous gleam in his eyes.

"Oh? How so?"

"I'm…not gay. Not even a little bit."

Chapter Three

Tomás's grandmother, Ruby, kept him company, sipping her nightly cup of green tea, while he washed up the dinner dishes and filled her in on his day just the way she expected him to—starting at the beginning and going straight through until the end. He'd just gotten around to explaining about the business arrangement he'd reached with Erica.

Lamplight mellowed the mango-colored walls to a peachy gold, and the air remained redolent with the smells of chicken and green chile. His daughter was, as usual, cloistered in front of the computer in her room, working on homework—he hoped. She had finals in a few weeks and was a conscientious student. In any case, he had every parental control known to man on the computers in this house, so he didn't harbor many chat-room nightmares about Hope. He still wished he knew a little more about how she spent her time on that darn thing sometimes.

"So, anyway, she thought I was gay," Tomás told Ruby, with a rueful smile.

"The event planner?"

"Yup."

For a moment, his grandmother just grinned. "Well, did she mean happy or homosexual?" She knew full well which.

Tomás snorted.

Ruby sipped, swallowed, then shook her head. "I don't know what possessed people to change the meaning of a perfectly acceptable word," she mused, mostly to herself. "It's confusing for everyone, and homosexual is as service-able a term as any."

"You're missing the point, Rube. A good-looking, single, twenty-eight-year-old woman thought I was—"

"You don't date. What's she supposed to think? And I didn't miss the point, I was just thinking aloud."

"How would she know I don't date? Today was the first time I've ever seen her in person."

"It's the vibe, sonny." She grouped the fingertips on one hand together and shook them. "You give off a vibe."

He pondered his reflection in the window over the sink. "Maybe I need a new style. Or a tattoo. Something manly, like a power tool."

"Oh, don't be silly. What do you care if she thinks you're homosexual anyway?"

"I…I don't." He wasn't truly bothered by Erica's mis-take, but it was fun to joke about it. If he'd given it more thought, allowing her to believe he actually was gay might've been smart. At least there wouldn't have been questions. Any time she sensed him watching her or felt his attraction, the attraction he couldn't seem to overcome, she'd have written it off as her imagination. But, for what-ever god-awful reason, he simply hadn't been able to walk out of that room without making his sexual orientation very clear to her.

"She's a looker, this woman?"

Sometimes Tomás wondered if Ruby could read his mind.

His maternal line had always been a little bit psychic. "Yeah. And a real go-getter." He tossed a sharp look at Ruby over his shoulder. "She's also hired help. Period. I hired her for what she could do for Hope, not what you might be thinking I want her to do for me."

"That would be the day," Ruby scoffed. "It's no wonder you have this reputation as a flamboyant homosexual."

"Flam—" Tomás twisted around to look at his grandmother, who he knew was simply goading him. She always did love a good debate. "You know how I feel about bringing another woman into Hope's life."

"Indeed. How could I forget?" His grandmother sighed, running fingers through her artificially magentaed locks.

"Are you saying you disagree with the way I'm raising Hope?"

"*Ay-yay-yay,* and they say women are bad." Ruby gazed heavenward, as though pleading mercy. "Men are tiring. Tiresome, too. Here." She held out her mug. Tomás took it, slipping it beneath the bubbly surface of the sink water. He knew when a subject had been dropped by his grandmother. He also knew she never, ever intruded on his parenting. He appreciated it most of the time. Every now and then, he could have used a dose of wisdom. He was sure his mother would have given advice periodically, were she still alive. Then again, she *had* been very much Ruby's daughter.

Tomás drained the sink water, hung the dishrag over the faucet and turned to face Ruby. She looked great, vibrant as ever. He knew only too well how deceptive MS could be, though.

"How are you feeling?" He didn't ask often, and only offhand when he found he couldn't stop himself. His grandmother was matter-of-fact about her condition and didn't want nor tolerate mollycoddling. A lot of people were worse off, she never failed to remind him. *Save your moonfaced sympathy for them,* she'd say. *I have a life to live and you're on my last good nerve.*

"Tired," was her only response. She waved vaguely toward the small glass vial resting atop the counter. Its cap had been punctured by a hypodermic needle, and the whole mess had to sit until the medication had liquified within the saline. "Let's get that shot over with so I can go to bed. It's been sitting long enough, I think."

Tomás quickly dried his hands, then rolled the small vial between his palms smoothly, so as not to bubble the mixture. Ruby, meanwhile, fished in her medication dispenser and popped a pain pill, dry.

"How do you think Hope's going to feel about it?" No need to elaborate—Ruby knew what he meant.

"You should ask her."

"Come on, Rube. I want your input."

"Hope will be fine," she said patiently, in a tone meant to convey her opinion that he spent far too much time worrying about Hope for no good reason.

He drew up a syringeful of Copaxone, then checked the chart they kept on the refrigerator to remind them which injection site to use. "Right arm," he said, then squatted next to her. She'd already begun to roll up the loose sleeve of her blouse. They'd both grown so used to the intricate routine of these shots, Tomás found it hard to believe he'd ever been nervous to give them.

Alcohol swab, one swift jab, pause, then depress the syringe. Tomás administered the medication, removed the needle, then slipped it into a sharps disposal box mounted in an out-of-sight spot on the wall next to the refrigerator. He handed Ruby a Band-Aid. While she put it on, he crossed to the freezer to retrieve an ice-pack. The first half hour after each injection burned like a snakebite, according to Ruby.

"What I mean is, do you think she'll be disappointed that a stranger is helping her plan this instead of her father?"

Ruby rolled her eyes. "For goodness' sake, sonny. I think she'll be overjoyed to shop for clothes with someone of the female persuasion for once, if you want the truth."

Tomás pursed his lips. He didn't know how he felt about that. He'd always tried his damnedest to be both parents for Hope, shopping for clothing with her and learning the purposes of all the various pots of makeup, in case she ever wanted to start wearing the stuff—which she didn't need, mind you. He wasn't some clumsy, clueless male. He was her father *and* her mother—had been since she was six weeks old.

He needed to think about this a little longer, come to terms with how he felt about letting a stranger replace him in Hope's life like that.

"Stop worrying so much," his grandmother urged, reaching out to pat his arm. "People would think you're the old woman in this household instead of me. Hope will be fine, like I've told you a million times. It's you I worry about."

He didn't need her worry. Hope was his concern. "You're missing the point, Rube—"

"You always think I'm missing the point," she said, aiming a gnarled finger at him. She smiled, to soften her words. "Someday you'll find out it's been you missing the point all along, *m'ijo*. But people learn when they're ready to learn." She shrugged, unconcerned. "I just hope I'm still around to witness the swan song. Good night." Without waiting for reciprocation, she deftly maneuvered her wheelchair around the table leg and sped from the room.

Poised to push open his daughter's bedroom door, Tomás checked himself, paused, and then knocked. He had to constantly remind himself Hope was a young lady now, an adolescent who deserved—and demanded—respect for her privacy.

"Yeah?"

He cracked the door and peered in. From across the room,

behind a computer screen, and beneath a purple baseball cap, Hope peered back. He didn't like her cloistered behind the desk, but she'd patiently explained that the new location of her desk was good feng shui, and he was lucky she didn't paint her bedroom door red. "Hi, baby."

"Hi, Dad."

A ribbon of melancholy twirled around his heart. He missed the days when she'd called him Daddy. She still did occasionally, but only when she was trying to get something from him. Like a puppy, God forbid. "What's up? Homework?"

She shook her head. "Already done. I'm just surfing."

A quick jolt of concern struck, but he repressed it. Tomás wanted to give his daughter his trust and the benefit of the doubt. Hope had common sense. "Any interesting sites?" He approached the desk as casually as he could.

In a few keystrokes and button pushes, Hope had the computer off. "No. Just…nothing."

He raised one eyebrow.

Hope sighed. "I'm not going in chat rooms, if that's what you're thinking. Those people are all creeps and idiots." She smiled, deepening the dimples in her cheeks.

Tomás's heart swelled. He chuckled at his daughter and tugged the ponytail pulled through the back of her cap, then took a seat on her bed. Why did he feel so nervous? "Have a few minutes to talk to your old dad?"

Hope kicked back, planting her heels on the edge of the desk. "You're not old, newsflash. But go ahead."

"You know I've been trying to plan your *quinceañera,* but I haven't been doing a very good job."

Hope twisted her mouth to the side, her tone turning almost plaintive. "It's okay, Dad. I don't need to have one."

"Nonsense. You'll have one. But I've hired someone to help us plan it. Help you. I think you'll like her."

He watched Hope's eyes widen before a line—worry? annoyance?—creased her forehead. As quickly as it had come, it disappeared. All of a sudden, her expression went bland. "Okay. Who is she?"

"Just okay?"

She bit her bottom lip a moment, thinking. "Oh, I meant, thank you."

Tomás sighed, hanging his head for a moment. "I wasn't looking for gratitude, baby, although I appreciate it. I'm asking—what do you think about that? About having help? And she's an event planner from Santa Fe."

Hope shrugged, picking at the remains of the sparkle polish that looked so out of place on her stubby little fingernails. "Oh. It's fine. Why?"

"I...don't know." He waited, but Hope didn't volunteer further comments. "Okay. So, we're going to have her over for dinner next Wednesday, so the two of you can meet. So we can start to plan this thing." He paused for comments that never materialized. Weren't teenage girls supposed to jabber? You wouldn't know it from his enigmatic daughter. "You have anything going that night I don't know about?"

"Nope. Nothing important." Hope offered a placid smile. "What should we have?"

A low-grade sense of dismay settled in Tomás's gut, and he didn't know why. It wasn't Hope—she was cooperative enough. Then again...maybe that was it. He felt as if she never really talked to him anymore, as if he didn't know how she truly felt, or what went through that fertile mind of hers. "I'll worry about the menu. You just be here at six next Wednesday. Deal?"

"Deal." She giggled.

Tomás watched her a moment, loving her with an intensity that nearly suffocated him, and at the same time feeling as though he hardly knew her at all. But, for no reason. She'd always been a good, obedient daughter. No changes there. Somehow, though, he felt...a distance. And a powerlessness to change it. "Is everything okay?"

She shrugged again. "Why wouldn't it be?"

"You'd tell me if something wasn't okay?"

"Dad!" she moaned. "You're bugging me. Stop being weird."

With a tired, put-upon chuckle, Tomás stood. "*Bueno.* Okay. I'm leaving. God forbid a father should try to have a little conversation with his best girl."

"I'm immune to your parental guilt trips."

He turned back and grinned. "Dinner Wednesday at six."

"I heard you the first hundred times, Dad." She rolled her eyes and saluted. "Be there or be square."

He stood and crossed to the door, then turned and studied her for a moment, his back braced against the doorjamb. "I love you, baby."

Hope dropped her feet to the floor and clicked a few buttons on her keyboard before flashing him a quick smile. "Love you, too, Dad."

"Don't stay up late."

"What do I look like, a vampire?" She bared her teeth.

A perfectly normal exchange, Tomás told himself as he left the room, his soft chuckle feeling a little choked off by the lump in his throat.

Perfectly normal.

So why did he feel so disconnected?

Chapter Four

Rule number one for leaving a good impression with a man: Don't assume he's gay within the first ten minutes of your introduction, and if for some ridiculous reason you *do,* for God's sake, *don't voice your thoughts.*

Sheesh, what a colossal mess she'd created for herself. There wasn't anything on earth wrong with being gay in her opinion, but experience taught her that straight guys didn't appreciate being mistaken for gay guys. That's all. And she'd done it, unabashedly, to probably the hottest man she'd encountered in months. Ugh.

It had been nearly a week, and still Erica couldn't get past the embarrassing exchange with Tomás. She'd replayed it over and over in her mind all week, cringing inside each time she heard him say, "I'm...not gay. Not even a little bit."

And now she had to face him again.

A fresh fist of humiliation punched Erica's middle as she guided her Honda Accord over the rolling hills and twisting curves of the Northern New Mexico back roads en route to Tomás's house. Soft flamenco-guitar instrumentals drifted out of her stereo speakers, and the scents of sage and May sunshine wafted in through her open window. The scenery in this area was beautiful, but try as she might, she couldn't concentrate on it. Instead, two distracting questions ran incessantly through her mind: One, how could she have been such a flipping idiot? And two—though she'd never admit having pondered this question—if Tomás was, as he claimed, a healthy, red-blooded heterosexual male, why had he assured her she'd *never* have to worry about him hitting on her?

Did he find her so unattractive?

Was she the polar opposite of "his type"?

Make no mistake, she knew it was fickle of her to even wonder. She herself claimed to have no interest in a relationship and to never date colleagues or clients. And she didn't. She really didn't. But that wasn't the point. She was human, and female, and when a drop-dead gorgeous, come-to-papa man flat out stated that he had *No Interest in Her Whatsoever,* well sorry, but give a woman and her still-bruisable ego a chance to wonder why.

The simplest and most palatable answer would be that Tomás was already involved with someone, but Erica just hadn't gotten that sense from their first encounter. After all, he'd hired her to plan Hope's party. Had there been an available girlfriend, logic said the woman likely would've planned the *quinceañera* herself. So, no girlfriend, and yet zip, zero, *nada* attraction. Yeah, she was fickle to the core, but still. She couldn't deny feeling judged and found lacking.

"Stop being ridiculous!" Erica told herself, smacking the side of her fist on the steering wheel. It didn't matter what Tomás Garza did or didn't think about her, and it wasn't worth the mental energy she'd been wasting on it for an entire week.

Interested, not interested, or full-on disgusted, facts were facts: the sum total of her association with Tomás was (1) his contribution to the Cultural Arts Festival, and (2) the *quinceañera* she would plan for his daughter, Hope—to the tune of five grand in her business fund. And the sole purpose of this dinner meeting tonight was to meet Hope and discuss preliminary plans. Period. She needn't obsess about anything else. So she'd taken extra pains with her outfit this evening, with her hair and makeup. Big whoop. She'd merely hoped to try for a second chance at an obviously poor first impression, despite the old adage that claimed no such chance existed.

Sometimes a woman just had to try.

Erica forced her mind on to the business at hand and gave one last glance at the directions Tomás had e-mailed her, hoping she was close. She'd driven so far into the boonies that his directions were now reduced to such landmarks as, "pass the blue-fenced property with a brown-and-white horse and a goat in the pasture, then turn left at the next dirt farm road adjacent to the large piñon tree." Thank goodness for cell phones or she might never make it, not that it would be such a bad thing....

Yes. Yes, it *would* be a bad thing. She was a business professional with a reputation to uphold, and this was a business meeting. She straightened her shoulders, tossed her hair. After a weekend of researching *quinceañera* traditions, she'd actually come up with some fun ideas, and she looked forward to running them by Tomás and his daughter and grandmother. She prayed Hope was an easy child to get along with and could only wish her first encounter with Hope and the grandmother would be better than—

Erica pressed her lips together in a resolute line.

Forget that. She was done thinking about it, done feeling humiliated, done apologizing. The last thing she needed in her life right now was a man, anyway, so the point was so moot it wasn't even a point. Meet the girl, plan the event and get out of this situation with her sanity and her independence intact—*that* was the goal. The only goal.

Spying the large piñon tree she'd almost missed, Erica jerked the wheel and made a bouncing turn onto the dirt farm road that would lead her to whatever lay ahead. As the dust cloud cleared, so did her head. Finally. She could survive this. No sweat. Well…not much, anyway.

Hope swung her stocking feet under the table and watched her father from beneath her lashes with a mixture of wonder and amusement. Something was definitely up. He bustled around the kitchen between the oven, the countertop and the bubbling pots atop the stove while she pretended to work on homework at the kitchen table. She was able to work here rather than in her room because tonight they were eating at the *dining room* table, believe it or not. Needless to say, she wasn't making much progress on her boring French conjugations. Watching Dad was way more interesting at this point and WAY distracting.

Who *was* this lady he'd hired to help plan the *quinceañera,* anyway? Hope hadn't seen her dad this…spazzed out for a long time, and they never ate at the dining room table unless it was, like, a holiday. Seriously, Thanksgiving, Christmas and their birthdays, period. Never on a regular old Wednesday.

Speaking of holidays—she inhaled, trying to pretend she wasn't actually sniffing him—was Dad wearing cologne? He smelled like Christmas, since the only time he seemed to wear his Gray Flannel cologne was for Christmas dinner each year. He usually just smelled like laundry soap and bleach, like the paste and paper in his studio. Comfortable, like her dad.

But he was wearing cologne now. She was 99.9 percent sure.

Not only that, but he was dressed UP. He wore his black microfiber slacks, the ones she begged him to buy because they were SO cool and he didn't want to because they weren't *practical,* and black shirt—with buttons! Like, a shirt for church, not one of his regular day shirts. Not only that, but the house was spotless, smelling of pine trees and lemons, and he'd been racing around all nervous, exactly like a guy preparing to impress someone on a hot, first date.

It so rocked!

The cologne, clothing, and cleanliness were definite clues that something was brewing. Business meeting? Yeah, sure. Maybe partly, but it was so totally more than that. Tonight's "meeting" was special, and she might only be fourteen but she knew why. Duh, can you say obvious? They were learning about variables in algebra, and the only variable tonight was this *Erica,* so it had to be her. Her dad was making all this effort for a woman, something he never, ever did. It was so completely romantic that Hope's tummy swirled with anticipation. She fought to hold back a giggle!

Biting her lip, Hope made a mental note to keep a close eye on her father tonight. She was pretty good at reading him, which wasn't saying much because he was a total open book. If he *was* interested in this lady, all Hope had to say about it was, like, FINALLY. Sheesh. Her dad always claimed he was happy without a wife or girlfriend, but Hope knew better. She was just in the way. She was! But maybe things were changing? From the looks of things, this Erica was the first woman in a long time who even had a remote shot at the title of girlfriend when it came to her stubborn dad.

Her tummy clenched and she fought back another nervous giggle. Hope had no idea what would happen after tonight— maybe nothing at all. But she knew one thing for sure: things in the Garza household were about to get WAY interesting.

By the time Erica pulled up the long gravel drive, her focus of anxiety had moved to Hope. She hadn't been exaggerating when she'd told Tomás she wasn't really a kid person, and yet she knew kids were far more intuitive than adults. They quickly recognized adults who were uncomfortable around them, and she knew she'd be pegged. Her only hope at this point was that the assignment wouldn't turn out to be horrid.

She glanced at the buildings up ahead, taking in this home, getting a feel for the animal in his natural habitat, so to speak. Tomás's low, smallish house looked to be authentic adobe; the setting sun washed it into shades of gold and peach that Erica found both beautiful and charming. Behind it loomed a newer, large wooden structure, probably a barn. A barn? She took in the property, saw no animals. Undulating meadows spread out around the house and barn, covered with scrub oak, sage, and piñon and juniper trees. Though she was a city girl at heart, she couldn't deny this would be a great place to raise children.

Okay, she'd stalled enough, avoiding that moment of truth when she'd have to face Tomás again and meet his daughter. What kind of person would be afraid of a fourteen-year-old girl? Idiot. Pulling in a deep breath, Erica stopped her car behind a black Ford pickup parked adjacent to the house and turned off the ignition. As the hot engine ticked, she resisted the urge to flip down her visor and check her makeup in the mirror one last time. Just nerves. She could beat them.

Alighting from the car, she retrieved a black-leather portfolio from the back seat along with her purse. She followed the small sidewalk up to the front door and then lifted her fist and hesitated only momentarily before knocking on the bright red door. As she stepped back and waited, she braced herself for the awkward moment when she'd face Tomás again, uneasy especially because she was on his turf this time.

When the door opened, however, Tomás wasn't on the other side. Instead, Erica faced a bright-eyed little tomboy who stood, one stocking foot atop the other, smiling shyly. The girl wore low-rise jeans and a baggy Buffy the Vampire Slayer T-shirt that sort of ruined the effect of the cute tummy-baring pants. She had Tomás's watchful, tiger's-eye gaze and a choppy haircut that was as bad as it was endearing. Erica wondered if the girl had cut it herself, and a pang of...something unrecognizable tightened her middle. Compassion? She smiled. "Hope?"

"Hi." The girl teetered on that precipice between girl and woman, gangly and unsure. "My dad's in the kitchen." She stepped back from the door and tilted her head. "Come on in, Ms....I don't know your last name."

"How about if you just call me Erica?" She stepped over the threshold into a warm, welcoming living room appointed with deep, comfortable mission-style furniture and bold colors. Intricate quilts shared wall space with Zarape blankets and artwork she recognized from some of the galleries in Santa Fe and Taos. Gorgeous black Santa Clara pottery and Jemez carved redware held places of honor on the lighted shelving adjacent to a huge fireplace. The shelves seemed to have been built just for the collectible Native American pieces, and the effect was stunning. This wasn't just a house, it was a home. Part haven, part gallery. Erica didn't know what she'd expected, if anything, but she was impressed.

She glanced over to find Hope studying her with a childlike intensity that caught her off guard. "It's beautiful." She indicated the room.

Hope stuffed her hands into her back pockets and turned her attention to the room as though she'd never seen it before. "Grandma Ruby made the quilts. There's one on my bed, too. It's a log-cabin pattern."

Erica couldn't help the smile that lifted the corners of her mouth. Leave it to a child to miss the significance of the artwork in the room and go straight for the comfortable.

"Is someone talking about me?"

Erica turned at the same time Hope did and saw a small,

elderly woman with a shock of almost magenta-tinted hair wheel deftly into the room from the archway behind them. She hadn't expected Ruby to look so vibrant, but then, she didn't know much about multiple sclerosis. "If you're the creator of these fabulous quilts, then the answer is, yes."

Hope pointed a thumb over her shoulder. "That's Grandma Ruby. You better just call her Ruby."

"Well, now. You must be Erica." Ruby came to a stop just before her and knotted her hands loosely in her lap, which was covered by another small quilt she no doubt made herself.

"In the flesh." Erica transferred her portfolio to her left hand and thrust out her right. "Thank you for having me."

Ruby shook Erica's hand. "Nonsense, it's our pleasure. Welcome to our home. I can't tell you how glad we are to have you helping with the *quinceañera.* Isn't that right, Hope?"

Erica glanced at the girl, sure she saw something move through Hope's expression before she bit her bottom lip and nodded silently, a placid smile on her lips.

Interesting. Erica filed that away for later.

"So," Ruby drew out, "I will admit Tomás has told me a bit about you." And then she chuckled softly and Erica knew.

Without a doubt.

Tomás had told his grandmother about their little mis-understanding at the Arts Festival meeting. Ugh, she wanted to kill him. Since that wasn't appropriate behavior for a guest, she tried another angle. "Yes. Well. I'm sure I know what little bits he shared. As his grandmother, I'm counting on you to share a few of his embarrassing secrets, as well."

Ruby's eyes sparkled. "You can count on that."

"What are you guys talking about?" Hope asked, baffled.

Ruby wagged a finger. "Mind your business, young lady."

"Erica."

So caught up in meeting Hope and Ruby, Erica somehow forgot that Tomás would be nearby. Her stomach plunged at the sound of his voice in the room, its depth and richness seeming to suck away all available oxygen. She looked toward the archway that led to the dining room beyond, and there he stood. Dressed all in black, wiping his hands on a strawberry-patterned dish towel, guarded laughter and welcome in his eyes.

God, but he was a beautiful man.

She forced a smile. "Tomás. I hope I'm not too early."

"Not at all." He tossed the dish towel over his shoulder as he crossed into the room, then wrapped Hope in a playful headlock. "You've met my girls?"

"Da-a-ad!"

Erica grinned at Hope then smiled genuinely at Ruby. "I have. We're all old friends by now."

"Good. Then let me get you all drinks." He smoothed those work roughened hands together, and Erica's gaze dropped to watch the mesmerizing motion. Why was it, with some men, you could simply look at them and imagine the feel of their hands on—

"Wine, Erica? A cocktail? What's your pleasure?"

Arsenic? These thoughts *had* to stop. "How about water?" She crinkled her nose. "Sorry to be so dull, but I'm not so sure about those dark, winding backroads after a drink."

"Backroads?" he teased. "Those are superhighways in these parts, city girl."

"I'll get the water," said Hope eagerly, and they all looked at her. Tomás with raw love. Ruby with pride. And Erica, with a sense of relief. She'd only been there for a few minutes, but if Hope was always so obedient and well-behaved, this job might turn out to be easier and more pleasant than she'd anticipated.

"Thank you, baby," Tomás said, as Hope bounded out of the room, all exuberance and no grace, like a retriever puppy. He looked at his grandmother. "Rube? How about you?"

"I will go with my great-granddaughter and fetch my own wine, thank you. I'm not an invalid who needs waiting on." She maneuvered one large wheel until she faced the kitchen and made her way swiftly from the room.

And then they were alone.

Erica fought the urge to avert her eyes, to look anywhere but at this man. She was no high school girl, and this wasn't a date. "They're wonderful, Tomás. Your grandmother is a pip."

"She's a handful," he said, but respect and love threaded through the statement. "God love her."

For a moment, they were both silent, and suddenly Erica knew she needed to say something about her gaffe. Anything. Or else the not saying would loom in the room with them all night long like a giant purple monster he and she would studiously ignore.

Garnering courage with a slow intake of breath, Erica splayed a hand on her chest. The words came in a nervous rush. "Tomás, can I just say one more time how sorry I am to have made the assumptions—"

"Ah, ah." Tomás stopped her, one palm forward. "We're past that, Erica. A simple misunderstanding. Let's just move on."

She hung her head, grateful...a little embarrassed, perhaps? But she wanted him to know it had been *her* mistake, not based on him, really, at all. "O-okay. I just...let me say that...you need to know my assumption was never because I thought you weren't..." She rolled her hand, realizing she'd just dug herself in further, wondering just how many times she'd wished for death since she met this man who stole her composure so easily, so completely, without even trying.

His smile widened. He was enjoying her discomfort, the rat. "That I wasn't what?"

"Well...not virile." Her face heated instantly. She held up her hands. "Wait, that didn't come out right."

Tomás laughed. "I think it came out fine. It's good to know my virility isn't in question." He blew on his fingernails and buffed them along the collar of his shirt. "Did you have any comments about machismo or handsomeness you'd like to share?"

Then he winked.

She managed, just barely, to roll her eyes. Her throat felt dry and tight, but she injected an illusion of friendly drollness into her tone anyway. "Don't push your luck, buddy."

"*Bueno.* No more joking, okay? I know what you're saying, even though you don't have to say it, and I swear to you it's in the past."

"Thank God. And thank you." A little more laughter, and then...silence. And what now? Small talk? She despised small talk. But it was either that or stand there stunned by how absolutely hot he looked with his hair hanging loose. A little bit rebel, a little bit artist. Hey, just because she wasn't interested in marriage didn't mean she wasn't interested in *men.*

And Tomás Garza was one verrrrry interesting man.

She cleared her throat and forced her thoughts from him before she did something stupid. "Your home is lovely. You're quite the art collector."

"Thank you. Ruby's the real collector, though. Most of these pieces are hers. I just build the display cases."

"You're a woodworker, too?"

"Hey, when you live out here, you become a jack-of-all-trades without even trying." He ran a hand slowly through his hair, his gaze on the thick black pottery Ruby bought at the last Pueblo Festival. "The Santa Clara is my favorite. So sleek and dark. Quiet. Beautiful in its straightforwardness."

Kind of like you, Erica thought, attuned to him in a way that frightened her. A lag in their superficial conversation ensued, and she was determined to fill it. She could pull her weight in most situations, but she absolutely couldn't sit in silence with Tomás. Not tonight. "Hope is a lovely girl."

"Thank you. That she is," he said, turning his attention from the pottery. "She's been looking forward to meeting you. At least I think." He quirked his mouth to the side. "To be perfectly frank, my Hope isn't a girl of many words."

"She takes after her dad." She wondered what traits Hope had received from her mother but knew it was a question she'd never ask. "Looks like you, too. Same eyes."

Tomás shrank back in mock horror. "Now, don't go and tell her that. The last thing a fourteen-year-old girl wants to hear is that she looks like her father."

They both laughed softly, and Erica felt herself loosen up a bit. Maybe it wouldn't be so bad, this dinner, this evening as an outsider with Tomás and his nontraditional little family.

Just then, Hope brought Erica's ice water and her own and claimed a spot on the chair, tucking one stocking foot up under her. Ruby pulled up in an empty spot next to an occasional table that looked to be there just for her.

"Are you going to make the poor woman stand all night, *m'ijo?*" Ruby asked, eyeing her grandson sharply. "My gosh, your manners. Raised in a penitentiary, I swear."

Tomás colored slightly but recovered just as fast. "Of course. Erica. Won't you sit. I'll leave you ladies to get acquainted while I check on dinner. Shouldn't be too long. I hope you're hungry, Erica."

She set aside her purse and portfolio, then claimed her spot in an armchair and laid a hand on her stomach. "You told me to come hungry, and I did."

"Excellent. Finally a woman who follows instructions."

"Don't make us hurt you, sonny," Ruby warned, giving him the eye. He just laughed.

Erica sat her water glass on a stone coaster, and as Tomás

moved out of the room, Hope asked her, "Do you have kids?"

Some non sequitur, Erica thought. "No kids. I'm not married. I have cousins," she offered, as a replacement.

"Oh." Hope twirled a finger in one choppy lock of her hair. "I wish I had cousins. My dad's an only child, and…"

An odd pause ensued.

Ruby sipped from her wineglass, and Hope gave Erica a funny little closed-lip smile. She never finished her statement, and Erica knew better than to ask, but she didn't quite know why. For a moment, the room fell silent. Then Ruby picked up a remote, pointed it at a stack of stereo components in a carved, wooden cabinet, and pressed the button. Soft native flute music wafted through the room, and Erica's gaze fell on her portfolio. Business. Yes. A convenient bridge over the chasms of the unsaid that seemed to flow through this house like canals through Venice. She reached for the zippered case, glancing at Hope while she did so.

"I've come up with a few ideas for your *quinceañera,* Hope. I'm looking forward to going over them with you."

"Oh." The girl's gaze lit on the portfolio before sliding away evasively. "Okay. Well…we'll wait for Dad, though. We can just…relax until dinner's ready."

"Of course." Erica abandoned the portfolio and reached for her water glass. So much for that idea.

"How about dogs?" Hope crossed her other foot up under her, then slipped into a lotus position in the chair, with the ease and flexibility of the young.

A sip, a swallow. "Excuse me?"

"Do you have dogs? Or cats?"

Erica shook her head.

"Any pets at all?"

Erica's expression was regretful. "I travel quite a bit, and when you live alone… I had a dog when I was growing up, though. His name was Spike. And a hamster, Morton. My mom has two dogs. Does that count?"

"Everyone should have a pet, right Grandma Ruby?"

The older woman shook her head, laughing tiredly. "I'm not getting in the middle of it, *m'ijita,* but nice try."

Hope giggled, and Ruby looked toward Erica. "This one has been trying to finagle a puppy out of her father now for months."

"I love puppies!" Hope threw her arms out with exuberance. "We have, like, a zillion fields. It's not like he wouldn't have any place to run around."

Erica lowered her voice, sotto voce, and leaned toward Hope. "Shhh. I'll tell you a secret. I love puppies, too."

Hope turned a beatific smile toward her grandmother—in truth, her great-grandmother. "See, Grammy Rube? It's so totally perfect."

Erica wasn't sure if Hope meant the puppy, the secret or something else. But she did know, finally and for sure, that she would make it through this evening. Tomás was right—his daughter was a wonderful young woman rather than the sullen, petulant teen Erica had feared she'd face. Childlike, yes, but definitely not a child. A budding teen, but certainly not an adult. Hopeful, effervescent and eager to please. She reminded Erica of herself at that age, and that she could handle. Easing back in her chair, Erica sipped her water and relaxed.

By the time he had served the flourless chocolate cake and poured coffee for the adults, Tomás was beginning to mellow out. Erica seemed to fit in fine, and Hope appeared to like her. Almost too much. A pang of jealousy tightened Tomás's middle, but he tried to ignore it. Ridiculous that he should resent the fact his daughter liked the woman, when that had been his goal in the first place. He needed to chill. It was just…he and Hope had been a team for so long, he found it difficult to let anyone else into the fold. Old story.

But Hope was fourteen. Four more years, and she could be gone. For a moment, the world and his heart jolted to a stop. Horrid, that thought, and disturbing in ways he hadn't even begun to contemplate. He didn't want to face them now.

"How about we talk a little about the *quinceañera?*" Erica said. Tomás blinked at her, only just dragging himself mentally back into the room, into reality. She glanced eagerly from him to Hope to Ruby, then bent over to retrieve her black-leather portfolio.

The *quinceañera.* Yes. It's what he'd hired her for, and yet they'd spent the evening eating, drinking and talking about art, mostly. Art and soccer and the godforsaken yearning for puppies, and with each bit of conversation, he'd found himself more intrigued by her. He cleared his throat. "Yes, let's. Hope, come here, *m'ija.*" He beckoned her with a sweep of his arm. "Sit next to me and we can look at everything together."

Hope stood, then dragged her chair noisily over next to him. He draped his arm over her bony little shoulders and pulled her familiar warmth against his side. Smiling into her innocent face, he asked, "You ready?"

She shrugged. "Sure. Whatever."

"Now that's enthusiasm for you," Ruby said dryly. "Ach, teenagers. Pillars of zeal, I always say."

"Great-*grandmother,*" Hope said, in a playfully warning tone.

"She only calls me that to get my goat," Ruby told Erica.

Smiling, Erica opened the pages of the portfolio turning them to face Tomás and Hope. "First of all, you're going to have to sign up for some reconfirmation classes at your church." She glanced at Tomás. "I'm assuming you do want religious instruction as a part of this? From what I've read, it's traditional to have a thanksgiving mass with the ceremony, but this is the twenty-first century and I'm all about being nontraditional. We can modify however you wish."

"Well, we belong to a church in town." His face heated. "I can't say we're there fifty-two Sundays a year—"

"Or ever," Hope quipped.

Erica waved that away. "I'll leave that up to you. If you decide to go the church route, though, you should get started." She turned a page. "Hope, you'll also have to choose some community service to do for the summer."

She looked baffled. "Like what?"

"Anything that interests you," Tomás said.

Hope looked at her grandmother. "I'd like to do something for people with multiple sclerosis."

Erica smiled. "Perfect. I'll search out some options, and you can do the same."

"There is a ranch around here that offers therapeutic horseback riding for people with MS. It's called hippotherapy, even though I think it should be called horse-o-therapy." The adults laughed, and she shrugged. "We learned about it in health class. I guess riding a horse can help some people with their MS symptoms. Maybe I could volunteer there?"

"That's beautiful, baby," Tomás said, kissing her cheek.

"Yes." Ruby reached over and patted Hope's hand. "But don't even think about getting me on a horse."

Everyone chuckled again.

"Other than that, assuming you'll have the mass and ceremony at your church...?" She looked at Tomás in question, and he nodded. "Then the most pressing details will be selecting and booking a site for *la fiesta,* the party afterward, and ordering the cake, choosing a menu and selecting Hope's *vestido.*"

"My what?"

"Your dress," all three adults answered at once.

"And you'll need to select your *damas* and *chambelanes,* in other words, the lords and ladies who will comprise your honor court." Erica winked. "In plain talk, friends who get to dress up with you and cute boys you all get to dance with. Seven of each is traditional, plus one special escort just for you.''

Hope blushed prettily.

Erica flipped another page. ''There are other smaller details…ordering the cake, deciding what *recuerdos,* or mementos you'd like for all your guests, learning the waltz—''

''What waltz?'' Hope shrieked.

Tomás chuckled. It's traditional for the *corte de honor,* your lords and ladies, to dance the waltz. Along with you and me, and I get the first dance.'' Hope pulled a look of abject horror. ''Don't worry, baby, if I can do it, you can do it.''

''Smaller details yet—'' Erica directed her comment to Tomás ''—you'll need to come up with a toast, Hope's godparents will present her with a gift. And then there is the shoe thing.''

''What shoe thing?'' Hope asked.

''At one point during the fiesta, before the waltz with your father, he is to replace your patent-leather flats with a pair of high heels. After that, all the younger children gather, and you'll toss the *muñeca,* your final doll of childhood. It's all meant to represent your move from childhood to adulthood.''

''It sounds so weddingish,'' Hope said, nose crinkled.

Erica tipped her head to the side. ''Well, it sort of is. It's an acknowledgement by your family and your community that you're no longer a child. A rite of passage.''

''Does that mean I get to date boys?'' Hope teased.

Tomás made a pained face. ''Unfortunately, yes. But no car dating until you're thirty.''

''Gee, sounds reasonable,'' Erica said, jokingly. ''You know, it is also traditional for Hope's godparents and other special people in her life to act as sponsors, defray some of the costs.''

''No need. I've got it all.''

Her eyebrows lifted on a careful inhale, but she didn't question it. "Whatever works for you."

He regarded her across the table. For an assignment she hadn't wanted, she'd sure done a lot of work already. He had been smart to hire her, despite the exorbitant fee. The portfolio pages held drawings, fabric swatches, lists, charts. They'd gone over each page, with Tomás alternating between nodding and watching her intelligent, beautiful face. Her full lips moved sensuously as she spoke. It was enough to distract him completely from the matter at hand. The working Erica and the having-a-friendly-dinner Erica were two parts of a very interesting, enticing whole. He had to remember, she was here for Hope. Man, he *had* to stop watching her mouth.

"So, what do you think?" The portfolio closed, and Erica tossed her hair. "I've been doing most of the talking."

"It's going to be so nice," Ruby said.

"It looks wonderful to me." Tomás looked at Hope. "Baby?"

She rolled her eyes, and he grinned, because she hated to be called that. But she was his baby, from the moment he'd held her tiny swaddled form when he was seventeen—alone, at once terrified of and awed by what he'd created, adoring and determined to protect her—to now, when she was on the verge of womanhood. Mysterious and edgy. She'd always be his baby, like it or not. Some things he wouldn't budge on.

Hope lifted a shoulder, her face emotionless. "It's fine."

"Fine?"

"Sure." Her eyes flickered uncertainly toward Erica. "I mean, the ideas are good."

"Do you have any other ideas?" Erica asked.

"Not really," Hope said, after a moment of thought.

Tomás sighed, pulled a put-upon face and hugged Hope closer. "What did I tell you about Little Miss No Help at All?"

Hope clicked her tongue. "Dad, stop it."

Erica rezipped the portfolio. "It's a lot to take in, but we have plenty of time, don't worry. Speaking of which—" she propped her elbows atop the portfolio and knotted her hands beneath her chin. "When do you get out of school, Hope?"

"In June."

"Okay. That's perfect. I think we can wait to do a lot of the legwork until after that. I'll spend the rest of this month planning. You concentrate on school. I've got the festival and some other assignments, too." She checked her PalmPilot, which she'd retrieved from her bag. "Does that work for you, Tomás?"

"Absolutely, if you think you can swing everything. But perhaps you and I...can we meet briefly, say, once a week for a progress update? Just a coffee or lunch in town—"

"Or dinner," suggested Hope. Ruby and Tomás turned to her, surprise in their expressions.

Erica made a notation in her PalmPilot, ignoring the dinner prompt altogether. "Coffee works. We can set some times...."

Tomás gripped the top of Hope's head in his hand and shook playfully. "Let me get this one off to bed and we can talk a few minutes before you leave, coordinate things."

"Dad," Hope groaned, standing up. "I can go to bed myself, you know. I'm not a baby."

"I know, I know, so you keep telling me." He smacked her playfully on the backside. "You run on then."

Hope blinked shyly at Erica. "Thanks for coming over, Erica. I hope you liked dinner."

"You're welcome, and it was great. We'll talk soon?"

Hope giggled. "Okay." She turned to her dad. "Erica loves puppies. She thinks everyone should have one."

Tomás smirked in Erica's direction. "Thanks a lot."

Erica just grinned.

Ruby wheeled back from the table. "If you two don't mind, I'll retire also. It's been a long day."

"Of course, Rube. You go on."

The older woman turned to their guest. "Erica, it's been such a pleasure. Do come back sometime soon."

"Oh, believe me," Erica replied, laughter in her tone. "I'm going to need your help on this *quinceañera*. I fear you'll see so much of me you'll be begging me to leave."

Tomás watched as the two women shook hands. Somehow, he couldn't imagine ever growing tired of Erica's company. He could tell by Ruby's amused, knowing stare that she agreed, and also that she knew what he'd been thinking.

On that note, what in the hell *had* he been thinking? After fourteen years of avoiding even the remote possibility of entanglements that might put Hope in a vulnerable position, he'd willingly brought a beautiful woman into his house, into all their lives, even if only for business reasons. She was here, and the memory of her, he knew, would linger even when she'd left.

Hope liked her. Ruby liked her.

He even liked her, maybe a little too much.

He avoided entanglements, sure, but he'd never claimed to be celibate, and right now his libido was in rage mode. Damn. What *had* he been thinking, indeed?

Chapter Five

After the Garza women, young and old, retreated to their bedrooms, Erica accepted one last cup of coffee and joined Tomás on the back patio to discuss their meeting schedule and some last-minute details. The rural night beyond the light of the stake lanterns loomed black and silent, save the steady insect symphony and the intermittent, far-off howl of coyotes.

Resisting the languor brought on by the ambience, they got down to business immediately. Once they'd plugged a few meeting dates and backup options into their calendars, they sat back with completion. The setting instantly felt intimate to Erica, the company at once comfortable and disconcerting. She found herself determined to keep things friendly with Tomás, to stop shying away from him. She ran her palm along the smooth-sanded armrests of the hand-carved lounger, reveling in her feeling of ease around Tomás and yet not trusting herself for it. She fell back, once again, on small talk.

"I'll give you one thing." She patted her stomach. "You weren't kidding when you said you could cook."

He smiled, and the play of torchlight on his face showed her that his beard was coming in. A gentle breeze tossed loose strands of his long hair against his cheek. He looked at once rough and serene, unguarded but still emotionally distant. Politely so. He looked…so sexy. Gorgeous and dangerous and inaccessible—an enticing mix no matter the circumstances.

"Well," he said, a little wryly, "I'm glad you enjoyed the meal. When life throws you into single fatherhood at the age of seventeen, you find the time to learn all kinds of skills. Cooking is second nature to me now."

Wow. It was the most he'd admitted about his rather enigmatic life since they'd met, and she didn't quite know how to respond. Luckily, she didn't have to. Before she'd completed one tight swallow, Tomás went on.

"On that note, there are a couple of things you should know, Erica, since you're going to be spending time alone with my daughter, which is something I don't allow many people to do." He slid her an almost apologetic glance. "I don't like to think of them as rules, but…"

A small pause. Her wariness returned like a shifting wind. She managed to remain still and keep the apprehension from her tone. At least she hoped. "Okay."

For a moment, all she heard were the crickets. When he started to speak, his voice was low.

"Her mother left us. We were never married, but then again—" a self-deprecating shrug "—we were kids." He leaned forward in his chair, elbows on knees, rubbing his palms together slowly. A myriad of emotions crossed his face. Anger, disappointment, sadness, resolve. "Hope doesn't know her, has never known her. And…we don't talk about it." His gaze met hers then, level and full of meaning, and the motions with his hands stopped. "I'd appreciate it if you'd respect that."

Her stomach tightened. Could she believe what she was hearing? "Ever?"

"What do you mean?"

"You don't discuss Hope's mother ever?"

He shrugged. "She was two years older than Hope is now when…when it happened." He seemed to go pale at the thought but shook it off quickly. "She left when Hope was still nursing, never looked back. Why talk about a mother who never wanted to be involved in my daughter's life? Who never was involved? What's the point?"

Closure? Catharsis? Erica could think of a lot of reasons, but none, she knew, that would convince this man. And really, was it any of her business? Still, she couldn't keep from voicing the questions swirling around in her mind. She moistened her lips, treading cautiously. "Hope's okay with that?"

He blew out a weary sigh, but his tension seemed to ease slightly. He smoothed one hand slowly down his face. "I don't know. She never speaks of her mother. Nothing to speak about. I mean, she doesn't know the woman."

But wouldn't that fact in and of itself be something to discuss, Erica wondered? Ah, well. It wasn't her family, definitely wasn't her problem. If Tomás wanted her to pretend that Hope had been miraculously born without a mother, she would. And she'd pass Go, and collect five thousand dollars—no problem whatsoever, she decided. "It's fine. Don't worry. It wouldn't cross my mind to probe the child about her parentage anyway."

But Erica knew herself too well. If Hope brought the subject up…? Ah, well, she'd face that problem if and when it arose. As he said, Hope never talked about her mother anyway. Smiling gently, to put him at ease about her time with Hope, she asked, "Is that all? The only rule?"

"I…I guess so." Sincerity deepened the color of his eyes as he watched her. "Thank you. For understanding."

"I'm sorry."

"Excuse me?"

She tucked her hair behind her ears, staring into the blackness rather than meeting the eyes of this emotionally damaged man. Somehow glimpsing a bit of his vulnerability rendered him an even bigger threat to her senses. "I'm…sorry you went through that. It must've been hard." Silence. She finally glanced toward him.

He took a long, slow sip of his coffee, watching her over the rim of his mug. Not so much suspicious as guarded. Always guarded. When finally he swallowed, he said, "We've made do."

"That, I can see. You've done a great job. But still, it must have been difficult for you. That's all I'm saying."

He hiked one shoulder. "Hell, no one ever promised life would be easy. And I wouldn't change one thing if it meant I didn't have Hope."

Erica smiled. She never knew a proud papa could be sexy but here sat a prime example. Family men had never appealed before, for obvious reasons. Ready-made mommy, she wasn't.

Tomás's expression turned troubled again. "One of the things I promised myself, though, is that she wouldn't be shorted. That I'd provide a good life for her, everything she needs and wants." His jaw ticked. "I've always dreamed of a beautiful *quinceañera,* a day just for her."

"What all fathers would want, I guess."

"Yes, but…" He pressed his lips together, seeming to struggle for the right words. "What I mean is, a send-off befitting a young lady who didn't have an impetuous teenage boy for a father…and no mother. A real…event. Something complete. Something…not lacking."

Her heart jolted, and she understood. She finally understood, once and for all, and it made her heart squeeze with compassion and empathy. She yearned to reassure him, to validate his efforts as a parent who'd overcome tremendous odds. *Oh, Tomás,* she wanted to say, *a party can't make up for a mother's absence, and you have nothing to atone for anyway.*

So many kids had far less than even one parent who loved them as Tomás loved Hope. But she could feel his guilt, his desire to assuage it, like a palpable presence. She wanted to help him, whatever it took. A good man shouldn't bear the burden of guilt he didn't deserve. "I will plan a night so grand, Hope's wedding will pale in comparison. Will that do?"

He smiled, wide and grateful, but laid a palm over his heart with melodrama. "Now, don't get carried away. I'm going to be paying for both events, you know."

"A woman's gotta do what a woman's gotta do."

He paused, and the mood turned serious again. "I'm so glad you're planning this."

His words resonated with husky sincerity, real gratitude. She took this in, absorbed the feel of it, and the truth of what she felt deep inside came out without warning. "I am, too. Really. Everything's going to be just fine."

Erica Gonçalves, great avoider of commitment, to the rescue.

Hijuela, what was she thinking?

Just as quickly as the fear rushed in, she pushed it away. She might be no great rescuer, but she could flat-out hold forth in the party-planning department. Hope's event would be a gala, it would be memorable, because she'd settle for nothing less. Not for Tomás, necessarily, but simply because her personal standards demanded it. As long as she could avoid getting too involved in the Garza family, she'd be fine. Safe, sane and absolutely fine. A few innocuous coffee meetings with Tomás, some shopping and coordinating with Hope, consulting with Ruby—there was nothing to it. She could hold her own against the draw of this man and his family. She could and would.

Their first few meetings went exactly as Erica had planned. She'd stuck to the agenda, received payment for the few expenses she'd incurred, and not a single iota of personal information had been exchanged. It felt exactly like business, and that's how she wanted it. Granted, it didn't keep her from noticing how Tomás's presence in a room seemed to mesmerize every woman around, or how unexpectedly sexy she found it that he didn't seem to notice or care. Her thoughts didn't matter, however. Only actions counted when it came to Tomás Garza and his overwhelming appeal, and she planned to take exactly no action whatsoever.

On the day of their third meeting, Erica had a full day of driving—from Albuquerque to Santa Fe, then finally to Las Vegas. Her schedule was crammed with business and she felt harried and overwrought, with no time to think of herself or her own needs. Thank goodness there were only twenty-four hours in a single day. Certainly she could survive anything for twenty-four hours…as long as nothing went wrong. She said a silent prayer to the patron saint of women on the verge, feeling as if she just might survive.

Then her cell phone rang. "Erica? It's Tomás."

She felt an instant tightening of her stomach brought on by the attraction she couldn't quite keep under wraps. But a wariness came quickly on its heels. She focused on that instead of the way her blood pounded through her veins just hearing his voice, trying to work herself back into the harried, annoyed state, which felt safer at this point.

And anyway, why was he calling now?

Experience had proven, whenever a client called on the day of a meeting, it usually meant something was about to go wrong. She sighed quietly, glanced at the dashboard clock and noted it was already noon. She had another forty-five minutes before she'd even reach Las Vegas and the mere prospect of food.

As if on cue, her stomach growled—a loud, petulant sound. This commuting frankly sucked, and it hadn't even been a month. She was hungry and sleep deprived, not to mention overbooked, overworked and less than overjoyed to hear Tomás's voice, because she didn't have time for problems. On the other hand, the sound of his voice had revved her heart, made her feel giddy and lacking control of her emotions. That bothered her, too. Maybe even more so. But, the business problem.

Focus on that.

She regularly fielded frantic calls from nervous brides at all times of the day and night, but those were symptomatic of what she'd deemed prenuptial psychosis. They went with the territory, and she accepted them as such. She'd hoped this assignment with Hope Garza would be more worry free, though. It wasn't a wedding, it was a teenage girl's coming-out party. That's it. Her jaw tightened in preparation for the bad news, while her traitorous stomach quavered at the sound of his breathing on the other end of the line.

"Erica? Hello? Can you hear me?"

Disguising her dread—and her desire—as much as possible, she punched her car phone on to hands-free mode, white-knuckled the steering wheel, and said, "Hi, Tomás. Sorry, I was in a cell phone no-man's-land," she ad-libbed. "What's up?"

"Don't worry, I'm not canceling our appointment."

His unexpected insight startled her, but, after a moment, she smiled. "So you're a mind reader, too?"

"Jack-of-all-trades, lady."

She heard playfulness in his tone, which eased her tension a bit. Her grip loosened on the wheel.

"Plus, I know you're swamped and I respect that your time is valuable. I wouldn't cancel at the last minute like this unless there was a real emergency."

Last minute? Yeah, right. She'd had brides cancel appointments forty-five minutes *after* they were supposed to have commenced, all the while making it seem like Erica's fault. Five hours prior seemed overly gracious in comparison, and she chalked up a mental point in his favor. "What's up, then?"

"Would it be too much trouble to change meeting locations?"

Was that all? Her anxiety dissipated completely. She almost laughed. "Not at all. I don't care where we meet." As long as it wasn't a secluded hotel room. Yeah right— she wished. She shook that unbidden thought away. "Where were you thinking?"

"Ever met at a kids' soccer field before?"

"Uhhh—"

His tone became apologetic. "I know. Not so conducive to productivity. Hope's coach requires one parent to be at each practice to monitor, so we rotate. It's not my evening, but I made a switch with the goalie's mom. She was desperate, Erica. I couldn't say no."

What a guy. Never penalize a single dad who came through for his daughter in a pinch—that was her new motto. And there was that whole single-fathers-are-hot theme again, tripping her up, making her tummy flutter. She fought the inevitable but unwelcome allure, reminding herself as she did so that it really didn't matter in the scheme of things. Actions counted; lurid thoughts did not. She could fantasize about Tomás all she wanted, so long as she kept her hands where they belonged.

"I can't say that I've ever conducted business at a soccer field before," she told him, "but the fresh air might do me good. I've spent so much damn time in my car the past few weeks." He made a sympathetic sound on the other end, which pleased her. "Let me pull over so you can give me directions."

Five hours or so later, Erica sat next to Tomás on the sun-warmed metal bleachers. The air smelled of freshly mown grass, and all around her swirled the sounds of exuberant team talk, the coach's whistle and the distinctive *toonk* of cleat against soccer ball.

They attempted to talk business, and *did* manage to get the location for the fiesta hammered out. They also discussed how much Hope was enjoying her volunteer work with MS patients at the hippotherapeutic horse ranch. She wasn't doing much more than mucking out stalls at this point, but the director of the program had praised Hope for her kindness with the clients and said she had a natural ability with the horses. By fall, he planned on having her participating fully with the riding. As interesting as the conversation was, Erica kept getting distracted by the action on the field. She'd never been much of a team-sport gal in high school, but watching Hope and the other athletes interact made her wish she had joined in. It looked fun.

When the coach called for an impromptu scrimmage, pairing his team with one practicing on another field, she and Tomás abandoned the business agenda altogether in exchange for watching Hope run roughshod over her competition. She really stood out amongst the others. Hope, a forward, Erica learned, had just scored her second goal, bounding back for the hugs of her teammates with her arms raised, when Erica turned to Tomás.

"She's really good. I'm talking, college scholarship good."

Tomás absolutely glowed from the compliment, his eyes fixed on his daughter. "Yeah, she is. She never runs out of energy." He crossed his fingers. "And here's to that scholarship idea."

"I'm serious. Where'd she get her athletic ability? Should I start calling you a jock of all trades?" she teased, jostling her shoulder against him, an uncharacteristic move.

For a moment, he was silent. Finally, he pulled the elastic from his hair—a nervous gesture, probably—and let the westerly breeze brush the loose strands back from his forehead. "From her mother, actually."

Her mother? He paused, but not long enough for Erica to

fill the silence with the stammered apology that immediately came to mind for prying into his personal life.

Staring off into nowhere, his gaze obviously focused inward, he said, "Racquel was an athlete in high school until…" He let that thread drop. "A natural. She played varsity soccer, volleyball. She probably would've played softball, too, if the seasons didn't overlap. Me, I've always been an art and music guy." He made a rueful face. "A geek, in other words."

To Erica's way of thinking, artists, musicians and scholars topped the sexy list and weren't even close to being geeky. But she knew better than to veer off onto that mental tangent. Not with six-feet worth of untouchable sexy sharing a bench with her in the warm, spring sunshine. No way, no how.

"Racquel," Erica repeated slowly, bypassing the geeky versus sexy debate altogether.

He turned to her, one eyebrow raised in question.

"You've just…never said her name before."

His jaw tightened, and he laced his fingers together slowly, his gaze tracking Hope's maneuvers on the field. "Well, it's not that great of a memory."

"Did you love her?" Dear God. Erica had no idea where the audacious question had come from and wanted to smack herself for having voiced it. Where was her brain?

She was a nosy idiot. But the thing was, curiosity had gotten the better of her. She *did* sort of…want to know. He'd fathered a child with Racquel and still considered their relationship a bad memory. Was it Racquel's leaving that had made it bad, or had it never been good? And if it had never been good, why had they made love?

Teenage hormones? Heat of the moment?

This was SO none of Erica's damn business.

But, at the same time, she found she really wanted him to answer. Something about the soothing spring warmth, the casual comfort of sharing the bleachers with him after a hellish day, made her want to know this man better, to gain insight beyond what he put out there for the world at large to observe and assess. He was so inaccessible, at the same time so present and engaged with his family, so completely *in* his insular life.

A tiny swirl of envy rushed through her. She reached up and tucked her breeze-tousled hair behind her ear, waiting for him to reply, worrying he would, instead, tell her exactly what he thought of her intrusive questions.

He shrugged, not meeting her eyes. "Puppy love, maybe. Lust, definitely. We thought we loved each other, but we were kids. Damn, we were so young. I didn't realize how young until Hope started getting older. Then it really hits you, no? I mean, think about it. When I was Hope's age, I was already…" He ended that thought with a shudder, then leaned back, elbows bent and resting on the bleacher level behind them. The pose looked casual, but tension had deepened the lines around his eyes. "You really don't want to hear this stuff, Erica. It's ancient history."

Time to backpedal. She flashed him a contrite, quick smile. "You know, I shouldn't have asked."

"Nothing wrong with curiosity."

A hot arrow of humiliation zinged through her. She had no right. "I know. But I'm well aware that it's none of my business. I just wond—"

The subject was effectively dropped when, on the field, Hope successfully stole the ball from an opposing player and made it down the field on guts and fancy footwork alone for a third, daring goal. A roar of cheering ensued. Tomás and Erica stood, clapping and whooping along with everyone else on the sidelines. Tomás placed his pinky fingers in the corners of his mouth and let go with a long warbling whistle. A distinctive sound.

It was as though Hope just realized her father was in the stands. She turned toward the sound of his whistle, all smiles and wind-whipped energy, then stopped short. Her eyes

widened, mouth forming an O shape before she broke back
into a grin and waved wildly. They raised their hands in
response, then once again took their seats. Hope returned
her attention to the game, stealing a peek toward them
whenever the ball wasn't in play.

Erica found it endearing that the girl couldn't keep her
emotions off her face if she tried.

"I didn't tell her you were meeting me here," Tomás
explained, clearly having caught Hope's expression, too. "I
didn't even tell her I would be here, actually. No time to."

"Ah. I wondered about the surprised look."

"I figured."

She looked at him sidelong. "You're very intuitive."

"Eh. I'm an artistic type. Goes with the whole right brain
thing, I suppose." A pause stretched between them, and
when he spoke again, his tone had lowered. "She really
likes you, you know." He sounded chagrined. Scared, even.

She wanted to set him at ease, to assure him that she
wasn't about to trounce on his precious daughter's feelings
or force herself into the girl's life. But she knew instinctively that words would never be enough to convince Tomás
Garza of her intentions. Life had taught him a few hard
lessons, and she knew only actions would make him believe.
Time would prove to him what words could not, and actually, it took the pressure off.

"She's a sweet girl." She hesitated, weighing her next
words before garnering the courage to voice them. Maybe
if he knew how she really felt, he'd relax. "I have to admit,
I was apprehensive she and I wouldn't get along."

Tomás pulled his chin back with surprise. "Why's that?
Hope gets along with everyone."

Erica shrugged, feeling a little ridiculous. She leaned
back, mirroring Tomás's pose, then crossing her arms beneath her breasts. "Oh, you know. It's not about her." She
flipped her hand, then tucked it back in the crook of her
other elbow. "I'm just never around kids. I don't know how

to treat them, or what to do and not to do around them. To gain their respect, I mean.''

A smile spread over Tomás's face. ''Why, Erica Gonçalves. You're afraid of kids.''

It wasn't a question, and Erica felt like a colossal fool. ''Um...yeah. Sort of.'' She closed her eyes and let the breeze cool her shame-heated cheeks. ''They *are* scary.''

Her admission of vulnerability seemed to endear her to him, and he chuckled, soft and low. ''I can't believe it.''

She scowled. ''It's not *that* unusual, Tomás. Especially for those of us who don't have contact with them.''

''What about nieces and nephews?''

She pulled one corner of her mouth to the side. ''Sorry. I'm an only child.''

''I am, too.'' He ran a hand through his hair. ''But truly, there is only one golden rule for dealing with kids.''

''Which is?''

''Keep it real. Kids can spot a phony from a mile away, and they're relentless with the punishment.''

''Good to know,'' she murmured, although the advice seemed a little too amorphous to be helpful. Keep it real? So she was supposed to tell Hope that she really didn't like kids, never wanted them and felt uncomfortable around them? Oh, yeah. Great plan. That would go over like a seven-thirty curfew.

''So, what about you, Erica?''

The question had come out of nowhere. She blinked in confusion. ''What about me, what?''

''I blurted out my fantastic track record in the romance department.'' He lifted one ankle to rest it across the opposite knee, his head cocked to one side. ''Tit for tat.''

''Oh. That.'' How had she set herself up for this one? And really, he'd told her what? The tale of Hope's mother? Surely one fourteen-years-past high school lustfest didn't comprise his entire track record. ''You actually only told me one thing.''

"So tell me one thing."

His request felt both intrusive and intimate. She felt anxious about sharing, but she didn't want to come off as a cold fish. Not to mention the fact that he seemed interested was flattering. Plus, she'd been around the Garzas enough to know that she needed to develop rapport with him, as well as his daughter, and it wasn't as if her love life held any spectacular secrets anyway, so what did she care? She had nothing to hide.

A single beat passed. "Pathetic as this will sound, there's nothing to tell. No hidden male versions of Racquel in my background, if that's what you're asking." Her arms tightened over her stomach, warding off the feeling of exposure. "Honestly, I'm your pretty dull career woman." She flashed a quick, brittle smile. "What you see is what you get."

His languid gaze swept her from head to toe, not in a leering manner, but more like a caress. "Nice advertising."

She glanced down, unsure how to take the compliment. Unsure if it had been a compliment at all. Inside, however, her body flooded with pleasure.

"No serious relationships?" he added, as though he hadn't just made a flirtatious remark. His focus was disconcerting. It made her recall the meeting when they'd first been introduced. As he had that day, he sat so still now, studied her with a sort of reined-in intensity that struck her low and deep. Tomás, it seemed, could unnerve her with one long glance.

"No great loves?" he added, when she still hadn't replied.

She swallowed tightly, feeling as if she needed, suddenly, to make herself clear to him once more. Maybe to herself. He'd said he would never hit on her, but things seemed to have shifted slightly between them. The ground beneath her felt unfamiliar now, unsteady, like a beach as the tide washed in and back out. This was a perfect opportunity to reiterate her stance, one she couldn't let pass by. "I do have one great love."

"Yeah?" His eyes squinted against the glare of the low, early-evening sun.

"Yeah." She steadied her gaze on him. "Independence."

A moment passed, and then realization dawned. "Ahhh, *bueno*. I understand. A renaissance woman. No men for you."

Erica stiffened. Although she certainly deserved a payback dig after the assumptions she'd made about him during their first meeting, his knee-jerk assessment sort of annoyed her. Why the all-too-common presumption that a woman who wanted her independence didn't like men? Because real women were supposed to want to become subservient to their men, as her mother had with her father? No thanks. "I never said no men. I just meant…no long-term."

"Well, well, well, Erica Gonçalves. The longer we talk, the more interesting it gets." He nudged her thigh with his own. His casual mood was in direct contrast to her prickliness. "Are you trying to tell me you're a player? You go, girl."

She scoffed, but her hackles lowered. She couldn't maintain her affront when his attitude was so playful, and really, why maintain it? Their relationship had never been acrimonious, and he was only teasing. "Very amusing, Tomás. Highly amusing."

"I do my best."

They were silent for a moment, watching the game. Her mind wasn't on it, and she had a feeling his wasn't, either. Suddenly, she realized she wanted to tell him why commitment scared her, to explain what had prompted her to value her independence so highly. She wanted this man to understand her, to really *get* who she was deep inside. "It's because of my mom, actually. Or perhaps my dad. Both of them."

"Excuse me?"

''My need for independence.'' She sighed. ''I don't think parents even realize what they do to you sometimes, how their choices ultimately affect your choices.''

Now he looked intrigued. But, of course. He was a parent—a father striving for that all-too-impossible goal when it came to raising children: perfection. Any insight he could get, it seemed, he'd soak in.

So she told him about her mom and her dad, about who they'd each been before they met, and after. About the pressure they sometimes exerted in relation to her desire for self-sufficiency, especially her mother. She told him everything, who knows why—a client, for God's sake—and when she was finished his expression softened with empathy and respect. Maybe even desire?

She wouldn't think about that. It was probably all in her mind anyway. Still, she twisted her mouth. ''You think I'm a big commitmentphobe now, don't you? A woman with issues. I should've kept my mouth shut.''

''No. Not at all. I understand all too well.''

''You do?''

He nodded, and his jaw tensed a few times before he spoke. ''After Racquel left, well…Hope was too young to understand, but I hurt like hell. For her.''

''For her?'' Erica raised one eyebrow, skeptical.

''Maybe for myself, too. Who knows?'' His eyes reflected remembered pain. After a moment, he blinked and shook it off. ''I discount it because I was *so* young. But really, I thought I'd hurt forever. I finally resolved my pain when I realized how drastically my priorities had changed. I suddenly had someone depending on me, someone to put first in life from there on out. And I vowed I would never again place Hope in the position of being abandoned by someone she loved.'' He shrugged. ''So, yeah, I understand your choices. I don't date much, either, and no one comes home to meet my daughter. No one.''

I did, Erica thought, but immediately checked herself. She was a business contact, not a date.

Business contact or not, Shallow Erica felt suddenly buoyed to realize exactly *why* Tomás said he'd never hit on her. Not because he didn't find her attractive, but because he was trying to protect his daughter. Misguided. But also understandable, admirable and truly sweet. And a relief, thought Shallow Erica, her fickleness rearing its ugly head again.

At the same time, Reasonable Mature Erica also wondered about Tomás, the man. Questioned his explanation in ways that were none of her business—to the extreme. He claimed to be protecting his daughter, but wasn't he mostly protecting himself?

None of your business. She swallowed, weighed her thoughts, took the middle ground. She had to make some comment, after all. "I respect how you've raised her, Tomás."

Let it drop, Erica. Don't say any more.

Her hesitation, unfortunately, spoke volumes.

"But?"

"But nothing."

"But?" he persisted.

"Well…" She scratched her cheek, buying time, searching for a diplomatic route, willing herself just to shut the hell up before she said too much. "I just imagine…it's got to be difficult at times. For you."

He hiked one shoulder, the motion defensive, almost evasive. "I've got Ruby. I've got Hope. I've got my art, which I love. My jack-of-all-trades stuff. What more do I need?"

What about sex? she wanted to ask. Adult companionship? He was a virile, sensual man. An insightful conversationalist. What about all that? She bit her bottom lip, a reminder to filter her thoughts, for once in her life, before she verbalized them. Tomás was a client, no matter what this deceptively casual yet intimate conversation made her imagine. Not only that, but she was drawn to him. Big time. The very last topic she wanted to broach with him was sex.

"I'm not celibate, if that's what you're thinking," said the mind reader. "My daughter comes first, but I'm no priest."

"I didn't—" She pressed her lips together, unable to lie.

He slanted her a sly glance, looking pleased that he'd read her correctly…and shocked her. "It's okay. Like I'm sure you do, I take care of my needs. Just…no long-term. No one serious." He thought about that for a moment. "Or maybe I should say, no one temporary for Hope to get attached to. It's pretty much a balancing act."

Her face instantly heated, and she glanced down at her hands, then out at the playing field. Unexpectedly, her middle clenched with something that felt remarkably like jealousy. So Tomás was getting his groove on with various willing women when the need arose. Okay. It made sense. It shouldn't bother her. It shouldn't…but it did.

"I don't put the…fulfillment of those needs ahead of my goal of giving Hope a good life," he persisted, as though attempting to reel her back into the conversation.

Fine, she'd bite. It would do them both good to lay all their cards out on the table once and for all. After a moment, when her heartbeat regulated enough for her to pull off a fairly believable rendition of nonchalance, she said, "Just like I don't put those needs ahead of my goal of independence, I guess. In answer to your suspicions, no, I'm not a player. But I'm no ingenue, either. I'm twenty-eight years old and single by choice, and I know my way around my own needs."

He studied her for one long, sun-drenched and intimate moment. "We're a lot alike, Erica. You and I." His tone was rough, deep. Sand-washed and warm at the same time.

She knew just how on target that assessment was, and she felt so surrounded by it, by him. The jealous feeling faded but didn't entirely disappear. How could it, with the mental images of Tomás making love to any number of faceless, nameless woman engulfing her mind? His wide, smoothly muscled back. Long hair sweeping over one shoulder. Ugh. She had to stop. Right now.

Picturing a client making love was *so* out of line, so dangerous, and yet oh so easy to do when that client was Tomás Garza. Those women might not have all of him, but they sure as hell had more of him than she'd ever have. Another jealous stab.

Forget about it, Erica. You don't want that, remember?

"I think, maybe, we are," she managed, finally. "Alike, I mean." A thoughtful, awkward pause stretched between them, and Erica stared unseeing at the soccer field, wondering just what images Tomás Garza saw in his head....

Chapter Six

Before their uncomfortably personal conversation could continue, Hope bounded up to the bottom of the bleachers, all clean sweat, adrenaline and innocence. Her appearance was like a bucket of slush on the heat of their revelations, and Erica had never been quite so grateful for an interruption.

"Hi, Erica!"

"Well, hello there, star player."

The young girl beamed, her cheeks reddened from wind and exertion. She looked utterly pleased to see them. "I didn't know you were coming to my practice. You neither, Dad."

Tomás reached out and tugged Hope's ear. "That makes three of us. I'm filling in for Becca's mom." He hiked his chin toward the field. "Looking good out there, baby."

"Thanks." Hope glanced furtively around, then leaned in. Her voice was a rasp. "Don't call me that in front of the team, Dad. I've told you a million times."

Tomás held up both hands in surrender.

Appeased, Hope tucked her choppy, messy hair behind her ears, her expression turning earnest and unabashedly hopeful. Grass stains marred her purple shin guards, as well as one cheekbone, and a small clump of sod clung to her hair. "Is Erica coming to pizza with us?"

"Ask her, baby. Oops. *Hope.*" He laughed as his daughter scowled at him. "She's sitting right in front of you."

The girl's expression filled with something winsome and needy, something that tugged at Erica's heart in a way she hadn't experienced before. "We always have pizza together after Friday-night practice. The team, I mean. It's perfect, because Grandma Ruby has her computer class so she eats there."

Erica raised an eyebrow at Tomás. "Computer class?"

He smirked. "That's our Ruby. If there's an information superhighway, by God, she wants to be behind the wheel of the biggest vehicle on it."

"Will you come with us?" Hope continued, moving forward to gently touch the sleeve of Erica's loose linen blazer. She rubbed the fabric lightly between her fingers. "Please."

Erica blinked in surprise at the earnestness in Hope's invitation, at the unexpected touch. "Oh…well—"

"Please? Pretty please? You like pizza, don't you? If not, we can go somewhere else, just you, Dad and me," she suggested in a rush, as though desperate to avoid a refusal. "I don't care either way. I love pizza, but I'll eat anything, mostly. Especially if I don't have to clean up. So if you hate pizza—"

"Oh, no. It's not that. I love pizza."

"Who doesn't?" Tomás interjected, lobbing the ball back into Erica's court. He looked at her with something like challenge.

Brave enough to join us, Ms. Single by Choice?

Hope's eyes positively sparkled. "Then you'll come with us?" Well, Erica had certainly backed herself into a corner.

She should've said she was allergic to pizza. Allergic to eating out in general. Then again—she cut a glance at Tomás's casually crossed feet—she was never one to back down from a challenge. Plus, the more time she spent with Hope now, the easier things would likely be when they spent time alone together. Familiarity would put the girl at ease. It would put Erica at ease, too.

Okay, nice rationalizations, but that's all they were. A silly front. The raw truth was, she had begun to enjoy the time spent with Tomás, to crave it. The prospect of dinner with him and his daughter was actually enticing. Wouldn't her mother be jubilant to hear that?

But, really. Now that Erica knew where he stood, and vice versa, she felt safer, too…from him, from her own traitorous feelings toward him. There was no risk of losing her independence when it came to Tomás, because the man wanted romantic entanglements even less than she did. So what did she have to fear? A night out with him and his daughter, more time in his intoxicating presence—what was the harm in that?

"I'd love to come." She toyed with her gold charm necklace and addressed Tomás. "If that's all right with you, of course."

He slid his sunglasses from the top of his head onto his face, then gave her a droll, mirrored-lens glance she couldn't read. "Oh, I think we'll muddle through." One corner of his mouth quivered as though he were trying to hold back a smile.

"Yay!" Hope danced around, then plopped unceremoniously and noisily onto the bleachers to remove her cleats, replacing them with plastic Nike flip-flops worn over her white socks. "What kind of crust do you like, Erica? Thick or thin?"

Erica tilted her head to the side, squinting as she considered the question. "Thin."

"Me, too." Hope smirked at her father. "Is that SO cool,

Dad? She likes thin, too, so two against one. We win. He likes pan pizza,'' she added, for Erica's benefit, sticking out her tongue with abject disgust.

"Shocking," Erica said, in a wry tone.

Tomás snorted.

"It's way too bready. Blech. Hello, *carbs!*" Hope said, as if that should be explanation enough. "Are you ready to go?"

They stood, their footsteps clanging loudly on the metal bleachers as they descended. When the adults reached the bottom, Hope moved between them and slipped one hand into her father's grasp, the other shyly into Erica's.

Surprised, but touched by the spontaneous and childlike gesture, Erica squeezed.

"Maybe you can come to one of my games, too, Erica."

"Erica's a very busy woman, Hope," Tomás said, in a bit of a growl. "Don't pressure her."

Hope's face registered the chastisement immediately, the light in her eyes dimming ever so slightly. "Sorry."

"It's no pressure," Erica said quietly, knowing Tomás was warning Erica herself as much as his daughter with that growly tone. "But I am really busy. I can't make any promises, but I'd love to see one of your games if it works with my schedule."

"Okay." Hope accepted the answer easily. In one of her more childlike moments, she swung their arms high, skipping.

Erica glanced over at Tomás over the top of Hope's messy head, but she couldn't decipher his expression behind the shades. His lips were in a straight line, though.

Concentration? Irritation?

Or was she reading more into his expression than she should?

She almost caught herself pulling away from Hope so she didn't annoy him by being too familiar with the girl, but she discarded the notion as quickly as it had popped into her head. No way could she let go of the small hand. She knew how Tomás felt about people coming in and out of Hope's life, but their relationship wasn't about that. One— she was a business associate. Two—she needed to develop rapport with his daughter. To release Hope's hand might relieve Tomás's fears, but it would hurt Hope's feelings, and Erica just couldn't do that. The girl was a star athlete, the apple of her father's eye and as uncomplicated as a teenager could be—which wasn't saying much—but she was vulnerable, too. Anyone with enough distance and perspective could see that. Erica simply wasn't willing to hurt the child just to appease the father.

And, really, wasn't that his biggest worry about letting people close? That Hope would feel the kind of pain he'd felt when Racquel left?

Erica wouldn't be a person who would hurt Hope.

If only Tomás could believe that.

If only he'd realize, on that particular issue, their goals were identical.

Hope smiled up at her, and Erica winked back, feeling embraced, feeling Hope's hand in hers fully, as though the moment were suspended in time due to its perfection. Her heart expanded, and she realized, right then, that she'd broken her vow to stay detached with the Garzas. Full-out.

Her stomach tightened, a physical warning sign of danger, but she pushed it away. What was a little hand-holding? One harmless pizza dinner? It's not like either one would change her long-held goals in life. For God's sake, Tomás Garza didn't even want her. He had Hope and Ruby and any number of inconsequential women to slake his more masculine needs. She was hired help, so that was *that*. No problems here.

She liked Hope. Hope liked her. Beyond that, nothing much mattered. Erica lifted her chin, undeterred, and held the girl's hand a little tighter.

* * *

They took separate cars to the pizza joint because, as Tomás was quickly learning, Erica was the kind of woman who always needed an "out." No problem. He could dig that, could respect it even. In the few short weeks they'd known each other, he'd learned more than he'd ever planned to about the woman who had unexpectedly turned his life inside out.

He knew now that she was afraid of his daughter, and yet so innately good with her that Hope was smitten like only a fourteen-year-old girl could be.

He also knew Erica was no threat to his way of life, because the last thing she wanted was a family tying her down. And he knew, for some reason, that knowing this about Erica Gonçalves bothered him deep inside, in the small place no one ever touched. Why? Because, if he fell for her, if he let himself be that weak, she would eventually leave. Just like Racquel had.

And that made Erica wholeheartedly off-limits.

The big problem…he *could* fall for her. He knew this instinctively, just from the contact they'd shared so far.

"Are you mad at me, Dad?"

Tomás started at the sound of Hope's voice beside him in the truck. He roused, as if from a deep sleep, replaying the few minutes since they'd left the soccer fields. They'd entered the truck as any other day. She'd punched the seek button on the stereo until she found a teenybop pop station she loved, and then she'd just sat back, humming softly to the music, right thumb hooked beneath the shoulder strap of her seat belt.

It was normal, everyday stuff. And yet it wasn't.

His body sat in the car next to his daughter, but his mind was in the red Honda Accord they were following. He just hadn't realized Hope had been attuned to him. Reaching over, he patted her knee. "Of course not, baby. Why would you think that?"

"I don't know. You're quiet."

A beat passed. "I have a lot on my mind is all. A lot of work," he added, lest she take it for a conversational opening he didn't want it to be. She took it anyway.

"Is it...okay that I asked Erica to pizza?" Her voice sounded small, forlorn. Almost as if she feared censure.

He glanced over at the winsome features of his daughter and melted. At the same time, his guard raised. Had Hope inherited a little of that intuitiveness that ran in his family? Had she guessed how attracted he was to Erica? God, he hoped not. "Of course. It's fine."

Hope smiled, the motion pulling dimples into her cheeks. "Good. I really like Erica, Dad. She's so cool."

"I do, too."

"You do? That's so awesome."

He paused, weighing his next words, but knowing they had to be voiced. Better now than when Hope had become completely hooked. "I like her, Hope. But I want you to keep in mind that Erica is someone we've hired to help plan the *quinceañera.* Okay? Don't forget that."

"I know, Dad. So?"

"So...so she's not a friend."

Hope clicked her tongue. "Geez, that's not very nice."

"I didn't mean it that way. She...she is a friend."

"You just said she wasn't!"

He pressed his lips together, frustrated, wishing he were better at this. "What I mean is... I'm trying to tell you not to get too attached to her. Once the *quinceañera* is over, Erica will move on to other jobs. Because we are a job for her." He paused, letting this sink in.

Hope's bottom lip stuck out a little bit. "She doesn't treat us like a job."

"That's what makes her good at what she does." When he spoke again, he softened his tone. Everything Hope had interjected was true, but it didn't alter the bottom line. "What I'm saying is that she's not going to be a permanent part of our lives, Hope. Do you understand?"

Hope's skinny chest rose and fell with a long, deep breath. She gripped the seat belt tighter and stared out the passenger-side window. "I understand, Dad. I'm not a baby, you know. I understand a lot more than you think."

She did. And that's what scared him. If Hope took cues from his feelings, she just might glom on to the elusive, unreachable Erica. Damned if he wasn't feeling a little magnetized himself. But he had to stop it now. If he wasn't careful, he and his daughter would fall for her completely, and then she would leave, because Erica Gonçalves didn't want a man and she didn't want children. Period. And he and Hope were a package deal.

"Let's just enjoy dinner, *m'ija*. Okay? Erica doesn't need pressure from…" Us, he almost said. Pressure from *us* to be more than she had any desire to be. He licked his lips. "She doesn't need pressure from clients. Okay?"

"Okay."

"I love you, baby."

Hope sat still for a moment, then slipped off the shoulder strap of her seat belt and scooted closer to nestle her head on his shoulder as she'd done since she was a tiny toddler. "Love you, too, Daddy."

He felt stronger, could see his priorities again instead of the distracting image of Erica Gonçalves clouding his vision. He had everything he needed right in this truck, and he'd done so well for the past fourteen years. He couldn't let a simple case of animal attraction get in the way of keeping his promises. If he never did a single other worthwhile thing in his life, he would protect Hope. He'd made that vow to himself fourteen years ago, and it was up to him to keep it. If that meant distance from Erica, except within the context of what he'd hired her to do, so be it.

God, give me the strength to stay away from her.

He reached over and wrapped an arm around Hope's slim shoulders, then planted a kiss on the top of her head. "We'll be fine, you and I, no?"

A pause. "Sure."

The word sounded bland, resigned, and a seed of fear sprouted within him. He squeezed her shoulders, swallowing back his worry. "Hope and Daddy against the world?"

For the first time in as long as he could remember, Hope didn't echo the words back at him.

On Wednesday of the following week, Tomás, Hope and their surprisingly enjoyable pizza dinner were the furthest things from Erica's mind. She generally worked half days on Wednesdays, but nothing was ever predictable in her line of work. Long after she was supposed to have been off duty, she sat in the quickly darkening apartment she'd rented in Las Vegas, making one frantic phone call after another and getting nowhere fast.

The problem? A wedding—scheduled in exactly three days, starring the uninvolved, whatever-you-want-honey groom and the high-maintenance bride who couldn't seem to grasp the concept of screw-the-details, enjoy-the-day— had just officially gone to hell. Erica'd been sure she had every last component of the event firmly in hand, and she'd been overjoyed that the end was in sight. She had even promised herself a spa day as a reward for the suffering, and when she closed her eyes, she could almost feel the full-body sugar scrub and mud pack, could smell the eucalyptus facial mask.

Then the band she'd hired for the reception canceled.

God, she was so screwed.

You'd think there would be one damn band available to fill in at the last minute, but so far, nada. Her list of options was quickly dwindling down to nothing, and she knew she'd have to alert the Bride from Hell pretty soon. Wouldn't *that* be a party?

Forget bands, she thought, pouring more wine into the jelly jar she'd snatched from the cupboard and fighting the panic that tried to seize her at every turn. Who said people had to dance at a wedding anyway? Why couldn't she just order extra alcohol, rent a karaoke machine, and call it a day? Why couldn't brides be flexible? Maybe she should flee the state.

And maybe she'd recover, eventually, from what this gaffe would do to her reputation in the biz.

Damn. So much for referrals.

She'd just hung up the phone—another no-can-do—and had threaded all ten fingers into the front of her hair, wondering how much actual force it would take to yank it out, when the doorbell rang. It was the first time she'd heard the noise since she'd moved into this temporary home, and, for a moment, it confused her. She glanced up. Long tendrils of golden afternoon sunshine reached in through the sheer-covered windows of the tiny, slightly shabby living room, reminding her that it would soon be evening.

T minus two days and a few hours to the wedding and no band. She sat immobile and stared at the door emitting Go Away vibes, but the annoying bell ignored her and chimed again.

Get up, Erica. Answer it.

She stood, glancing down to realize that she'd only half changed out of her workday clothes before all hell had broken loose on the wedding front. She still wore the black silk skirt, sheer hose and pumps, but instead of the single-breasted, shawl-collared jacket that went with it, she wore a sports bra under a tattered Curious George Rides a Bike T-shirt, her favorite garment in which to work out—something she'd planned on doing before the blasted phone call had screwed up her day.

She looked like a half-dressed slob, and yet she just didn't care. It was after six o'clock. She didn't need to look pulled together anymore. She didn't *feel* pulled together—far from it. This was her time, and she could wear what she damn well pleased, especially since her professional life was in the garbage anyway. Wait a minute—after six?

Erica stopped short in the middle of the living room, fist clutched against her mouth. Oh, no! Her heart took up a rapid, dread-laden thudding in her chest. She and Tomás had a meeting scheduled for five o'clock. She was almost ninety minutes late already! Damn. She had to rid her porch of whoever had fallen against her bell and then immediately call Tomás and grovel.

Two referrals lost in one afternoon. That was a record!

Disgusted with herself, she threw back the dead bolt, twisted the knob lock and yanked open the door prepared to say she didn't want whatever they were selling, she gave at the office and her priest didn't encourage the acceptance of door-to-door religious paraphernalia.

Instead she saw Tomás.

Her palm flew to her chest, and her breath whooshed out of her. "Oh, God, Tomás. I'm so sorry. I had a minor crisis arise and completely forgot about our appointment until just now."

He held both hands up to stop her apologetic barrage. "No sweat. I just wanted to stop by and make sure you were okay."

"I'm fi—actually, not so fine, but that's another story. I'm so sorry. Please come in." She stepped aside, sweeping her arm out in invitation. She had to admit, it was good to see a friendly face. It was good to see *his* face. "If you have time, I can give you a quick update. Though I've been working on other assignments and I don't really have much to report."

Tomás glanced back at his black truck, and Erica tracked his gaze. Hope sat in the passenger side of the idling vehicle and raised her hand for a wave. "Actually, I just picked up—"

"She can come in, too. Of course." She peered down at herself and then helplessly into the room behind her. "You'll have to forgive the state of things. Today has been nuts." Erica beckoned Hope in with hand signals. Hope reached over toward the driver's side of the truck, and the big black machine stopped idling. She jumped from the car, keys clutched in her palm, and started up the sidewalk with a huge smile on her face.

"We don't want to intrude," Tomás said, softly.

"Please. Intrude. I've had the worst day—but no, you don't want to hear about that." Erica closed her eyes and shook her head quickly, rattling out the stupid and trying to focus. "Hope's party. We can discuss that."

His eyes clouded with worry. "If you need to talk…"

"Oh, I don't know." Her stomach growled, and she pressed her palm against it. "Oops, sorry."

Tomás laughed. "Hey, I have a plan. You might be happy to know that we picked up some take-out dinner before stopping by." He aimed a thumb toward the truck over his shoulder. "There is more than enough to share if you'd like. We can bring it in."

"Hi, Erica," Hope said, breathless from bounding up the sidewalk. "Cool T-shirt."

"Thanks." She refocused on Tomás. "What about Ruby?"

"Ruby's actually in the hospital—"

"What? Oh, no."

Tomás shook his head. "Don't worry. It's for an IV steroid treatment. Five days, and today's the fifth one. She has them periodically. It's a good thing, really gives her an energy boost. We're going to visit her after dinner, actually, and she'll come home tomorrow morning."

"That's good, then."

Tomás smiled at her, and then to Hope, "*M'ija,* go get the bags. We're going to eat with Erica."

"Really? That rocks!" Hope loped back toward the truck.

Moments later, she returned, and Erica glanced at the white bags the girl held, smelled the enticing odors of *posole* and green chile emanating from within their waxy interiors. "Bless you, you're a lifesaver. I hadn't even thought about eating but my stomach obviously has other ideas.'' She pre-ceded them into the house, glancing back over her shoulder. ''Give me a minute to clean off the table. I've been work-ing.''

''We don't mind,'' Hope said, boldly crossing the thresh-old and peering around the interior. She set the bags on the kitchen counter and turned toward Erica. ''Where are your dishes, Erica? I'll set the table.''

Erica waved vaguely toward the cabinets. ''You know, hon, I haven't lived here long enough to know, and the place came fully furnished. Feel free to look around.''

Tomás, meanwhile, had moved toward the table and was studying the label on the wine bottle. He glanced up and tilted the bottle toward Erica. ''May I join you?''

''Of course.'' She pointed at her makeshift glass, her cheeks flaming. ''You'll note I'm going the high-class route and drinking out of a jelly jar, but there may be more ap-propriate glassware in one of the cupboards.''

He grinned. ''I'm not too good for a jelly jar.''

''Here's one, Dad!''

The jar was passed off, and the simple gesture of Tomás choosing it instead of a wineglass charmed Erica. Flustered and happy, despite everything, she aimed Hope toward the refrigerator which held a selection of sodas.

Within minutes, they'd sat at the table, and their plates had been filled with steaming selections from a local res-taurant.

Tomás took a sip of his wine, then raised an eyebrow at Erica. ''So. Tell me what happened today.''

''Trust me, you don't want to know.''

''Oh, but I do. I didn't think anything would frazzle Erica Gonçalves. It's actually a relief to know you're human be-neath all that intimidating efficiency. Plus, it makes me aw-fully curious.'' He lifted his chin, indicating her T-shirt. ''Just like old George, I suppose.''

Erica looked down at her tattered top, then back up at

Tomás. She became aware of her muscles relaxing, one by one. It felt so good to be able to share this, to bring life back to a simple meal and conversation with people who cared. About her, not about what catering service she'd hired or how much money they could shave off a bill by using carnations rather than roses. She missed that simple intimacy. For one acute moment, she ached for dinners with her mom and dad so much it was a physical pain. Her growing up years *had* been wonderful.

"So?" Tomás sipped.

Following suit, she took a drink of her wine, too, then ran her tongue over her top lip. What the hell? Maybe it would help to vent. "You asked for it. I have a wedding this weekend with a bride who is…the spoiled youngest daughter and, shall we say, a little high maintenance."

"Sounds wonderful," he said, his comment laced with sarcasm.

Erica nodded. "We're down to the wire, and the band I'd hired for the reception had to back out at the last minute. A family emergency."

He winced. "That's rough, Erica. I'm sorry."

"Tell me." For a moment, guilt assailed her for focusing on her own inconvenience rather than the band member with a family emergency. She did, however, have a business to run. She sympathized, but that didn't negate her need to move on.

"The big problem is, I can't find a single band who can fill in on such late notice. I've even called as far away as Trinidad, Colorado. June is the traditional month for weddings, but this is late May—close enough—and everyone's been booked for months."

"My dad's in a band," Hope said, matter-of-fact. She blinked blandly at Erica, taking another bite of her *posole,* completely unaware of the ray of hope she'd just thrown on a very dark and dismal situation.

Stunned, Erica looked from the girl to the man. "She's kidding me, right? Is this another jack-of-all-trades thing?"

"It is, and she's not kidding." He quirked his mouth to one side. "Hey, when you're an obscure artist living in rural New Mexico, you do what you have to do to get by. It's a side thing for all of us, but we enjoy it."

It was too good to be true. Erica almost couldn't ask the question for fear her hopes had been raised for nothing. She set her fork gently against the edge of her plate before clasping her hands into a knot in her lap. "Does your band play weddings?"

"Weddings, house parties, you name it."

A tension-wrought pause ensued. "Are you…or I should say, is your band free this weekend?"

He raised his shoulders. "I can't speak for everyone, of course. I'd have to call the guys, but there's a good chance we could pull something together."

Without hesitation, Erica handed him the cordless phone. "Please. Make as many calls as you'd like. The wedding is in Santa Fe, and I'll need you for five hours plus prep. How many musicians in the band?"

"Three."

"I can pay you $1,500, plus a stipend for travel. I'll even put you all up in the hotel since it will be a late night."

"Can I come?" Hope's tone sounded plaintive but hopeful.

"Not now, Hope. Eat your dinner." Tomás started to dial.

No more than fifteen minutes later, their impromptu dinner had been eaten, and Erica had a replacement band. Her sense of relief was so strong, she poured a third jelly jar of wine and topped off Tomás's jar, as well, then raised hers for a toast. "You," she said, "are a lifesaver. I don't know what to say."

He clinked the threads of his jar against hers. "Here's to another successful business arrangement. What good is it being a jack-of-all-trades if you can't fill in at the last minute?''

"Daddy," Hope said quietly. "Can I please come?"

He pressed his lips together, reaching out to cover her small hand with his own. "I don't think so. This is work, and you should stay with Grandma Ruby, babe. She needs someone to look after her, and don't you ever tell her I said so."

"Why don't Hope and Ruby both come along?" Erica heard herself suggesting, unable to believe the words had come out of her mouth. She paused, hoping she'd just thought the suggestion instead of voicing it.

"Really?" Hope asked, astounded.

Damn. Erica swallowed. She had spoken aloud; no backing out now. "Sure. I'll put the band members up in the hotel, like I promised, but—" to Tomás "—Ruby and Hope can stay at my house where Ruby will be more comfortable."

Hope positively bounced in her seat. "Oh, Daddy. Can we? Can we please?"

Tomás studied Erica warily. "Are you sure?"

No. She wasn't sure at all. In fact, the only issue she felt sure about at this moment was her own insanity. "It will give me time to go over some traditions for the *quinceañera* with Ruby," Erica explained, selling the idea to herself more than to Tomás. "We haven't had much time to sit and talk, and I really need her input. This way, we can kill two birds with one stone."

"Please?" Hope said.

He smiled at his girl, and Erica could see that the man couldn't resist her if he tried. Did he ever try? Could anyone blame him if he didn't?

"It depends on what Grandma Ruby wants, but I'll ask her. If she isn't up to coming, you'll have to stay home. No complaining, okay?"

"Okay." Hope beamed. "I know she'll want to go, though. Staying home all the time is boring."

"Not when you're seventy-nine, baby."

"Hmph." Hope brushed off his comment, slanting a sly glance Erica's way. "Erica, maybe we can go visit the puppies in the pound while we're there."

"No puppies," Tomás said, his tone playfully stern. "Hope, we are not getting a dog, and that's final. Besides, this isn't a vacation for you or for Erica. She needs to work and you'll have to stay out of her way."

Hope dimmed for a moment from the no-puppy edict, but quickly recovered. "Okay, I will. I promise."

Tomás's gaze met Erica's, and something pulled between them. Something warm and sweet and connected. "I really owe you," she said, wanting to touch his hand much as he'd touched Hope's.

Tomás shook his head, denying the debt. "My pleasure. We haven't played a gig for a while. And instead of paying me my part, you can apply it to the balance I'll owe you for Hope's *quinceañera,* okay?"

"Whatever works for you. I'm just…really grateful. You have no idea."

He kept hold of her gaze, the moment hanging between them like an unanswered question. A question that had never and would never be asked. The corners of his mouth raised slowly into a soft, private smile that nearly did her in. Her tummy tightened, as did her throat. She found herself thinking she'd like to show Tomás just how grateful she was, to find out exactly how soft and talented those smiling lips could be, to touch him, to know him like none of his faceless, nameless, taking-care-of-his-needs women ever could.

Oh, God.

Her heart jolted to a stop, then immediately jump-started itself into a machine-gun rhythm. How had it happened? More to the point, why had it happened? And when? She was full-out infatuated with this unattainable man. Not good. Neither she nor Tomás had any interest in a relationship, probably not even in a fling. They were too close for that already. His world was way too complicated and she didn't have time—

She sighed inwardly. Okay, for a fling with Tomás Garza, she'd *make* the time, if it weren't completely outside the realm of possibilities, but it was. And yet, she still wanted him. Was that so unbelievable?

He was a beautiful, sexy man. Not only that but he was a good person, an amazing father. Hell yes, she wanted him. Not forever, but for now would be nice. *Joke's on you, Erica.*

Averting her eyes, she vowed to herself she must never, ever let on how she felt. It would complicate things beyond her level of comfort, and it could cost her a job. A referral.

"Seriously," she told him, her tone brisk and businesslike once again. She tossed her hair. "You're getting me out of a bind here and I appreciate it so much."

As if he'd read her illicit thoughts and wanted to make his position crystal clear, to reiterate his life goals so she wouldn't make the mistake of thinking she could change him, Tomás said the words she just didn't want to hear right then: "*De nada,* Erica. Stop thanking me. What are friends for?"

So that's how it's gonna be. Friends.

Nothing more. Nothing ever.

She'd known that all along—in fact she'd pushed for it. So she shouldn't feel let down. Yet, she did. More than she ever would've imagined. More than she'd ever admit.

Chapter Seven

Tomás had been sequestered in his studio all day, trying his best to complete his third historic-building piñata for the Cultural Arts Festival—a depiction of the Carnegie Library—before the unexpected weekend trip to Santa Fe. Built in 1903, the library's neoclassic revival design typified the Carnegie Park District and was a proud part of Las Vegas history. He had two traditional star piñatas to make for a children's party, too, not to mention a whole hell of a lot of work to do on getting Erica out of his mind.

The piñatas, he had a handle on. The other? Well…

Don't think about her.

But that was his problem. His hands stilled over the row of beige paper he'd been carefully gluing to the piñata before him. He couldn't stop thinking about her. He forced his hands, which were white and sticky from paste, back into action. He had deadlines, for God's sake. He couldn't sit here all day and moon over a woman he would never have.

He didn't know what he'd been thinking, agreeing to having his family spend the weekend at Erica's house in Santa Fe. If he was serious about keeping Hope from getting too attached, he'd screwed up something awful with that particular decision. But he hadn't been able to help himself. He was drawn to Erica with a strength that shook him. The very reason she attracted him, however, was the same reason he desperately needed to avoid her. She understood his aversion to bringing a new woman into their lives, indeed agreed with it as far as he could tell.

Which would be great, except…he really liked Erica.

Too much.

He hadn't been able to pinpoint when or how it happened, but he wanted her. In fact, if she walked out of his life right then, as little contact as they'd had, it would already hurt. That was how vulnerable he'd let himself become. How much would it hurt if he allowed himself—and his daughter—to become even more used to Erica's company, more dependent on her presence?

The pinking shears he held slipped and sliced his finger.

''Damn it.'' He tossed the shears aside disgustedly and pressed a scrap piece of tissue paper to the cut. After a moment, he lifted the paper and checked the cut. It wasn't bleeding much, but this lack of attention to detail wasn't like him, and it pissed him off.

He glanced around his studio, a large, airy barnlike structure he'd built himself, with the help of neighbors and friends. The wall facing away from the house was almost completely glass, drawing in the natural northern light he so loved to work by. He also liked to look out over the land his parents had worked so hard for, the legacy they'd left him. After all they'd done, the myriad ways they'd suffered to provide for him, he could not screw up his business, his life, his daughter's life over a woman.

Not even a woman so special as Erica Gonçalves.

Tomás closed his eyes and took in a deep breath through

his nose, blowing it out slowly as he fought to regroup, to focus on his craft, on the calming pleasure of working with his hands. It had always helped before when he had problems on his mind.

But not today.

Today, damn it. Now. Pull yourself together.

He let his eyes drift open slowly and he took in his surroundings, brought himself back to the touchstone of craft. Afternoon sun slanted through the glass wall, and his back and arms ached from the work. He liked to make his piñatas the old-fashioned way he'd learned from his own father, mixing a paste of starch and water by hand, until he could discern the proper consistency by feel. He still fashioned most of his piñatas around red clay pots he imported from Mexico, too. The shape of the historic buildings he was making for the Cultural Arts Festival lent themselves to more of a box shape as the base. Since they were display pieces rather than piñatas to be broken, he chose to use sealed fiberboard cubes as the foundations.

The first two sat finished on large sawhorse and plank worktables that stretched the full length of the studio at the far end. His first, based on the Benigno Romero house, built in 1874 and representing the Old Town Residential district, had turned out beautifully. He felt he'd done a fair rendition of the James H. Ward house, too, which had sat proudly in the Lincoln Park district of Las Vegas since 1883. It was one of New Mexico's finest examples of an Italianate villa, and transforming it into a recognizable replica in his medium hadn't been easy. But he'd pulled it off.

Las Vegas might be a small town, but its historic districts, which spread out from the Old Town Plaza like spokes in a wheel, boasted fine, well-preserved examples of nearly every important architectural style of home built in the United States between 1840 and 1940. Narrowing his choices down to seven hadn't been easy. But, so far, the art piñatas were coming along magnificently. It gave him pleasure to look at them, to know he'd be representing Las Vegas well in the festival. He'd done good work. Work he'd be proud to display.

Work he'd be proud to show Erica.

But, that wasn't the point now, was it? He snapped out a long strip of tissue angrily, disgusted at his own lack of self-control over the situation.

Behind him, the door creaked. He peered over his shoulder, keeping hold of the tissue. Ruby stopped in the doorway, smiling from her chair. She had a thermos in her lap, and she lifted it, waggling it toward him. "Fresh coffee."

"Bless you. Come on in."

He'd carefully planned the studio to be wheelchair accessible so Ruby could get out of the house whenever she felt the urge. He picked up the stereo remote and pointed it to the system, lowering the volume. Even Stevie Ray Vaughan guitar riffs pounding out from his speakers hadn't been able to block the incessant and disturbing thoughts in his head.

Ruby wheeled over to his table and then took in a deep breath, peering at the work in progress. Tomás had never been the kind of artist who hid his work until it was finished. The process was most of the beauty to him.

Finally, Ruby smiled. "Looks wonderful, sonny. The library, no?"

"Exactly. I'm glad you recognized it. *Gracias, Abue,*" he said, softly. Every so often she let him get away with calling her *Abue*—Grandma. When they were alone, when they allowed their affection to show. "It's coming along." He accepted the thermos from her, pouring himself some of the rich, steaming brew. Holding the thermos aloft, he cocked his head toward Ruby, asking her without words if she'd join him.

She shook her head. "You've been working far too long, Tomás. Come in now. Eat with us and sit with your old grandmother and talk."

From his perch on the work stool, Tomás stretched his shoulders, clasping his hands behind him, lifting them as high as he could. He did ache. But sitting idle left him far too much time to think, and lately that hurt more than any muscle ever could. "Soon." He brushed some dried paste off his cheek with the back of his wrist. "I want to get as much done as I can before the weekend."

"Ah, yes. The weekend." Ruby steepled her hands, tapping her forefingers on her lips as she considered him.

He did not want to get into this with Ruby. She'd been enthusiastic enough about going, but she'd also been trying to milk him for info he didn't feel ready to give ever since Hope announced the invitation. He'd successfully avoided her innuendos and subtle probes for information thus far, and he'd do anything to keep it up.

Ignoring this latest conversational prompt, he cleared his throat and chose a safer route. "It's good to have the gig." He picked up a strip of charcoal-colored tissue and frowned down at it too intensely. Gripping the pinking shears in the other hand, he went to work making neat little wavy snips about half an inch apart, all along its length. "It ought to knock about five hundred bucks off my bill for the *quinceañera*. It will be good for Hope to get out of Rociada, too. Something new." He glanced up at her sharply. "Unless you've changed your mind. If you're too tired—"

"Tired? I feel great. You are the one who looks like you haven't had a decent night's rest in a good while."

He pressed his lips together, but tried not to show any other outward signs of his desperation. Ruby would have been his only out, but there went that lifeline. It looked as though his family *would* be going to Santa Fe, like it or not.

"Plus, Hope is really looking forward to a weekend at Erica's." Ruby's gaze could penetrate like a nail gun sometimes. "We couldn't disappoint her, Tomás, could we?"

No, he didn't want to disappoint Hope, and that was the whole point. On a much larger scale, he did not want to disappoint Hope. Tomás decided the time had come to have a little conversation with Ruby. He set down the strip of tissue and the pinking shears and regarded her somberly. "Rube, listen." He paused, chewing on his thoughts for a moment. He didn't know how else to say it than just…saying it. "I don't want Hope to…get too attached to Erica."

"Why not?" She gestured vaguely toward the house. "The girl has been more animated in the past few weeks than I've seen her in ages. What can it hurt?"

"What can it hurt?" He stared at Ruby with disbelief. "Erica is a hired party planner, that's what it can hurt. Next September, after the *quinceañera,* we'll probably never see her again. How animated do you think Hope will be then?"

"Well, I think that's up to you."

He didn't follow. "Come again?"

"You say Erica is hired help, and yet you treat her like a friend, Tomás. She acts like a friend to you. To Hope and me, too." She pursed her lips and shrugged simultaneously. "What is Hope supposed to think? What is your definition of a friend?"

A beat passed. "And you want me to do what, then? Fire Erica? Treat her rudely?"

Ruby shook her head, wearily. "*Hijuela,* so thickheaded. That came from your father's side."

He smirked, but it was humorless. "Your point?"

"Okay, fine. You want my point, I'll get right to it." She leaned in and aimed a finger at him. "What is so wrong with having Erica Gonçalves for a friend, sonny? You're acting like a fool. She's a fine woman. You two have a lot in common."

He spread his arms. "What? What do we have in common? She's a certified single city girl, I'm a country boy, a family man. She lives in Santa Fe, I live here. What exactly do we have in common, Rube?"

"You're both afraid, that's what." She twisted her index

and middle fingers together. "Two peas in a pod, both un-willing to accept what you see right before your eyes."

Tomás cocked his head to the side, squinting. "What are you talking about?"

Ruby rolled forward, her expression softening. She patted Tomás's knee and then let her bony, age-spotted hand remain on his leg. After a moment, he covered it with his own. "Tomás, I'm talking about you. And Erica. It's okay if you like this woman. We all like her. It's not the end of the world."

"No. You don't understand. I'm not looking for…" He couldn't talk about this with his grandmother, for God's sake. He shoved a hand through his hair and shook his head.

"Nobody said you were looking for anything. Not every decision is life or death, black and white, forever or never." She paused for effect. "Life has a lot of gray area, *m'ijo*. I know you've had a lot of black-and-white decisions in your life, but you're still a young man."

"I'm a father," he said, stiffly.

"Yes," she said, her tone rough. "And a damn good father. But you're also a young man. Although, God knows, you act like you're older than I am, sometimes. Set in your blasted ways. Your life didn't cease to exist when Hope came into the world."

His jaw worked, and he hated the direction this conversation was taking, but eventually he looked up and met his grandmother's eyes. She was stern, but she was kind. And she didn't preach. Every so often, she said something because it needed to be said, and he'd always known to listen to her before.

He felt a yearning, a deep need for some of her wisdom. His parents had always worked so long and hard, it had always been Ruby he'd turned to. He felt the same right at that moment as he had at age seventeen, the day Racquel came to him, shaky-lipped and doe-eyed, and handed their infant to him, all wrapped in a pink cotton blanket.

''Take her, Tommy. You…just take her. I can't…do this. I don't want to.''

That afternoon, after Racquel had turned and walked away forever, he remembered sitting on the porch of his parents' house until the sun hung low and gold in the sky. He'd sat for hours, staring down into Hope's little face feeling so goddamn terrified, so overwhelmed by the prospect of her, by his love for her, so much so that he'd wanted to run. Just set her carefully on the porch and run, fast and far.

But he couldn't. He never would have, and he hadn't.

On the contrary, he'd fallen more in love with his daughter in those few paralyzing hours on the porch than he'd ever thought possible. He hadn't loved anyone or anything as much before or since. He'd done right by her, in the end. But that day on the porch, he'd needed guidance. He'd needed reassurance, desperately, that he was up to the daunting task of fatherhood even though he hadn't reached adulthood yet. He'd needed Ruby.

He was older now. Wiser, sure. But his need for guidance and reassurance hadn't waned. He still needed Ruby, and his desperate expression must have told her so.

''It is okay for you to have a friend, *m'ijo*. It's good.'' Ruby smiled, kind and knowing. Her voice softened, catching every now and then with emotion as she continued. ''Listen to your *abuela*, now. Your daughter has seen that you love her, every day of her life. She knows that she hung the moon in your world, that she makes the sun rise for you every day. She knows, sonny. Our Hope knows she's valued, deep in her soul.''

Hot, unshed tears stung Tomás's eyes. He swallowed thickly and tried to smile. ''Thank you.''

''Now, *m'ijo*.'' Ruby's tone grew more urgent. ''Now she needs to see that you love yourself just as much.''

He thought on that a moment, caressing the paper-thin skin on the back of Ruby's hand. ''I…I don't know how to show her.'' He didn't know if he did love himself as much, frankly. He'd spent so much time atoning for his sins, feeling guilty for his compulsiveness, his shortcomings. Trying to make up for all that Hope hadn't had in her life because of poor choices he'd made. "How, Rube? How do I show her?"

"Let yourself feel. Let yourself be a man. It's okay. It's okay to have a friend, even if she is a woman."

Maybe so, but it was still no good, this…thing…with single-by-choice Erica. Tomás pressed his lips into a regretful line. "Not Erica. She's hired help, Rube. She's not a friend."

"Only if you keep her in that role."

"No. You don't understand how Erica—"

"Yes, I do understand. I really do. Like I said, you and Erica are two of a kind. I can see that." She slipped her hand from beneath his and reached up to touch his cheek. "Erica will remain—" she made quotes with her fingers "—hired help only if you put her in that box and seal it."

Ruby was wrong. She had no idea about Erica's feelings, her goals in life, or how directly they opposed everything about his life. "She put herself in that box. She doesn't want…long-term. She doesn't want—"

"Did I tell you to marry her?"

His face heated. "Well…no."

"I said, be her friend. Take that small risk, is all I'm saying. Everyone needs friends, no matter what walls the two of you have thrown up, what denials you whisper to yourselves all alone at night."

"What if Erica doesn't want a single father as a friend?" His lips twisted in a cynical smile. "Ever thought about that?"

"How will you ever know if you don't try?"

"If I don't try, I don't have to worry about getting hurt."

Ruby stared at him balefully for a long time. "And what a damn fine way to live your life, Tomás. Never hurt, sure. But will you ever be fully alive?"

On Saturday, Erica rose at five in the morning in her beautiful room at the Inn at Loretto and immediately wondered how Hope and Ruby were doing alone at her house. Just fine, she decided. They'd been settled when she'd left the previous evening, comfortable and reassuring that she needn't worry about them, so she wouldn't. God knew, she had other things with which to occupy her mind.

The wedding wasn't until three that afternoon, but she had loads to do before the first notes of the wedding march played. The power of a memorable wedding was in the details, and those were her jurisdiction. She needed to be like Gepetto—invisible, but pulling all the right puppet strings to assure the show ran smoothly. She'd pull it off, she always did. But she couldn't wait to clear this assignment off her desk and, after all the headaches, she wanted everything to run like a well-oiled machine so there'd be no more problems. That took diligence.

She showered and dressed, power-guzzled some room-service coffee while flipping through her notes, then met with the caterers at seven for a quick check-in. After that, she awakened the bride, her three attendants and the mothers of both bride and groom, and escorted them to the Inn's spa for massages, facials, manicures, pedicures and hairstyling—the whole deal. A concierge accompanied the men to a round of golf at Pueblo of Pojoaque's Towa Golf Resort, a fifteen-minute drive from Santa Fe proper. With the wedding party taken care of, the rest of the morning and early afternoon belonged to Erica. Well, sort of.

She spent the time combing through details, checking that everything was in order at the Loretto Chapel where the ceremony would be held, and basically willing away all of the zillion or so problems that could arise during any wedding.

The chapel, she noted during her visit, was perfect. Its gothic architecture, stained glass and famed spiral staircase were perfectly complemented by the mixed-white floral sprays and bouquets, tied with turquoise-and-silver ribbons that decorated the pews and altar. No doubt the bride would be pleased, even as difficult to please as she'd proven herself over the last year.

Back at the Inn, which shared beautifully manicured grounds with the chapel, Erica popped her head into the Tesuque Ballroom, where the reception dinner would commence. This space, too, was so gorgeous in its own right, with fourteen-foot vaulted ceilings, skylights and a stunning kiva fireplace, it hardly needed any decoration. Hence, the turquoise, white and silver table settings that were simple and elegant.

Two white calla lilies stood in a silver keepsake Nambé vase at the center of every table. Around them, pieces of polished turquoise had been scattered. The effect was stark, modern, very New Mexican and in keeping with the bride's wishes. Everything seemed ready. Indeed, perfect, but Erica didn't want to jinx herself with that kind of thinking. She rapped her knuckles lightly on the wooden door for luck.

Glancing toward the stage, she noted with a rush of unexpected pleasure that Tomás and the band had their instruments and equipment already set up. They were here. More to the point, *he* was here. She didn't want her heart to soar at the mere knowledge Tomás was nearby, but it did, and she didn't have the time nor the inclination to fight it today. Erica couldn't wait to hear the band play that evening, taking it on faith that their music would be good, their presentation professional. What other choice had she had?

Closing the doors to the ballroom, Erica hesitated, then decided to call Tomás, since obviously he and the other band members had made it to their rooms. She'd gotten approval from the hotel manager to let them check in far earlier than normal, so they could rest up before the reception. Granted, she really didn't *need* to speak to Tomás at the moment, but she'd just make a quick phone call, ask how their rooms were and make sure the band didn't need anything before show time.

She pushed away a needle of self-derision. A wedding planner was sort of like a general contractor. It was perfectly within her purview to touch bases with all the subcontractors, one of which was the band. Rationalizing it like that, it really made sense that she *should* call Tomás.

Right. Flimsy excuse.

Truly, she just wanted to hear a friendly voice. Okay, complete honesty—it was *his* voice in particular that she yearned to hear, not just any friendly voice. Ever since she'd admitted to herself how she felt, she couldn't seem to evict thoughts of him from her mind. No one needed to know about her infatuation with the emotionally unavailable lead singer of Soul Searchers, especially not the man himself.

But they had seemed to make a little progress with each other recently, and that cheered her. He'd even allowed Ruby and Hope to ride to Santa Fe with her, so he could drive over with the band. She'd been astounded by the gesture and happy, too. Was he finally starting to trust her?

Her high heels clicked purposefully on the tile floor as she moved toward a house phone in a nook off the lobby. She picked it up, dialed, panicked and almost hung up, but he answered on two rings before she'd had the chance.

"Hello?"

Her throat closed, but she cleared it immediately and adopted her supremely businesslike voice. "Tomás? It's Erica." She wound the curly cord around her finger. "I'm glad you're all checked in. How are the rooms?"

"Fabulous." She could hear the smile in his voice. "I have a view of the sculpture garden and pool from my balcony."

"So do I." How close were their rooms to each other? She knew they were on the same floor, but it wasn't a topic she wanted to contemplate too closely. She switched the phone to the other ear after removing her pearl earring. "I was just in the ballroom. I notice you're all set up."

"No worries, Erica."

"I—I'm not worried." Suddenly, talking on the phone didn't feel like quite enough. She needed to see Tomás, to be in close proximity to him. It was a visceral need, not an intellectual one, so she tried not to analyze it. Instead, she forged ahead in an all-business tone. "Are you busy?"

"Are you kidding? I'm lounging on my balcony, drinking hot tea with honey so my voice will last five hours tonight."

She smiled, leaning against the wall. How could simply speaking with the man ease the tension in her jaw, lower her shoulders into relaxation mode? "That's just what a harried wedding planner loves to hear. Anyway, if you've got a few minutes, I would…" She would what? Like an excuse to see him? "I'd like to…run the schedule by you one last time." She cringed at how trumped-up it all sounded. Would he realize she was stretching for excuses to be in the same room with him?

He didn't seem to notice. "That's cool. Come on up."

"Oh." The suggestion startled her. She bit her bottom lip, uncertain. What was it she'd told herself about never meeting him in a secluded hotel room?

His tone sounded tentative. "Unless you'd rather me come down. If you can give me a few minutes…."

Geez, she was acting like a seventh grader. Of course she should go to him. *She* called *him*. And he'd been minding his own business, relaxing his voice, resting for the evening. She did have a vested interest in his vocal cords lasting, and she owed him the consideration of bending to his needs. "N-no. That's fine." She flipped through her book, her "wedding bible"—she had one for every wedding—and read his room number from the list, even though she'd just dialed it. Flustered by his invitation, the number had slipped from her mind. "I'll be right up. Do you need me to bring anything? More tea? Honey?"

"Just you. Honey," he teased.

Her mouth went dry with something that felt suspiciously like desire, and she fought the urge to stammer her apologies and skip seeing him until he was at a safe distance from her, on the stage holding a microphone. Then again, when did a stage ever render a dangerous man safe? Everyone knew you could take an absolute frog of a man, hand him a microphone or a guitar and put him on stage and BANG, he was hot. Tomás was already hot.

How much hotter would he be that evening?

How would she react to seeing *him* on stage, she wondered? Not to mention, how would the other women at the wedding react? Her stomach contracted with something sour and unproductive, and, had she been a cat, her claws would've come out. This line of thinking was a bad idea all around. She could not, for her own sanity, start being possessive over Tomás Garza.

"Erica? You there?"

"Yes, sorry. I'll be…actually, can you give me half an hour? I need to check on something." Just her sanity.

"I'll be waiting."

She murmured a quick goodbye and hung up before this impromptu meeting started to seem like a tryst in her delusional mind. Ha, she thought, moving toward the bank of elevators and punching the up button. In her dreams. She couldn't have handpicked a more unattainable man to fantasize about.

She squeezed the thick portfolio to her chest and leaned her head back, watching the illuminated numbers above the doors as the elevator slowly descended from an upper floor to the lobby level where she stood waiting. She needed to pull herself together, and quick, if she had any hopes of maintaining a reasonably professional demeanor when she finally reached Tomás's hotel room.

Tomás had given the conversation with Ruby a lot of thought over the past several days, and he'd come to realize she was right. Not such a surprise. The woman had four decades-plus of life experience on him.

Why was he fighting this friendship with Erica so ferociously? They didn't have to be a love match for her to remain connected to Hope's life…even distantly. Friendship, for now, was enough. Then again, considering they shared similar outlooks on life, perhaps hooking up wouldn't be so unwise.

He could satisfy his thirst for her and leave her sated, too. Ruby had a point—he wouldn't know what would happen if he didn't risk it. And now he had the perfect chance to test the waters. Erica was coming up to his room in half an hour. He'd just test her, see if she had even a quarter of the attraction for him as he had for her. See if, perhaps, she had any interest.

Smiling, Tomás picked up the phone.

Tomás's door opened, and he looked completely relaxed in a pair of worn blue jeans, a University of New Mexico sweatshirt, and bare feet. What was it about the sight of a sexy man's bare feet that seemed intimate? Decadent?

"Hey."

"Hi there," she managed. He stepped aside, and she skirted around him into the room. It was decorated in a nearly identical motif as hers, but she took a moment to glance around anyway. Anything to keep her gaze from settling on him, on the casual confidence so much a part of him that made desire pool low inside her. Finally, she turned to him.

Hands loosely on his hips, he gave her a once-over. "You look…organized."

She lifted her chin with playful confidence. "Please. Did you expect anything less?"

He chuckled. "I just got off the phone with Hope and Ruby. They're having a great time at your place." His expression took on an air of ruefulness. "Although Hope wanted me to tell you that the feng shui is all wrong in your house, and she'd be glad to work on your baguas if you'd like.''

So that explained the problems in her life. Bad feng shui. Bogus baguas. Erica smirked, shaking her head. ''You know, I might just take her up on it.'' A light breeze from the open balcony door blew a strand of hair across her face. She brushed it away. ''Incidentally, she asked to use my computer while she was there, and I told her she could as long as she stayed off any bad Web sites. I hope that's okay.''

''Hope's a trustworthy girl.'' He nodded. ''It's fine.''

Erica crossed toward the balcony and pulled back the already opened curtain, gazing down on the sculpture garden for a moment. ''I'm really glad she and Ruby came along.'' She turned back toward Tomás, knowing she was resorting to small talk once again but unable to stop. ''Since you're riding back with your band, we're going to have lunch tomorrow before I drive them home so Ruby and I will have an opportunity to talk. We spoke on the way here, of course, but it will make things easier once we really get going on the *quinceañera* to have things hammered out.''

''Okay.'' He watched her curiously for a moment, then sank into one of the two chairs settled around a small, round table in the sitting-room corner of the oversize room. He smoothed his palms together slowly. ''So. What about these last-minute details you needed to discuss?''

''Oh. Well.'' She glanced down at her wedding bible as if she had just realized she held it, then crossed the room and took the seat opposite his. She crossed one leg over the other, fire moving through her belly when she noticed his gaze caress the length of them before jerking away.

Opening the book, she leafed through the pages. She could smell him, she realized. It was as if the room had become an extension of him, and she felt cloaked in the essence of…him. He smelled both like man, and uniquely like Tomás. She couldn't place the scents of him, but she found them utterly intoxicating.

Breathe through your mouth.

She cleared her throat. ''To recap. Sound check at—''

''Five.''

She hesitated, blinking up at his steady gaze before continuing with considerably less confidence. ''Yes, and then the actual dancing portion of the reception—''

''Starts at seven. Although you'll want us there at six to add a little musical drama to the entrance of the bride and groom.'' He cocked a challenging eyebrow, his attention never wavering. After a moment, he steepled his hands beneath his chin and waited patiently for her to go on.

Her cheeks grew warm. ''Y-yes, and you'll play—''

''Five fifty-minute sets, wrapping up at midnight. If the party is still going strong, the bride and groom may opt to keep us for an extra two hours at five-hundred dollars an hour. Right?''

She gulped, feeling sheepish and obvious. She closed her schedule. ''Well, then. I guess that's all I needed.'' She stood, tucking the thick, black leather-bound book under one arm, but Tomás reached out and grabbed her hand. She froze.

''Erica.''

''Yes?''

''Sit down. You're nothing but nerves.''

She managed to settle back into the chair and give him a wan smile. ''Am I that transparent?''

He grinned.

''Don't get me wrong, this is nothing unusual. I'm always high-strung on the actual day of a wedding.'' She hiked one shoulder. ''It's my job. I have to make everything perfect.''

He pursed his lips, nodding. ''Did you check on the chapel?''

''Yes.''

"And the caterer?"

"Him, too. Full staff. No disasters. It's all good."

"The ballroom? The wedding party?"

"All in perfect order."

"Of course they are. You're in charge." He leaned forward and squeezed her knee. It was an "I'm on your side, buckeroo," kind of a squeeze, but he let his hand linger for a moment after, and effervescent sensations zinged through her.

"Look, you've got enough on your mind. You don't have to worry about the band. We're experienced in this sort of event."

"I...I know."

"And it looks like everything else is under control."

"Yes. I guess it is." She blew out a sigh, her shoulders sagging. "Look, I'm sorry to have wasted your time, Tomás. If you want the truth, I just wanted...to talk to someone not necessarily wedding-related. I mean, you *are* related to this wedding, but you're also..."

"A friend?" he suggested.

Little warm fuzzies overtook her, and she smiled. "Yes, Tomás, you are a friend. And so I'll return the favor and leave you to rest up." She went to stand again, but he touched her. Stopped her. She swallowed carefully, then gave her most efficient smile. "Really. I'll get out of your hair."

"What if I don't want you out of my hair?"

She couldn't respond. Inside her, everything felt shaky.

"You should relax for a few minutes. Chill." He lowered his chin, and his tone. "Have lunch with me."

"Oh, I couldn't. I don't have time—" Just then, a knock sounded on the door. Erica tossed a quick glance over her shoulder. "Are you expecting someone?"

"As a matter of fact, yes." He stood. "Room service."

At her questioning look, he continued. "I haven't known you too long, Erica, but long enough to know that you tend to put work before everyday necessities like…eating.'' He raised his eyebrows and paused, giving her a chance to deny it. She didn't. ''So I took the liberty of ordering us lunch.'' He traversed the room toward the door, opening it and exchanging pleasantries with the bellman while she stood there in a daze. After a linen-covered table had been wheeled in and Tomás signed the form and sent the smiling man off with a generous tip, Tomás turned toward Erica and swept his arm toward the spread.

He cocked his head in question, and God did he look sexy.

She blinked over at the table. All the dishes were covered with metal domes, but a single rose stood proudly in a glass vase. A yellow rose. For friendship. Had he specified the color? Of course not. She was overthinking the details.

Everything smelled wonderful, and she really was hungry, not to mention touched by the gesture. Erica was used to taking care of everything, not used to being taken care of. It felt nice.

When she hesitated, he said, ''You need sustenance or you aren't going to make it through the night.''

Erica's heart squeezed. He was so thoughtful, so nurturing. These years of being both father and mother to Hope had paid off. Tomás Garza was the quintessential catch who wouldn't be caught. But that didn't mean she couldn't eat a meal with him. She'd survived them before.

She flipped her hands up, a helpless gesture. ''I don't know what to say. Thank you.''

''So, you'll dine with me?''

''Yes, Tomás. I will dine with you.'' She held up a finger, a stern look on her face. ''But then—''

''It's back to work.''

How did he always know what she was going to say before she said it? In a way, it was disconcerting. But it also felt comforting. ''Y-yes. Back to work. I have a lot to do.''

He shook his head, amused. "Man, had I known you were this driven, I would've packed a Curious George T-shirt and a couple of jelly jars for the wine." For emphasis, he uncorked the bottle that had come on the room-service cart. "That would've lightened you up."

Wine. The man ordered wine. Not only that, but he'd noticed her favorite T-shirt the other night and had picked up on the fact that wearing it comforted her. Thoughtful and insightful, an alluring combination. But she could not, absolutely would not have any wine during her workday. "Thank you for lunch. I *am* hungry and you're right—I would've skipped it. But I can't—"

"Yes, you can, Erica. One glass of wine will take the edge off. I'm not trying to get you drunk, you know."

He was right, damn him. She had more edges than a faceted diamond right now. She crossed to the table and snatched the glass of wine he offered. "Would you stop reading my mind?"

He tapped her glass with his own, took a sip and then winked as his mouth spread into a smile. "I can't help it. It runs in the family. Watch what you think around Ruby, because believe me, she will know."

For a moment, Erica just stared at him, feeling the pull. Finally, she sighed. They were adults. They could talk about this. So much was going on in this room just below the surface. She couldn't take the filled silence. "What are you doing, Tomás?" she asked softly. "What are we doing?"

His expression turned serious, and he moved closer, stood in front of her until she could feel the warmth from his body like an embrace. "We're having lunch. Together. I'm helping you with a wedding. You're planning my daughter's *quinceañera*."

Her mind screamed for her to step back, get a little distance. At the same time, her heart urged her forward. Caught up in the fight between logic and emotion, she simply stood her ground, staring into his eyes, willing him to be honest with her about this. "You know what I meant."

"Do I?"

"Don't you?"

A long pause ensued, but their gazes never unlocked. Finally, he reached out and touched her cheek. One soft sweep of the backs of his fingers down her skin. Involuntarily, her eyes fluttered closed as her insides seemed to melt at his touch.

"I don't know what's happening, Erica. I can't say. All I know is, I'm glad to be here, and I'm glad you're here with me. Can that be enough?"

"Yes. I'm…glad, too." She opened her eyes, and the moment of genuineness boosted her confidence enough to tell him what she'd been holding in for so long. "I want you to know… I'm not going to hurt your daughter. I would never—"

"I know." His eyes clouded for a moment, but he recovered quickly. "I do know. It's just been…fourteen years of living the way I live." He sighed, raked his hand through his hair. "Sometimes it's all I know. But, how about we eat now and worry about all the questions later?" His eyes moved over her face with care, with appreciation. "I know I've got way too many questions to tackle today."

She felt relieved. Close to him, and bolstered by the knowledge that it wasn't just her, this attraction that stretched invisibly between them like an intricate spider's web. He felt it, too. They wouldn't talk about it, might never explore it, but just knowing the yearning wasn't one-sided eased her stress more than she could verbalize. So she didn't. She took a seat, snapped the crisp linen napkin over her lap and smiled at him.

He uncovered the plates, revealing chicken-cordon-bleu sandwiches and thick, golden fries. "Looks good," he said.

Teasing him, she tilted her head side to side. So-so. "Hey,

it's not a Tomás Garza home-cooked special, but it's better than starving to death. I say we go for it.''

"Indeed, Erica Gonçalves." He sat, his gaze never leaving her face. His lips pursed thoughtfully. "Perhaps we should.''

Chapter Eight

Hours into a long, stressful day that was turning out beautifully after all, Erica breathed a sigh of relief. The wedding ceremony had gone off without a hitch, the bride seemed to be enjoying herself, the food had been consumed, cake cut and served, and twenty minutes into their first set, Tomás's band, Soul Searchers, was a smash hit.

Erica had a hard time keeping her eyes off the stage. Tomás didn't just perform for the crowd, he connected with them, made each person feel as if he was singing just for them. Indeed, all through the evening, she kept getting the feeling he was singing just for her. To her. And every moment she watched him she found herself more attracted.

Laughing couples crowded the dance floor, and others sat at tables nodding or tapping their feet to the music. She'd just made a mental note to add Soul Searchers to her list of regular bands when the father of the bride approached her.

Rogelio ''Roger'' Roybal was a short man, but his prodigious belly made up for the lack of height, giving him an odd sort of presence. Mr. Roybal and his wife had produced five daughters, and today's bride was his last to marry off. It was no surprise he'd gone prematurely gray—white actually. She almost felt bad charging the man, except she knew he was an extremely successful art dealer in Santa Fe and beyond. He had more than enough money to see his daughters off in style.

He smiled, hoisting his tuxedo pants a little higher and rocking back and forth on his feet. "Ms. Gonçalves. I believe we have some business to take care of?"

Ah, the bill. It was an archaic ritual, this habit of waiting for the father of the bride—or other responsible party—to approach before discussing payment. Erica reached out and shook his hand, discreetly passing him an embossed envelope that contained her invoice with the other hand. "Mr. Roybal. I trust you're enjoying the day?"

His guffaw sounded as if it should come from a much larger man. "To be honest, I'm mostly enjoying the fact that the rest of my pension will belong to the wife and me, yes. But the wedding has been beautiful." He looked toward his daughter, beautiful in a Vera Wang gown that had cost the earth. "I know my little one can be a bit of a handful, but you've done such a wonderful job…well…handling her. Thank you."

"It was my pleasure," she lied, touching his forearm. "Have you had a chance to dance yet?"

"Not yet, but the wife is after me to limber up. She won't let me get away without dancing, no matter how hard I try." He glanced up at the stage, a pleased, well-fed ruddiness to his face. "The band is particularly good."

Erica tracked his gaze and found Tomás watching them. She smiled, and he winked in response. Her response was immediate; blood thrummed through her ears and heat suffused her flesh. She felt infinitely alive, right on the brink of something both exciting and dangerous.

It all hinged on Tomás. But right now wasn't the time.

She forced the pleasant memories of their lunch and her omnipresent fantasies about the man out of her mind, then turned back to Roger Roybal. "Yes, I'm happy with them." She hesitated, weighing the prudence of revealing her secret, then decided this man would appreciate her quick thinking in time of crisis. She leaned a bit closer. "I didn't want to worry your daughter, but to be perfectly candid, Soul Searchers is a fill-in." His bushy eyebrows shot up, and she nodded. "The original band backed out." She paused for emphasis. "Three days ago."

"You're kidding."

She shook her head. "Tomás—the lead singer—came to my rescue, and I think they're an even better choice than the first band. We lucked out."

"Indeed." He appraised her appreciatively. "I must say, you certainly keep your cool under fire."

"Well, that's my job." She smiled, then indicated Tomás and the other musicians. "They are willing to stay an extra two hours, as we've discussed."

He nodded, pursing his lips. "Let me run it by my daughter and her new husband, see how they're feeling. In the meantime, I'll just excuse myself for a few minutes and take care of this." He waggled the envelope she'd handed him.

She patted his arm again, feeling truly grateful that at least one member of the Roybal family was pleasant to deal with. Receiving payment meant the end was in sight, and this would be one hell of a good check. "Thank you. And if you have any friends whose daughters are getting married—"

"Don't you worry. I'll sing your praises."

She breathed a sigh of relief. "Thank you."

"While I'm dealing with the bill, why don't you take a spin, Ms. Gonçalves?" He nudged his chin toward the dance floor.

"Oh, gosh no. There is still too much for me to do."

"Nonsense. It's all been done. We're over the hump.

They're married. They're dancing. They're smiling. Besides—'' he shared a knowing grin ''—the band is taking their first break, and the way he's been watching your every move, I have a hunch a certain singer wouldn't mind a slow loop around the floor with the likes of you.''

Stunned, Erica turned toward the front of the room just in time to see Tomás and the two other members of Soul Searchers step off the stage to a round of applause from the wedding guests. Almost immediately, recorded music filled the space. Some guests continued dancing, others took the opportunity to cool down and have a little champagne. Her eyes met Tomás's, and his expression was anything but cool. It smoldered, and it was directed at her.

She turned back toward Mr. Roybal as though grasping for a life preserver in stormy seas, but he'd already ambled off toward the lobby. Unsure what she felt, unsure what to do, Erica simply stared after the benevolent man. Her fingers made their way to her gold charm necklace, and she toyed with the small heart-shaped charm given to her by her best friend, Rita.

When she'd confided in Rita that she hoped to launch a successful wedding-planning business, her friend had given her the heart to remind Erica that the whole point of weddings was to celebrate love. Rita had always accused her of being too jaded and thought it ironic that Erica, of all people, would want to plan weddings.

Erica smiled at the memory, feeling a little melancholy. Gosh, she missed Rita. Rita's husband was in the navy, and they'd left six months earlier for a two-year tour in Okinawa, Japan. She'd have to e-mail her from the room tonight. If she ever got back. She'd place bets on the fact that this party would run well into the middle of the night.

''How's it going?''

Tomás's rough-soft voice sounded just over her left shoulder, his warm breath tickling her cheek. She jumped, then spun toward him. He stood close, way too close. A light sheen of sweat glistened in the V of his crisp white shirt and at his temples from the exertion of playing guitar and singing for nearly an hour straight. He smelled of spicy soap and his own essence, that all-Tomás scent that beguiled her with its primitive mystery. With the back of his hand, he swiped off one temple, then the other, his amused gaze never leaving Erica's face. "Earth to Erica. Have you finally gone over the edge?"

"Sorry." She placed her thumb and index finger together and held them up. "I'm still this far from the edge, luckily."

"Good to know."

"I'm just…distracted." *By you,* she thought, but she didn't want them to veer off on that dangerous train of thought. Instead, she cleared her throat. "You guys are truly wonderful."

"Gracias."

"I mean it. Absolutely fantastic. The bride's father is thrilled. Do you have a problem if I add you to my database of bands for future weddings?"

He laughed, a rumble deep in his throat. "Now that's a silly question." A circulating waiter offered him a flute of champagne, and he looked to Erica for confirmation.

"Go ahead."

He accepted the glass, sipped, then made a low moan of pleasure that weakened her knees. "Good champagne." He raised his glass. "My compliments to the woman who selected it. In answer to your question, we'd be more than happy to be added to your database, Erica. But…how many of these moonlight assignments do you take?" He shook his head in wonder. *"Hijuela,* you work more than anyone I know."

She lifted her chin, a little defensive. "Except you."

"Even me."

She twisted her mouth ruefully. "If you want to know the truth, I'm saving money to start my own event-planning business."

"Ah. Time to stop working for The Man, huh?"

Maybe she shouldn't have said anything. He was an artisan with the Cultural Arts Festival, after all, which was being handled by her firm. She didn't want to sound like a malcontent. "It's not that I don't enjoy working for my firm, but—"

"You want the independence of working for yourself."

She settled into a sigh, her eyes smiling up at him. "I should've known you'd understand."

"Well, you've made your position on things pretty clear."

She didn't know what to say to that. Did men speak in subtext, or did women just read too much into their straightforward comments? She decided to consider his words benign. She felt too good just being in his presence and didn't want it to change. Turning, she tilted her head toward a set of double doors which led to a hallway that ran between the Tesuque Ballroom and the kitchen. "Walk with me, Tomás. I need to check on the caterers. I'll even get you some hot tea with honey for that throat."

"Yeah? A bribe I can't refuse. But you know, I only have a ten-minute break."

She scoffed. "Well, gee, I wasn't planning on holding you captive in the backroom."

He drained the champagne glass and set it on an empty serving tray as they started toward the hallway. "Now *that*," he said, in a sexy drawl, "sounds like my loss."

Well into their sixth set, Tomás sang his heart out, trying his best to knock off all the requests that came from guests smiling up from the front of the stage. Most of them were women, and several of them were more attractive than the average joe—definitely flirtatious—but he didn't care. His eyes had tracked one woman all night long, and no one could come close to her magnetic draw. Erica. Even the syllables of her name sounded sexy to him. He itched for her.

They'd just finished up a Tony Bennett cover, especially for the older guests who'd stuck it out past midnight. Tomás swung his Taylor Jewel Kilcher signature model guitar to the side and reached for his tea, taking a sip. When he'd set the mug back down on the stool adjacent to his microphone stand, he looked out at the still applauding crowd and immediately sought Erica.

Had she gone? His heart squeezed.

No, there she was. Dressed in that form-hugging but not tight dove-gray dress that stopped just above those sexy knees of hers and fit her in a way that made him want to rip it off. She stood toward the back, unobtrusive and in charge. She'd been awake since the crack of dawn, he knew, and yet she still looked fresh and lovely, good enough to eat.

Apparently one of the wedding guests thought so, too, Tomás noted, with a sudden, violent tightening of his gut. The man, well-marinated from whatever he'd chosen from the open bar, stood next to Erica, talking, flirting, invading her personal space. Tomás could tell from her rigid body language and polite but brittle smile that Erica was merely tolerating the man because her position dictated it.

The drunk leaned in, she leaned subtly back.

More than once, Tomás saw the man's eyes drift down into Erica's demure yet blindingly sexy cleavage, and each time Tomás's vision actually blurred with anger. How dare the drunken clown take advantage of Erica's politeness? Like the guy even had a shot at a woman like Erica who was pure class.

Tomás continued to sing by rote, but his eyes never left the tense exchange at the back of the room. Relief flooded him when Bruce Springsteen's "Born in the U.S.A." came to an end, because he'd watched Erica try to walk away from the man at least three times during the song, and he'd seen the snake's preventative grasp on her arm grow tighter with each attempt.

Blood pulsed in Tomás's temples. That's it. He couldn't stand by and watch this any longer. The crowd cheered for more, but Tomás barely heard them.

He lifted the guitar over his head and set it gently in its stand, then gripped the mike and leaned the stand toward his mouth. "We're gonna take ten, folks," he managed, through gritted teeth, "but then we'll be back for one last set."

Without a word or a glance directed toward Manny and James, his other band members, Tomás jumped down from the stage and stalked through the crowd, turning his shoulders this way and that to avoid knocking into folks. He saw no one, felt nothing except a burning need to get to Erica. His jaw felt tight, and he knew his fists were clenched. But he couldn't walk up and punch the guy. Erica would never forgive him for that. He slowed, unsure for a moment what to do. Then it came to him.

He tempered his pace and made a conscious effort to loosen up as he moved closer. To adopt a placid expression. Finally, he broke through the back of the crowd. Nothing stood between him and the situation.

Walking straight up, he placed himself between Erica and the interloper and slid his hands around her waist, pulling her lush curves against his body, settling her rounded hips inside the V of his wide stance. Their eyes met briefly, his half-mast, hers wide and surprised. Her mouth opened, but she looked so utterly stunned, nothing came out. Thank goodness.

"Hey, baby girl," Tomás half drawled, half growled, before she could say something to blow what he was trying to pull off.

And then he kissed her.

This was no chaste, public peck. Oh, no. He took her mouth with his, tasting, probing, invading her with his tongue. This was a *damn, I can't wait to love you,* full-body kiss, with contact from their chests to their knees, including all the interesting places in between. He smoothed his palms up her back and threaded all ten fingers into her satiny hair, and she felt like a dream, tasted like wedding-cake frosting. What he hadn't expected, however, was the explosion of emotion inside himself. It could be from the satiny-smooth texture of her mouth or the intimacy of tasting it. Perhaps it was the boldness of her own tongue as it connected with his. It could be the fact that she tasted like dessert. He didn't know.

He'd felt angry, watching the drunk manhandle her. Maybe even a little jealous. But now his mouth was on hers, and all he could feel was the unexpected desire for more. He deepened the kiss, cradling her face in his hands and thoroughly exploring her sweet, satiny mouth, probably more than was necessary to fend off the drunk. But all of a sudden, this kiss was about more than protecting Erica. It was about a woman he'd watched and wanted and denied himself for so long, she'd become like a Christmas gift he wasn't allowed to open, and he was a wide-eyed child in front of the tree. God, how he wanted to tear off the wrapping paper and sample the surprises he knew he'd find inside. Erica's mouth, lush and soft, was the type that inspired and tormented a man. He'd known it would be.

He felt her stiffen, then melt into the moment, then stiffen once again as she no doubt regained her senses. Before she could push him away and ruin their cover, he broke the kiss, smoothed away her smeared lipstick gently with the rough pad of his thumb, and then turned back to the startled slime who'd been bothering her. Tomás slid an arm possessively around Erica's waist, pulling her against him, feeling as if anger and jealousy and the unexpected punch of knee-weakening, all-encompassing, blow-his-mind desire might make him explode before he finished this thing.

''I don't think I've met your friend, sweetheart,'' he said, in a calm, even tone that a woman might take for polite conversation, but any man in his right mind would recognize as the dead-on threat it was. Tomás stuck out his hand.

The other man, mumbling apologies, scuttled away.

And then they were alone.

He could feel Erica trembling slightly next to him, and he didn't know if she was scared, relieved or ready to blow. He knew he had to face it sometime, and anything was better than facing the confusion he felt inside at the moment. Taking a deep breath, he turned toward her, cradling her arms at the elbow and lowering himself so he could look straight into her eyes. He hoped his confusion, his rush of wanting, wasn't obvious to her. "Are you okay?"

She stared at him, incredulous, mouth slightly opened. "Do you mind telling me what in the hell just happened?" she rasped, finally. "Need I remind you I'm working?"

He released her arms and stepped back, raking both hands through his hair, over the crown and down to the back where he removed the elastic and shook it out. "I'm sorry, Erica. I know. It was out of line, but I saw that guy…grabbing you, and I just… I lost it."

As though just regaining control over her composure, Erica blinked a couple of times and then looked away, around, anywhere but at him. She smoothed her already smooth dress with shaking hands, then lifted her chin. "Well…thank you. I guess. Your methods are—" she shook her head, releasing a monosyllabic scoff of laughter "—a little…disconcerting. But he *was* bothering me and I couldn't get rid of him. So…thank you."

Tomás raised his face to her, relief raining through him. He hadn't expected that, not at all. He'd expected her to be angry with him, and he damn well deserved it after taking liberties to which he wasn't privileged, but he hadn't known what else to do. And yet, she wasn't angry. "I really am sorry. I was in a think-fast situation, and it was that or punch him."

Color rose to her cheeks, and a smirk quivered one corner of her mouth. "Well, thank God for your decision-making process. One punch would've cost me a referral, I'm sure."

What did one kiss cost her? he wondered.

Their gazes met for a moment before hers skittered away. She got a distracted, flustered look again, and through that soft gray dress, Tomás could see her nipples were hard. He hadn't meant to look, but he couldn't seem to help himself. Erica Gonçalves, without even trying, stole all his control.

But, damn it, he didn't want to be in control around her. Right now, he wanted them to be out of control. Free from fear, completely present and out of their minds with passion.

"I...I need to check on...something."

Tomás watched her spin unsteadily on her gray suede pumps and head toward the double doors that led down the same hallway they'd walked together earlier, toward the kitchen. The one that had been empty last time. She was walking away, and with a flash of insight, Tomás knew he didn't want her to. He had been fighting his attraction to her for weeks, fighting the feeling of absolute rightness he felt every time he was around her. Why?

Ruby had told him to take risks, and he suddenly realized he wanted to. Had to. This moment, this woman was worth taking a risk. They wouldn't have forever, of course, but maybe for now was enough. And this was his chance. He couldn't let it pass.

After a split second of hesitation when she'd disappeared from his sight, he followed, striding long, throwing open the door to the hallway like a man on a mission. He saw her ahead of him, hurrying down the hallway, her hand running lightly against the wall as if for support. "Erica, wait."

She spun to face him, her back against the wall, chest rising and falling with rapid breaths. She said nothing, but her dark eyes assessed him warily, the pupils dilated with what looked to him like arousal, just as he was sure his were. He might not always be honest with himself about his feelings, but his body never lied, and he wanted her.

He moved slowly, but when at last he stood before her, he reached out a hand to touch her face. No. Not yet. He pulled back before contact, curling his fingers into his palm as he let the hand fall to his side. "I'm sorry I kissed you." His voice sounded husky to his own ears. "I didn't mean to offend you."

Her pink tongue darted out quickly to moisten her lips, lips swollen from his kiss and half-free of lipstick. So damn sexy, so self-possessed. She hesitated over her words, it seemed, but when she did speak, her voice was steady and quiet. "The last thing you did, Tomás, was offend me."

Lust, pure and hot, knifed through him. God. How could he want the woman a hundred times more than he'd wanted her just moments ago? She wasn't some jittery virgin. As she'd told him, she knew her way around her own needs.

"Yeah?" he asked.

"Yeah."

He did reach out that time, running the backs of his fingers down her smooth, firm, sexy arm from shoulder to wrist, and then back up. Slowly, a smile pulled the corners of his mouth upward. "Well, the truth is…I'm not really sorry I kissed you."

Erica rested her head back against the wall, exposing a neck so long and creamy-tan, he could scarcely keep himself from leaning down to taste it, from pressing his lips lightly to the pulsing vein there, feeling the life within her. It seemed as if his whole life had narrowed down to this sharp pinpoint of need, this moment in time. This woman.

"It's almost time for your next set," she half whispered, but her expression told him she didn't want him to leave.

"They can wait." He moved closer, until the only thing separating them was their body heat.

She pulled her bottom lip between her teeth for a moment, worry clouding her eyes. When she released the plump lip, it was moist, and he wanted to lick it, pull it into his own mouth. To taste her, starting at the mouth and moving down until he'd tasted all of her, until he knew all of her by touch.

She reached out, hesitantly, and straightened the collar on his shirt. A woman's touch. A signal of possession. "You have a job to do, mister."

"I have a lot of things to do, but right now I'm here." He leaned in, his chest just barely grazing her breasts. "With you. Just where I want to be."

A beat passed, and she looked directly in his eyes. "Don't play with me, Tomás."

He lowered his face until it hovered so close to hers that his lips tingled with the anticipation of tasting her once again. "Oh, I'm not playing." Her throat worked around a tight swallow, but she didn't pull back or look away. He liked that. "I'm looking at you, and I like what I see."

"Meaning what?"

"You know where I stand. I know where you stand."

"True," she breathed.

"And that's good."

"Yeah?"

His face came even closer. He could feel puffs of her warm breath on his mouth, tingling his lips, and his body responded, tightening, firing to life. "To my way of thinking, it could be all good. You and me. This thing."

"Are you absolutely sure you know what you're doing?"

He ignored the voice of reason, her offering of an escape route. Right then, he didn't want it, repercussions be damned. He'd watched her from afar all night, and he was aroused. Plain and simple. The time for caution, at least for this night, was over. "I'm pretty sure I'm making my interest clear to a very beautiful, very sexy woman, but you'll have to let me know if my message is coming across."

She lifted her chin, challenge in her eyes. "The bride's father said you've been watching me. All night."

He braced one forearm against the wall above her shoulder, then leaned in and ran his tongue lightly along the bottom of her earlobe, gratified when she shivered. "He's an astute man, the father of the bride."

"Why, Tomás? I need to know why."

He caught the soft skin of her neck between his teeth, then let go. "Because you're the best view in the room."

"That's it?"

"That's not even close to it." The rest of the world disappeared as he stared into her big, dark, liquid eyes. He could barely think for the need pulsing low and hot in his body, didn't want to think.

He knew it would happen, but he still felt a shot of disappointment when she slid her palm in between them and pressed against his chest. She lowered her tone to a private near whisper. "Tomás, as persuasive as you are, I'm working. We're both working. You need to get back out there and—"

"Shh. I know." He covered her hand with his own, pressing her slim fingers more tightly against his chest. "Trust me, I've been singing for six hours now. I'm not going to ruin your gig at the last minute. But this party can't last all night long, and this...thing between us..." He pressed his body into hers slightly, letting her know how hot he was for her, how stunningly hard she made him without even trying. "Just tell me, can you ignore it any longer?"

She hesitated, closing her eyes for a moment before opening them and shaking her head slightly, almost with regret.

He smiled. "Yeah. Me neither. So, we're alone tonight, you and I. Despite the wedding, despite the work. And we're both adults." He let that sink in. "You know what I'm saying."

She did know, he could see it in the high color of her cheeks, the arousal so apparent beneath her dress. "What are you saying? Just to avoid confusion. I want to be sure we're—"

He laid one work-roughened finger across her lips, stilling

her words. When she'd gone silent, he traced that finger across her top lip, then back across the full, luscious bottom lip. "Go work. Do your thing. All I'm saying is, after the reception, if I'm not the only one feeling what's between us...if I'm not the only one who wants to find out what's there..." He eased his finger against the seam of her lips until he felt moisture, then he stepped back. "You know where to find me."

Chapter Nine

Erica tried her best to retrace her steps through the surreal evening, hoping to figure out how in the heck she and Tomás had inadvertently reached the combustible point. But it was no use. In her mind, one moment she was vowing to stay businesslike with the man, and the next he was kissing her neck in the back hallway and she was loving it. Boom, just like that.

She shivered a little at the memory but forced herself to focus on the reality of the situation rather than the complete *un*reality that comprised most of it. She wasn't sure of a whole lot by the time she'd tied up all the final strands of the reception, but she was absolutely certain about two things:

One. She wanted Tomás. Badly.

Two. Acting on that desire would lead to nowhere good.

So, what was she to do?

She rode the elevator up to her floor—her and Tomás's floor, she reminded herself—and hesitated just as she exited.

She peered first one way, then the opposite way down the long hallways, biting her bottom lip with indecision. No earth-shattering insights came to her. With a tormented whimper, she focused on the floral display perched on a table across from the elevators and pondered her dilemma objectively. To turn left would take her to Tomás's room. Right, and she'd reach the safety of her own.

Left or right.

Heart or logic.

Danger or safety.

God, this shouldn't be so damn difficult. She'd taken her pleasure from a lot of men over the years without this level of angst. It should be simple. He wanted her, she wanted him. Enough said. Go to the man's room and have him. But it wasn't simple, and she wouldn't do herself or Tomás any favors by kidding herself that it was. It was the most complicated mess she'd faced in a long time, because she really liked this guy.

Disgusted with herself, she came to the sudden conclusion that she wasn't the least bit sure of anything, so she absolutely could not turn left, no matter how much she wanted Tomás. With more than a little reluctance, Erica swiveled to the right and headed toward her room. With each determined step, she ticked off the reasons she should lock her door and stay there.

Tomás was a client.

Tomás was a father.

Tomás didn't want a woman in his life.

Actually, to be more specific, Tomás *had* women in his life to take care of his sexual needs, and, ridiculous as it might seem, she didn't want to become just another body in the long line of them.

And then there was Hope. Ruby. Erica's own mother.

Her mother? She shook her head, emitting a less than ladylike scoff. Sheesh, she was way overthinking this if Susana entered the picture. It was almost…creepy. Sighing,

Erica slid her key card into the slot at her door, waited for the green light, then pushed into her dark room. She kicked off her shoes as she walked through, stopping to flip on the bedside lamp. Was she in for the night?

She hesitated, undecided still. She peered down to the book she'd been reading, but it held no interest for her. The image of an embracing couple on the front blurred, and when it came back into focus, the characters looked like her and Tomás. God, did she have *any* self-control at all?

She sank onto the edge of the bed, then fell backward with a groan, her hair fanning around her on the bright bedspread. Her legs dangled off the edge as her eyes stared unseeing at the ceiling. Meanwhile, her mind raced with the pros and cons, and her heart pounded with anticipation…or warning.

But deep inside, in her most secret spot, Erica knew she wanted Tomás with a ferocity that could easily undo her. The size of the wanting had begun to eclipse the magnitude of the fear, and his…pull was almost more than she could resist. As he'd said, she knew where he stood, he knew where she stood. So what was the problem?

Other than the fact that she could really fall for this guy.

This guy who wanted nothing to do with a woman in his life.

No. Forget that. She wouldn't fall, and she didn't want to be "a woman in someone's life" anyway. She had her eye on her goals, and nothing, especially not a man, not even Tomás, could distract her from those.

So what in the hell was she waiting for?

A steely determination flooded Erica, and she jolted up. Damn it, she wanted this. She wanted one night with him, if nothing else. And there would be nothing else. She accepted that. But the point remained, Tomás was waiting in his room on this very floor, waiting for her, waiting to make love to her.

Sure, it could be disastrous, but it could also be amazing.

It *would* be amazing, if that kiss had been any sort of a preview, and creating an amazing memory was enough for her. The thought of that kiss was the deciding factor, and suddenly Erica burned with an urgency to go. Immediately. To knock on his door, to feel his arms around her, his lips on hers. She stood, hurrying to put on her shoes and stopping quickly in the bathroom to check her appearance and rinse with mouthwash.

She was a grown woman with complete control over her emotions, with a steadfast determination to reach her goals, to live life on her terms. She would have one perfect night with Tomás. The consequences, she decided as she entered the hallway, could be dealt with later.

It was after 1 a.m. when Tomás heard the light knock on his door, but he'd been wide awake and waiting, hoping. His heart leaped, and his body went on full alert, sensations zinging and bursting through him like fireworks through a dark Fourth of July sky. Up until this moment, he hadn't been sure she would show. In fact, he'd begun to have serious doubts. Flirtations in a back hallway were one thing, but they still left Erica that all-important ''out'' she seemed to thrive on. Despite that, she had shown up, and coming to his room meant one thing, and one thing only: she wanted him, at least half as much as he wanted her. That spelled nothing but good news if you asked him.

One lamp burned in his room, washing everything in a warm, dark gold glow. He thought about buttoning the camp shirt he'd thrown on after his shower, but decided it didn't really matter. With any luck, he'd be taking it off soon anyway. Why compound the work? When he snicked back the dead bolt and opened the door, a cone of bright hallway light spilled into the room like a brash glare of reality, but they both ignored it.

There she stood, looking unsure and scared and turned on all at once. Boy, he could relate. He leaned his forearm against the metal doorjamb and studied her, letting all his emotions show, hiding nothing. "Hey."

She didn't respond for a moment, just traced his body with her eyes, from his face down to his torso, bare between the flaps of the shirt, and back up. She blinked a couple times and chewed on the bottom corner of her lip. Good. They would start on equal footing in the nerves department, a piece of insight that comforted him. Finally, she swallowed. "Hey." A tiny smile played on her lips. "You going to let me in or do I need a secret password?"

After a brief pause, he eased the door open wider and stood aside, dipping his head slightly in welcome.

Her gaze dropped to the carpeting as she crossed the threshold past him, and directly toward the chairs they'd sat in that morning, going over a schedule that hadn't needed to be revisited just so she could spend time in his presence. He'd known it then, and it both flattered and baffled him. Right now, though, the memory of it turned him on.

His studied the sway of her rounded hips as she moved through his room, his space, into his world in a deeper way than she'd ever done before. He watched her toe one gray pump and then the other off her feet, and then she turned, the heels of her hands braced on the table behind her. She looked so much tinier with her shoes off, so much more vulnerable. So much more…relaxed. Even though she wasn't. That much was evident in the way she white-knuckled the table's edge, which he found both amusing and endearing.

His gaze traveled slowly up her body, taking in all the scenic spots along the way. When he reached her face, that familiar sexy challenge shone in her eyes. He swallowed thickly, past a lust so strong it temporarily immobilized him. This lust felt somehow different from others he'd felt over the years. Deeper, more alive, brighter. Riskier and more frightening.

Finally, he remembered himself. He closed and locked

the door, then ran his hand through his just-washed hair, feeling lost for words, unsure of the next step. He didn't want to just…jump her, but she was so damn sweet. So damn…

Everything I've ever wanted.

He brushed the disturbing thought away, grasping for the banal. He was not going to make this…encounter more meaningful that either of them wanted. "Can I…get you a drink?"

One corner of her mouth lifted, sardonic and sexy at once. "I didn't come here for a drink, Tomás."

Instantly, all of his pistons fired. He pinned her with his gaze, cocking one eyebrow. He had to be certain. Had to know. "What did you come here for?"

A beat passed, and her bravado faltered. "Something that probably indicates I have finally gone around the bend." She tossed her hair, and her dark eyes pleaded with him. "Are we insane? What are we doing?" She flipped her hand, a helpless, confused gesture. Sweet vulnerability.

"Erica," he whispered. He closed the distance between them in three strides and she was in his arms, breasts against his chest, mouth his for the taking. Oh, but she took, too, and he found it so meltingly sexy. So hot. She wasn't a woman to be had, as so many others had been. She was a woman who gave as much as she got, who knew what she wanted and took steps to get it. She was so completely different from the women with whom he'd been…acquainted over the past decade, and he couldn't get enough of her.

He molded his hands to her waist and around, up and down her strong, lean back, pulling her in, deepening a kiss that was already so deep it felt like making love standing up. Her hands explored him just as hungrily, from his back around to his bare chest, her thumbnails flicking over his taut nipples without a single iota of shyness. God, he was so hard for her. So physically controlled by every little thing she did.

That should scare him.

It should terrify him.

Why didn't it?

He groaned, then used every remaining scrap of his strength to lift her and set her on top of the table. She was light, but his desire for her had weakened him. "I'm glad you're here," he whispered, against her lips, desire thickening his voice.

"How glad?"

"Let me show you. I...I want to show you, Erica." He studied her for signs of doubt, of refusal, but saw none. His hands pushed her dress up a bit higher, allowing him access to her firm, soft thighs. He was gratified to learn that she wore thigh-high hose...and a thong. He was also startled to realize that he wouldn't have cared if she'd worn support hose over white cotton briefs. This was about her—the woman she was—not about her choice of garments. It wasn't about some preconceived fantasy with all the right props.

He cupped her face in his hands, leaning his forehead against hers for a moment, his eyes closed. "God, Erica. Forgive me, but I've wanted this...wanted you for so long."

She slid her hands around his wrists until he tipped his face up enough for her to kiss his lips. "Me, too." She sounded almost ashamed to admit it. "But I hope you realize we're probably making a mistake."

"Could be a huge one."

"But we're both clear on where we stand, so who cares?" She looked at him, a worry line bisecting her forehead. "Right?"

"At the moment, not me." He kissed her deeply, his tongue and hers in an intimate dance. After a moment, he pulled back. "I didn't want to admit to myself how much I wanted you."

"Me neither. But, I'm admitting it."

"Me, too."

She grabbed the front of his shirt and pulled his mouth back to hers, moaning her pleasure into a new kiss.

He reached around behind her and unzipped her dress, their lips never breaking contact, tongues touching, tasting. He eased the dress off her arms and let it pool at her waist, and then he stepped back just to look at her, to burn this beautiful image into his memory for the long, lonely nights ahead.

She sat before him half-dressed, hair disheveled, lips moist and swollen from his kisses, nipples hard beneath a little scrap-of-nothing lace bra, and her chest rising and falling rapidly. For several heavy moments, they stood staring at each other, breathing hard. He couldn't believe this moment had come. He didn't want to waste time standing immobile in his own disbelief, however. He wanted to make love to her, wanted to prove to himself that this night was actually real. That Erica Gonçalves was here. With him. For him.

He watched Erica's shaky hands slowly, so slowly come up to meet at the middle of her bra, between the lush, promising curves of her breasts. Swift fingers unclasped the bra and then she shrugged it, first off one shoulder, then the other.

Her breasts were high, round and tipped with rosy caramel-brown nipples, taut with arousal. His reaction was immediate, feral. He clenched his fists to keep himself in check. "You're…unbelievable," he said, his voice husky and amazed, feeling so lucky for her trust.

"In a good way?"

He nodded. "The best way."

She held her arms out to him, and he came forward, feeling so fortunate. He took her breasts into his hands, molding them, lifting them, feeling the hard peaks against his palms. Such a delicious dichotomy, the soft mounds and then the hard tips. He took her mouth, swept his tongue inside then pulled back and bit her bottom lip gently.

Their eyes met.

He released her trembling mouth. "This okay?" he whispered.

"It's okay."

Unable to hold back a moment longer, he bent, lifting one supple breast and taking the nipple into his mouth, nipping and pulling on it while he caressed her other breast with his free hand. Erica let her head loll back, hands splayed on the tabletop behind her for support, her chest lifted toward him. She moaned and strained toward his touch, his tongue, and the sound shot directly to his groin. Her thighs subtly squeezed his hips, quivering with an unmet need and he cautioned himself to go slow, to make it perfect for her. He wanted to feel her, wet and warm around him, squeezing him intimately, taking him in. He wanted to bury himself in her in the most private way possible, but he also didn't want to rush.

Pulling back from her breasts, he stared down at the glistening, taut, moistness of them, and then he watched her. He couldn't help himself. She was beauty in a way he hadn't seen beauty in…maybe forever. Open and brazen, sweet and unsure. They shared a soft smile, and then he could watch no longer. He kissed his way down her soft stomach to her legs, exposed above the delectable thigh-highs. He absolutely crackled with sensation, physical and—hard to believe—emotional, too. He needed more of her, and he needed it now. He slid his hands behind her knees and pulled her to the edge of the table, then knelt before her and hooked his finger inside her thong to pull it to one side.

He rubbed his whiskered face side to side, along the tender insides of her thighs and against the soft, moist black curls between them. One sharp intake of breath told him she liked what she was feeling. She smelled like clean, sexy woman, ripe and musky and pulsing with readiness for him. He couldn't think of a better scent, a more enticing taste. Slipping his hands beneath her buttocks, he lifted her to him, glancing up at her face for a moment before bending down to indulge in her fully, to feel her most private pulse against his tongue, to taste her excitement.

With one slow, measured sweep of his tongue, he parted her. She bucked gently and moaned. He didn't need further encouragement. Pressing his mouth to her, he stroked, suckled, and nipped her warm, wet center with his tongue and teeth until her thighs shook and her moans came with abandon. She couldn't hold them back. He didn't want her to. Reaching up, he slid one, then another, finger inside her body. So hot, so slick, wet and ready for him. Her body tensed, closing around his fingers, and he smiled against her wet curls. He increased the pressure with his tongue, probed her more deeply with his fingers, until her body contracted around them rhythmically and she cried out—even laughed a bit—with her release. He savored the gush of moisture her climax had brought and knew, without a single doubt, that he *had* to be inside her. He couldn't wait much longer.

She'd sunk down to her elbows on the table, head hung back, razored tips of her black satin hair brushing the polished wood. He could look at her like that all day, all month, all year, but right then, she looked up at him, eyes half-mast with satisfaction. "Tomás," she whispered.

He reached out a hand, and she took it. He helped her to stand, then slipped that dress all the way off until it puddled at her feet. The thong went next, then the thigh-highs. A momentary thought intruded; he couldn't believe this was happening. She moved in on him immediately, her hands pushing his shirt off his shoulders as her mouth lifted to his. He smelled of her, he knew, and she moaned with pleasure as she tasted him, tasted herself on his lips.

He hadn't thought he could grow harder, and yet he did. His erection pulsed, almost painfully so. They broke the kiss for a moment as he yanked his shirt over his head and then they came back together, as though magnetized. He felt her small, agile hands on his belt, his fly, and then on him, warm and tight and unafraid to take what she wanted.

A groan broke loose from deep inside his throat as she stroked him, up and down, her thumb brushing gently over the drop of moisture at the head.

"My turn," she whispered, pushing him backward. The backs of his legs met the bed and he sat automatically. He kicked off his pants and briefs, then lay back. Almost before he regained his bearings at the change in direction, her sweet mouth closed over him, an onslaught of hot pulling moisture, that wicked, wicked tongue. He wanted her to stop before he lost it; he wanted her to never stop. He swirled in a vortex of physical sensation, an unexpected quicksand of emotion he didn't want to ponder too closely.

He reached down blindly and threaded his hand into her slick, soft hair as she tasted and suckled him, brought him just to the brink over and over before backing off each time.

Finally, he gripped her shoulder. "You've got to stop."

She chuckled, then reached for something. With effort, he lifted his head. Her purse? From inside, she extracted a foil packet. Leave it to take-charge Erica to remember protection. He'd brought his own, of course, but it pleased him that she'd thought ahead, too.

He heard the package tear, then felt her deft fingers rolling the condom into place, making even that feel like a caress. She stood and started to climb onto the bed above him, and he emitted a low, playful growl in his throat. He liked a woman on top sometimes, but not this time. Not this woman, not this night. As give-and-take a lover as Erica was proving to be, he needed to love her, to capture her, to show her that she wasn't just another body, that she was more. He was consumed with an overwhelming need to claim, which he didn't want to examine too closely in the heat of this unexpected night.

Reaching up, he pulled her body on top of his, feeling the softness of her breasts compressing into his chest. In one quick motion, he rolled her over until he was on top, on his knees between her willingly spread thighs. He looked at her, studied her facial expression for a moment. ''Problem?''

''None whatsoever.'' She raised to her elbows and then eased herself all the way up onto the bed, her full breasts bouncing with the effort. Tomás crawled after her, soaking her in with his eyes. All that soft, creamy skin.

The tops of his thighs nudged up against the backs of hers as they lifted for him. He could have simply plunged into her, had sex, focused on the physical. But his damn, traitorous, romantic heart wouldn't let him. He paused, locking his eyes with hers for one eternal moment. He needed to know, needed to understand how this had happened and why. Needed to be absolutely sure it wasn't just okay with her, but that she wanted him as much as he wanted her.

He needed it to be for the right reasons. His erection teased against her, the heat and wetness engulfing him. It was all he could do to speak, and, when he did, the word came through gritted teeth. ''Erica?''

''Please,'' she whispered.

''You're sure? I want you to be sure.''

''Tomás, don't make me beg.''

Enough said. With one swift, deep thrust, he entered her. Hands beneath her buttocks pulling her body onto him, he held her there. He felt a hot, fast pulse but didn't know if it was his or hers, didn't care.

''So right, Erica,'' he murmured. ''So right.''

She hooked her legs around him and raised her hips. The motion was enough of an invitation. He started moving. This wasn't a slow, tender version of making love. Oh, no. Neither of them had the patience for that, not on this night, not after all the weeks of unstated wanting. Her hands grasped at him, nails digging in, as she pulled him into her body, rising to meet his hard, steady thrusts.

He moaned. She moaned.

She cried out and he pulsed harder inside her.

He reached out and grasped the headboard for leverage, pulling himself deeper, deeper into her, until he knew he couldn't hold on a moment longer. He felt dizzy with the restraint, but he wanted her to find her pleasure first. "Come on, sweetheart. Let go." He reached down and swirled the pad of his thumb over her small, distended nub. He felt her body start to quake around him and knew he was going to lose it.

"Erica?" he groaned, jaw clenched to maintain control.

She threw back her head, exposing that long creamy neck, her pounding pulse visible. "Now. Please, now, Tomás."

His hands spanning her waist, he pulled her body once, twice, three times onto him, so hard, so far inside her he was sure he felt her heart beating against him as he released. Her body convulsed and tensed and gushed around him as they both cried out in unison. Time froze for a good long moment, and then he fell forward, covering her with his body but careful to keep the bulk of his weight off her.

After a moment, everything in the room stilled around them, and it was as if reality had shifted. He dropped one forearm next to her head, then the other, his lips against her forehead. Their breathing came rough and ragged. A sexy sheen of sweat glistened between her breasts.

"Oh, Erica," he whispered, knowing he was in trouble.

"It was good?"

"It was good," he assured her, through gasps, his tone gentle. Then wondered the same thing about her. "For you?"

"For me, too." She smiled softly, and his heart clenched.

Trouble wasn't even the word. The realization struck him suddenly that he'd fallen over an edge he hadn't even known was there. "Oh, God," he half groaned, knowing it was too late for regrets, for backtracking. No sense scrabbling for the edge, trying to pull himself over the top to sanity. He'd lost himself to this amazing woman, just like that. And part of him never wanted to be found.

She stroked his back, his waist. Tipped her mouth up to kiss his lips. "It's okay. It's good, yeah?"

It's better than good, Tomás thought to himself. He'd never felt anything like it, and he knew with a flash of white, dangerous fire that he never wanted to feel another woman beneath him, around him, connected to him again. No one except Erica, the woman who never wanted a long-term man. And *that,* he knew with a death knell of certainty, was one hell of a problem. Oh sure, he hadn't wanted long-term, either, but he'd never been inside this woman before. All he knew was, he wanted her.

"Tomás?" she asked, her face showing a bit of concern.

"Oh, God," he whispered again. Could he get his heart back now that he'd inadvertently given it to a woman who wanted nothing to do with it? Again. "Yeah, it's okay." He kissed her, and then kept kissing her. He closed his eyes and told himself it was okay, praying he could make himself believe it, deciding that, even if he couldn't, he wanted this magic with Erica for as long as the spell could last.

They'd made love twice more that night before ordering room-service hot-fudge sundaes—which led to a fourth round of lovemaking as tasty as it was messy—all she could say was thank God for frozen maraschino cherries—and then falling into a sated sleep in each other's arms. There had been a point after the first time when Erica felt like Tomás might be having second thoughts, but his shift in mood dissipated as quickly as it had appeared. After that, nothing but bliss.

Oh, she knew this wasn't the real world, but she didn't care. For this moment, on this night, in this man's arms, things couldn't be better if she'd planned them. Erica had drifted off surrounded by a sense of peace, of safety. Her last lucid thought was, she could get used to waking up next to Tomás Garza. The smell of his skin, the sound of his breathing. The promise of making love to him, feeling his arms holding her. It all felt magical and safe. She could get used to it, indeed.

She awoke sprawled on her stomach next to Tomás with an incessant and annoying noise in her ears.

Loud. Obnoxious. Persistent. *Brrrrrrrrrring!*

She lifted her head and squinted through the bright sunlight slanting through a break in the curtains, across Tomás just as he'd turned from her and picked up the phone. God, who would call at the crack of freakin' dawn? She glowered at the clock, which read…9:26 a.m.? That gave her a start. Not exactly the crack of dawn after all, and Hope and Ruby would be expecting her at any minute.

Hope and Ruby. She and Tomás. Real life. Oh, God.

She rolled onto her back, then sat up, leaning against the headboard and pulling the covers up around her naked breasts to ward off the glare of the sun and the brash reality of The Morning After. Her skin still felt a little sticky from the ice cream and chocolate sauce, and a rush of fresh desire hit her, but it was tempered by a wave of unease.

Nine twenty-six in the morning.

She smeared her tangled hair away from her face and tried to quell the sensation of things being not quite right. The outside world had intruded, and she could already feel the spell breaking. They'd connected, she and Tomás, in a frighteningly real way. If only they could stay in this fantasy room forever.

"Hello?" Tomás mumbled into the receiver, propping himself on one elbow and clearing the sleep from his voice. His back was to her, and the sight of that sleek, muscled expanse of skin, his long hair disheveled and black against the white bed linens, struck her low and deep. She could look at that every day.

Stop it, she ordered herself, trying to focus on the here and now. It was probably Manny or James, from the band, wondering where the heck their lead singer was. They all had places to be, people to see, including her. She would only hear one side of the conversation, but she'd known Tomás long enough to discern between the tones he used with different people, so she listened.

"Well, hello." He stretched, then settled back against the headboard next to Erica, offering her a quick warm smile when he noticed she was awake. His hand slipped beneath the sheets and rested possessively on her stomach.

Her insides melted at his touch. She wanted to pull away…and yet she didn't want to.

"What are you up to this morning, baby?"

Oh, God. Erica's heart kicked into instant overdrive. It wasn't Manny nor James. It was Hope. Erica made frantic hand gestures toward Tomás meant to convey that he shouldn't let on the fact she was in his room. He nodded, giving her a "calm down" motion with his hand, looking relaxed and at ease, almost as though he'd been there, done that, many times before. Gulp.

"Yeah, you did," he said into the phone. She felt electrified, her world tunnel-visioned down to the contact between his hand and her skin. But he just went on talking to his daughter as if everything was status quo. Freaky. "We ran over a few hours, so I didn't get to bed until really late."

And then spent four straight hours making love, Erica thought, sure that he was remembering, too. Hoping he was.

He smiled at something Hope had said. "It's okay. I don't mind if you wake me up. You know I always love hearing my best girl's voice." A pause ensued, and Tomás gave Erica a wink. She gave him a reproachful look.

"Stop it," she whispered, indicating the phone receiver.

He simply shook his head no. "Oh, she's not there yet?" he asked in an innocent tone. He glanced pointedly at Erica and her stomach plunged.

She scrunched her face into a grimace, covering it with both hands. Hope was clearly asking about her whereabouts, completely innocent to the fact that Erica was presently naked in her father's bed. It was all *way* too much. How did people ever manage to have sex after kids were in the picture? Reason number 1,000,031 why she would never be cut out for family duty. She bit on her bottom lip to stifle a morose groan.

"Well, she worked later than I did, baby. I'm sure she'll be there just as soon as she gets stuff wrapped up here, okay?" A short pause. "I know you want to see her, but have patience."

Erica slid her hands from her face and peered over at Tomás. She found it both charming and a bit disconcerting how dadlike he could sound after the erotic night they'd shared. Probably honed during years of practice getting his needs met without ever letting his daughter know. Double gulp.

The visual image that followed was like a cold splash of water to the face. She didn't want to think about Tomás with other women, and she absolutely didn't want to contemplate the reasons behind the aversion. It's not as if she and Tomás had any ties to each other. It was *one* night. She wouldn't get hooked on a man who went against every goal she'd ever set for herself, no matter how good he made her feel.

Okay, her train of thought was *so* not erotic.

She removed his hand gently from her body and swung her legs over the edge of the bed, needing to get up, get dressed, get her head together and get the hell home. Tomás might be riding home with his band mates, but Erica had to pick up Ruby and Hope at her house and drive them all the way back to Rociada. In order to face them, she needed a few minutes to erase images of last night from her brain, and she certainly didn't need any fresh visions to torment her.

Something had happened when she and Tomás had made love. Something scary and threatening and real. She could feel herself becoming hooked on the guy, and that wouldn't work. On that lovely note, she started to stand.

Tomás's hand on her shoulder stopped her. She peered back at him, knowing it was a mistake. The pleading welcome in his eyes reeled her in, and, against her better judgement, she eased back under the covers, nestling close, resting her head on his shoulder. She laid her palm on his slim, muscled torso and closed her eyes. If only it were as real as it felt.

Try as she might, she couldn't get back to that place of rightness that had lulled her into false security the night before. By the light of day, all their obstacles popped up in front of her like ugly puppets, reminding her why she'd vowed to avoid this man in the first place. He was emotionally inaccessible. He had a family. He was exactly the type to steal her independence if she fell for him, however unplanned that might be on both their parts, and the thought terrified her.

At the same time, though, the smell of his skin, the light touch of his fingers on her spine as he talked with his daughter—a conversation tuned out by her own racing thoughts—made her want to curl into him and never let go. Never.

And that was a problem.

The man didn't want a permanent woman in his life.

She didn't want to *be* a permanent woman in any man's life.

And yet she wanted Tomás, so much.

Erica sighed. Was she ever in a world of hurt.

After the phone conversation, that seemed split-second short in retrospect, Tomás hung up. He sighed, the sound as heavy as the thoughts burdening her. "I don't know what to make of that."

"What?" Tipping her head, she pushed aside her own misgivings and peered up into his troubled face.

"You didn't hear?"

"No." Her heart thumped in her chest. "I wasn't paying attention. What's wrong?"

"Well…I'm not saying anything's exactly *wrong*—" But

his gaze slid away, and she knew something was definitely wrong.

Her uh-oh radar went on full alert. "Are they okay?"

"Yes, they're—"

"Did something happen with the house?"

He smoothed her hair absentmindedly with one hand. "No, Erica. Chill. It's not the house, it's…" He cringed.

She jolted to a sitting position. "What?"

He blew out a breath, casting her a guarded look. "Well, it's probably nothing, except after what you've told me…"

"Tomás!" She clenched his forearm. "Tell me."

He grabbed her hand and held it pressed against his bare chest. The words tumbled out in a rush. "Ruby and Hope had an unexpected visitor this morning, and she's still there. Hope slipped and said you were staying here…with me."

"Oh, God!"

"She didn't mean it the way it sounded, of course, but—"

"Who?" The blood pounding in Erica's ears made her fear she wouldn't hear the answer. But it didn't matter, because she knew who'd dropped by, just as she knew her life had just gone to hell. "Who was it, Tomás? Who's at my house?"

His gaze slid back to meet hers, sympathetic and apologetic at once, as though he knew how she'd react once he told her. As if he sensed it would be an issue. He reached over and stroked his fingers down her cheek. "Your mother."

Chapter Ten

Well, so much for the fantasy.

The monster, known as reality, had burst into their dream-world, stomping all over whatever magic lingered from the amazing night they'd shared. Erica groaned inwardly, but resigned herself to the new status quo. Last night was last night, after all, and she had to keep it in perspective, no matter how many new feelings for Tomás swirled around inside her. The unexpected morning wake-up call was a clear and present reminder that recess was over, and it was high time to get on with the business of her life. A life which did not, unfortunately, include leisurely days in bed with the very sexy, very talented Tomás Garza.

Deal with it. Your choice. Your mess.

She gave a resigned sigh, flinging the blankets off and snatching her dress up from the floor. She used it to cover her nakedness as best she could, then spun back to Tomás, feeling suddenly shy. "I'm so sorry about that."

"Sorry? Why?" He lunged across the bed and tugged the

dress away playfully, tossing it to the other side of the room where it settled, like a parachute, over a lamp shade.

She stood there stunned. And so very naked. "Tomás!"

He took hold of her hand before she could cover herself, his smile coaxing, his golden eyes full of promise, his body so ready for her. The sheet had slipped away, exposing every delicious inch of him, but he clearly wasn't bothered by his own nudity. Tomás, she'd learned, was a man completely at ease in his own beautiful skin, a fact that made him just that much sexier.

"Forget your mother," he said, his voice full of promise. "They're having a nice visit. Come back to bed."

She avoided looking at his body. Doing so seemed inappropriate somehow this morning. She focused, instead, on his face, the strong planes and angles roughened by morning beard. His eyes looked soft and sleepy, full of desire. He was so lethally sexy, and when he'd been inside her, she'd felt something special. Something like…belonging. How was she supposed to resist him?

She stole one moment to appreciate the broad, golden-brown expanse of his chest, the lean muscled stomach…and below, before reality struck her once again. She could not stand here leering when the world was crashing down around them. *Her mother,* lest they all forget, had been chatting up Ruby and Hope for God knows how long while she—Erica, the confirmed bachelorette—slept naked next to Tomás. Who knows what havoc Susana had wreaked, what assumptions she'd made, what kind of impression she'd left with Hope, with Ruby.

It was all wrong. Disastrous, in fact. She did not have the patience for her mother's pressure and innuendos, which were surely in the offing after this. She needed time and space and privacy to mull over the knowledge that Tomás had spun her world on its axis. The only remedy was to rush over there and head off any suspicions at the pass. Hence, the leering simply *had* to stop, and no way, no how, no chance in hell could she get back in that bed. A long moment passed, her hand still in his.

So, why wasn't she moving?

"Erica," Tomás teased, in a low, sexy purr. "Come here. You know you want to."

Oh, she wanted to. You bet she did. Too bad it would be damn near the most irresponsible decision she'd ever made. A bad choice. Bad juju. Bad idea all the way around, as a matter of fact, probably even bad feng shui. Bad, bad, bad.

"Are you nuts?" Erica managed, finally, though her own words sounded weak to her ears and her skin tingled where he'd touched her. She cast about frantically for another garment, feeling so exposed, so vulnerable to him. Her dress, she noted with dismay, was Way Over There. Call her a typical woman, but she didn't relish the idea of streaking through the broad daylight—in front of him—to retrieve it.

As luck would have it, she spied his shirt in a wadded heap near the foot of the bed and grabbed it, slipping her arms through the sleeves and wrapping it quickly around her nakedness. No time for buttons. One fist clamped the shirt closed at her chest, the other at tummy level. His shirt was redolent with the scent of him, the pull of his sexuality, his masculinity, and—unable to help herself—she lifted the shirt's collar and took a deep breath of that intoxicating scent.

He chuckled, as though reading her mind. "Tell me again how you don't want to get back into this bed with me."

She shook her hair and raised her chin, determined to grasp firmly on to her dignity and resist him. Enough of this nonsense. "Do you have any concept whatsoever how capital *B* bad this situation could be? Stop laughing. My mother is at my house with your daughter and grandmother, need I remind you."

His lips quivered. "I'm aware of that. So what?"

"So what? You think we have time to lounge in bed?"

His expression turned almost pensive. "Erica…does reality have to intrude so soon? Who knows when we're going to have this chance again. We're both aware of all the…issues with…''

''With me losing my senses and getting back in that bed with you?'' she offered.

He smiled. Maybe a little sadly. ''Yes. With you being in my bed at all. But I want you here. Please. At least one more time before life gets…complicated.''

''Complicated?''

''You can't deny it is.''

''Of course not. Which is why I need to leave.''

''No. Please. I want to be inside you again, Erica.'' He held out a hand. ''I know I'm being shortsighted, but at the moment, I don't care. All I can see is you.''

She sighed. He was persuasive, and damned if it didn't stir something inside her. She'd always played by the rules, and now was no time to stop. Right? ''Don't do this, Tomás.''

''Yes.''

''I really…have to go.''

Tomás smiled. ''Don't go. Forget the world and all its 'have-tos' with me, just for a little while.''

Incorrigible. She opened her mouth to protest, but he stopped her, reaching out his hand to touch her thigh, bare beneath his shirt.

''Just for a minute, then. For a goodbye kiss.''

He looked so sincere, so innocent. So completely delectable. She was wrapped in his shirt and drowning in his eyes. The smell of him was all over her body. She was a goner.

''Come on, Erica,'' he coaxed, deep and sexy. ''Aren't we both a little too caught up in the rules? The world is out there. We are in here. Let's take advantage of it.''

She felt her body respond to him immediately, pulsing, opening, swelling with desire. He must have sensed it, because his expression turned a bit less playful, more feral.

"Come to me," he urged, his voice husky. "One kiss."

Her mouth quivered into a half smile. "Yeah, right."

"Please?"

She bit her lip, her eyes pleading with him to be reasonable, her heart pleading with *her* to do what the man suggested. It might be her last chance, and she wanted him so badly. "But—"

"Pretty please?"

She groaned. She shouldn't. She couldn't! But she did. "One kiss," she told him, in a stern tone, as she climbed back into the bed, into his arms.

"I promise," he said, making the Boy Scout sign of honor.

Forty-five erotic minutes later, Erica pulled out of Tomás's embrace, ignored his protests and headed for the bathroom in search of her sanity and her self-control. They seemed to have run off together somewhere. A quick shower, packing, checkout. She might still have time to run herd on her mother's imagination if she hurried, and she felt an urgency to do so. She intended to make the nature of her relationship with Tomás crystal clear to her ever hopeful mother.

Erica frowned at herself in the mirror over the sink as she started the shower. Problem was, the nature of her relationship with Tomás, thanks to last night, had grown murky in the extreme. She supposed she'd best reset the parameters in her mind, get things straight. She tested the temperature with her fingers as steam began to fill the bathroom, then stepped into the tub. As the water sluiced over her, she worked on mind control.

Bottom line? Sadly, last night had been a fluke.

A wonderful, amazing spectacular fluke that she absolutely did not regret...but a fluke nonetheless. From here on out, things would return to normal between them. They *had* to. Because she could fall in love with this guy in a snap, and that wouldn't do for either of them, considering their goals.

He's only a client. Erica repeated this in her mind like a mantra as she washed the scent of their lovemaking from her skin with the small bar of complimentary soap that smelled of almonds. Her fingers lingered of their own volition on her lips, her neck, her breasts. The places Tomás had last kissed and nibbled.

A pang of desire struck low and deep.

He's a client. Yes. A client. She absolutely *had* to convince herself of those words before she'd ever have a chance in hell of convincing her mother. Susana had always been able to read her like a book, much to her chagrin.

Client. Client. Client, she whispered to herself, eyes closed, hands braced on the shower wall. She tilted her head back so she could take the water spray directly on her face.

He's a client. Nothing but a client.

She repeated the word client in her mind so many times, she'd almost begun to convince herself. And then Tomás slipped into the shower behind her....

As it turned out, Erica's mother had already left by the time she escaped Tomás's lure and made it back to her apartment. She maintained a remarkable semblance of normalcy as she made lunch for Ruby and Hope. They discussed *quinceañera* plans while they ate. After that, they packed up and hit the road. And the whole time, all Erica could think about was Tomás.

It was hours before Erica returned to her apartment in Santa Fe for good, after the trip to Rociada and back. She hadn't planned to make it a round trip, but after the whirlwind of emotions she'd experienced with Tomás, she needed some distance to reassess her priorities. She also needed to squelch any romantic fantasies her mother might be entertaining about the two of them, and the sooner the better.

Not that she wasn't entertaining them herself, but for now—maybe forever—they were private. And impossible.

She bathed in stress-relief salts, put on sweatpants and a T-shirt, then took some chicken out to thaw. She poured herself a glass of Pinot Grigio, drank it, poured another, and only then was she fortified enough to dial her mother's number. Susana picked up on the second ring. "Hello?"

"Hi, Mama."

"Well," said Susana, in an overly bright tone, drawing out the vowel. "I take it you're home at last?"

Erica rolled her eyes. "Yes, and I was wondering if you wanted to join me for dinner. We need to talk."

Her mother sounded smug when she said, "I'll be right over."

Twenty minutes later, Susana stood at the counter next to Erica, tearing greens for a salad. Her own glass of wine stood nearby. Erica was on her third. "So tell me about this Tomás."

Ding! Round one. Erica stopped sautéing the chicken and faced her mother squarely. "I knew it was only a matter of time before this came up. Mother, you have the wrong impression."

"And what is the right impression, dear?"

Indeed, Erica thought ruefully, remembering the way he'd held her, the way she'd fallen into those eyes of his and drowned in the feeling of him watching her, loving her. She set her jaw. "Tomás is a client. He got me out of a bind with the wedding, and he wouldn't have been able to do so if Ruby and Hope couldn't be nearby. Ruby had just gotten out of the hospital."

"Yes, I know. Lovely woman."

"So I offered to let her stay here where it's more comfortable instead of at the hotel. That's all. Tomás and the other band members stayed at the hotel, and, because I know you're wondering, no, Tomás and I did *not* share a room."

That much was true. Sort of. They *did* technically have separate rooms.

"Mmm-hmm. Whatever you say." Susana sipped her wine. "What does he look like, this Tomás?"

"That's not the point, and you know it."

"Point? I'm asking a simple question."

Was it actually that simple? He looked simultaneously like danger and like home. He kissed like a dream. And he made her feel as if she were perfect, just as she was. Erica lowered the fire beneath the chicken, then sank into a chair at the table and pondered it. Tomás was…masculine. Beautiful. Virile. There really weren't enough superlatives to describe exactly how hot the man was, so why bother? "Mama, Tomás Garza is a single father of an almost fifteen-year-old girl. He does not want a stand-in mother for his daughter, and even if he did—" She pressed her lips together, frustrated. "Do I even have to launch into the myriad reasons he would be wrong for me even if I were interested? Which I'm wholeheartedly not."

Susana stirred the chicken. "Is that a no? You won't tell me what he looks like?" She cast Erica a knowing look, adding gently. "Because that is, after all, the question I asked."

Oops. After a moment of self-recrimination, Erica flung her arms out to the side, knowing she'd pretty much given herself away and somehow not caring so much. "He's absolutely gorgeous. Is that what you want to hear?"

"Is that what you think?"

Trapped. Screw it. She needed someone to talk to, even if it was her mother. She wouldn't tell her everything. "Yeah, that's what I think. I have eyes in my head, you know." She ran a weary hand through her hair, still damp from her bath. "But there are a lot of gorgeous men in the world, and that doesn't change the fact that I am not interested in marriage." Boy, this spilling her guts thing had been a bad idea. As quickly as the urge to talk had come over Erica, it faded. She would have to deal with this problem all on her own, like it or not. "Or in him. I've had a long week, Mama."

"Okay, *m'ija*. I hear you." Her gaze softened. "My goodness, you invited me for dinner, not for World War III." She indicated the chicken with the spatula. "And I think it's done. So, if you don't want to talk about this man who is so wrong for you in so many ways, then what do you say we eat?"

Momentarily stunned, Erica simply stared at her mother, searching for ulterior motives. She couldn't identify any right off the bat. Well, okay then. An unexpected reprieve. Strangely, she almost wished her mother had pushed her to talk. She felt so confused about everything since Tomás had entered her world, and she didn't know how to make things right again. "Thank you, Mama." She stood, and the women dished up their plates at the stove, carrying them to the table.

"What about Hope?" Susana cocked an eyebrow sardonically, a few bites into her meal. "Are we allowed to talk about her?"

Erica eyed her mother drolly over the rim of her wineglass as she sipped. "Sure. Go for it."

"I think she's a wonderful young lady."

Erica smiled, genuinely this time. "So do I."

Susana tsk-tsked. "That abysmal haircut."

"Yes." Erica's tension eased. "It's pretty awful, I agree. Poor little thing."

"But endearing."

"Isn't it? I think she cut it herself."

"He seems to have done a wonderful job of raising her, despite her mother's absence." She raised her glass in a salute to Tomás, Erica supposed. "Except in the hair department, but what can you expect from a man alone?"

"He's an amazing father," Erica said, a tad defensively.

Susana took a bite of chicken, chewed and swallowed.

She sipped her wine, then wiped daintily at the corners of her mouth with a napkin. "It would take a very special man to do what he's done. But, can I tell you something? One thing, and it's not about the father this time," Susana added, before Erica had a chance to become annoyed. "Just something you might want to know as you complete your assignment with the family."

"Sure," Erica said, warily. "Tell away."

Susana planted her elbows on the table, threaded her fingers together, then rested her chin atop them. "I think you should talk to that little girl about this party, honey."

"Mama, I have. On numerous occasions."

"No. I mean, alone. She's too sweet to say what she really wants in front of her father and grandmother." Susana shrugged. "That's my impression, anyway."

Erica recalled all the times when Hope had seemed less engaged in the whole process than she probably should be. Her mother was probably right. "I knew something was wrong, but I hadn't pinpointed it. Do you think…there's a problem?"

Susana shrugged, taking up her fork again. "I doubt it. And I don't mean to interfere in your work. I just…get a feeling about that little girl. She's a pleaser."

Erica gulped. "What should I do?"

"Plan the event, Erica. That's what the man hired you to do. But never forget that it's Hope's party, not his."

That evening, Tomás sat on the side of his daughter's bed, tucking her in with their usual chat time. It used to be story time until Hope had grown old enough to read on her own. Now, they just shared odd bits about their day.

"Did you have fun at the wedding, Dad?"

Boy, what could he say to that? He'd glimpsed something during the night he'd spent with Erica that he hadn't believed existed—the possibility, indeed the risk, of falling in love again. Even more disconcerting, the knowledge that he could be lured, that he could set both himself and Hope up for another emotional fall if he wasn't careful. It had him spooked.

Which meant, he had to be extra careful.

Which meant, he should avoid Erica for a while, no matter how desperately he wanted to be near her, just to watch her, to listen to her breathe. He looked into his daughter's innocent, trusting face and pulled himself back to the here and now, to what was important. Hope. And Daddy. Forever.

Hope crisscrossed her hands in front of his face. "Yo, earth to Dad. Come in, Dad."

Laughing, he grabbed one of her hands and kissed the back of it, then held it between both of his. "I had a great time at the wedding. They loved us. We played for seven hours."

"Did Erica have fun?"

He slid his glance away, hating himself for the evasiveness. "Well, she was working, *m'ija.*"

"The whole night?"

He nodded, not wanting to remember *the whole night.* Not wanting to discuss this any longer. He needed some time alone to get his own head straight first. "How about you and Ruby? How was Erica's place?"

Hope rolled her eyes. "You mean, other than a full-out feng shui nightmare? Pretty awesome, actually. Erica's mom is really nice, too." His daughter's face flushed with excitement. "Did I tell you, Erica has a DSL line, Dad. You wouldn't believe how fast it is. I wish we could get one. But I know—"

"—we live in the boonies," he finished for her. They both smiled. "If I could get you one, baby, I would."

"I know." Hope glanced down at the quilt covering her, tracing her fingers around one of the small red square centers of the Log Cabin design. "Daddy? Can I ask you a question without you getting mad at me? I'm just curious."

He leaned in and smoothed her hair back off her forehead, dreading a probing question about him and Erica. "Of course. You know you can talk to me about anything."

"What was my mother's middle name?"

His stomach plunged from the unexpectedness of the query. It wasn't that he refused to talk about Racquel. It was just that there had never been anything much to say. The woman—okay, girl—deserted them. Enough said. He swallowed past the knot in his throat and worked on making his tone sound light and unconcerned. "Maria. Why?"

She hiked one shoulder. "I'm just curious, like I said. And her last name was Silva, right? Racquel Maria Silva?"

"Yes."

"Do we...do we have any pictures of her?" Hope added, her voice hesitant and so childlike.

He pressed his lips together and stood, bending to plant a kiss on Hope's forehead. "No, baby. I'm sorry. We don't."

"Why not?"

"Because—" he broke off with a frustrated sound as guilt riddled through him. This was territory he didn't want to broach. A child wouldn't understand. "We just don't, Hope. But enough questions for tonight, okay? You go to sleep." He'd made it all the way to the door before her small voice stopped him.

"Daddy?"

He gripped the doorjamb, unsure how much more he could handle. "Yes?"

"Do you like Erica?"

Finally. Something he could answer sincerely. He turned back toward his daughter, crossing his arms and leaning his shoulder against the jamb. "Yes. I like her very much."

Hope smiled. "Good. Me, too." She reached over and snapped off her bedside lamp. From the shadows, he heard, "But I love you the most of all people, Dad."

He recognized the statement from a little private game,

one they hadn't played in at least eight years. His heart squeezed with emotion. He really missed how close they'd been when Hope was little. "I love you the most of all people, too, baby."

"And animals!" she added.

"And bugs," he replied.

"And aliens," she said, laughing.

"And monsters," he said, moving back to Hope. When he reached her, he began tickling her. "The ones under your bed."

She squealed, and his soul warmed with love. He sat and pulled her into a hug. "You'll always be my best girl, Hope."

"Someday, you're going to have to share me."

"What if I don't want to?"

"What is this, a prison?" Hope joked.

He hugged her tighter and realized, with consuming regret, that he would have to share Hope someday. But not yet. He wasn't ready. He thought of Erica with a small pull of sadness in his heart. Truth be told, no matter how deeply he felt for her, he just wasn't ready to risk more than he already had.

Erica's other assignments, and a little bit of diligence, had kept her away from Tomás for a couple of weeks. He left messages on her machine. She left messages on his. Neither of them tried too hard to see the other, and for this she was grateful…and wistful, in equal parts. Initially, she'd been relieved. Their night together had been physically and emotionally intense, and it had thrown her off-kilter. As the weeks went on, though, she started to feel as though Tomás was truly avoiding her, and she wouldn't deny that it hurt.

Apparently she had been just another woman in a long line of them. Temporary and unimportant. She should be relieved, but she wasn't. And yet, nothing could be done about it. She'd known his wishes going into their brief affair, and she wouldn't play the damaged female for any man. His messages would have to be enough to tide her over, she supposed. She consoled herself with the knowledge that she could hear his feelings in his words, even when the messages were straightforward and businesslike.

Still, she yearned to see him with every fiber of her being. But, distance, she finally convinced herself, was a good thing. She'd begun to feel like her old self again, immune to his charms, resigned to their intrinsic incompatibility, intent on her goals. But when she'd picked Hope up at the house on Friday evening and he was sequestered in his studio, Erica couldn't hold back the wave of melancholy. Facts were facts.

Their night together had meant nothing to him.

Clearly, he wanted her to get the message.

Ah, well, she needed to snap out of it. She had his daughter for a weekend of *quinceañera* planning, and she couldn't waste time in a romantic funk. Plus, it wasn't everyone, she reminded herself, who Tomás trusted with Hope. He might be denying that their lovemaking meant anything, but the fact that he'd allowed Erica to take her for the whole weekend spoke volumes about his true feelings for her. Didn't it?

That weekend, Erica and Hope were hot on the trail of the perfect *quinceañera vestido*—gown, and she also hoped to pin Hope down on which friends she'd like in her honor court. Hope would spend the night with her in Santa Fe, and they planned to shop all day Saturday and Sunday morning. She would return Hope to Rociada Sunday night, hopefully with a lot having been accomplished. With any luck, she'd actually see Tomás in person upon their return. One look in his golden eyes and she'd know, once and for all, his true feelings. She could wait.

Halfway into Saturday, unfortunately, things weren't going quite as Erica had imagined. Hope had been enthusiastic enough on the drive to Santa Fe, and they'd had a lot of fun Friday evening eating pizza and working feng shui magic on Erica's beleaguered baguas, but it quickly became clear that having fun was all Hope wanted to do. In the dress shops, Hope's attitude had gone from subdued to sulky in fifteen dresses flat. By the time she'd emerged from the dressing room in potential dress number twenty-seven, Erica's teeth were on edge.

This was why she hadn't wanted to work with a teenager. She adored Hope. She really did. But it was a dress, for goodness' sake. *Just freakin' pick one,* she wanted to snap. She could tell by the way Hope sulked out of the dressing room in the current offering that this gown didn't make the cut, either.

Annoyance flowed through Erica, hot and sticky. She pressed two fingers to the stress point between her eyebrows and spoke through clenched teeth. "Okay, so what's wrong with this one?"

Hope shrugged listlessly, staring down at the white lace gown. "I don't know. I look like a cupcake."

"You do not look like a cupcake. Everyone knows cupcakes have sprinkles and those little paper things."

Hope cast her a droll glare.

Erica pasted on a strained, humorless smile. "It would help if you could tell us exactly what kind of dress you envision, Hope. Can you do that, at least, to narrow it down so we don't waste the rest of the day combing through every rack?" She glanced pointedly at her watch. "We have a lot to get done, and we've blown four hours here already."

To her utter horror, Hope's chin started to quiver, and she burst into tears. Hauling up the dress's heavy skirts in her fists, she fled toward the dressing room. Erica jumped to her feet and pressed a palm to her stomach, guilt flooding through her. Maybe she'd been too hard on the girl, maybe she'd spoken too sharply. She had to remember, Hope was little more than a child, and this was probably overwhelming for her. "Oh, gosh."

She started unsteadily toward the dressing chamber, but the sales assistant stopped her. "Why don't you let me help her out of the gown," the woman said, smiling sympathetically. "Give her a little space to cry it out. It happens."

Erica had no clue, but it sounded good. "O-okay."

A few moments later, the sales assistant returned, looking a tad more worried. She angled her head toward the dressing area. "You'd better give it a try. She doesn't seem to want to come out, and she sure isn't letting me in."

Erica gave the woman a grim nod, then moved soundlessly over the gold carpeting into the back, where a warren of expansive dressing rooms flanked both sides of a long aisle that ended with a carpeted dais and a massive three-way mirror. She could hear sniffles and hiccups coming from behind the closed door at the end, on the left. Sympathy and regret tightened her throat. And fear. She didn't know how to handle heartbroken teens, and she hated being the one who had made Hope cry. She reached the door, stood for a moment feeling way out of her element, then knocked softly. "Hope?"

A pause. "Yeah?"

She swallowed. "You okay, honey?"

"I'm sorry, Erica. I'm not trying to be a jerk, honest. I just…can't decide."

"I never thought you were being a jerk." Erica crossed her arms and leaned against the framework of the slatted, white door. This whole shopping trip had been pretty whirlwind in nature. Hope, after all, was a small-town girl. Erica was accustomed to working for society brides, who had known what type of wedding gown they wanted since girlhood, but she couldn't lay that rap on Hope. "Listen, I'm sorry I snapped at you."

"I-it's okay."

Erica remembered what her mother had told her over dinner a few weeks earlier. "I have an idea. Want to hear it?"

Hope hesitated. "Sure. I guess."

"Let's forget all these stupid dresses and go out for burgers and shakes. I think we both could use a break."

Silence. A few sniffles. "Really?"

"Really. I know just the place. They make the milkshakes in old-fashioned metal shakers and even bring you the extra on the side. You'll love them."

After a pause, Hope sounded more hopeful. "Okay."

"Great. I'll just go out front and wait for you, okay? Come on out when you're ready." She started to leave.

"Erica?"

"Yes."

"Are you…mad?"

Erica smiled at the vulnerability in the girl's tone. She might not have the maternal instinct, but she knew the feeling of being an awkward fourteen-year-old and wanting to be liked. Yes, she'd been annoyed. She'd had an agenda, and items listed on it weren't getting ticked off at a steady pace, but how could she be angry with the girl? Before jumping into this thing any further, they needed to have that heart-to-heart her mother suggested. She softened her tone. "Of course I'm not mad. Let's just go eat and forget about it for a while, okay? We'll have some girl talk. Everything will be fine. I promise."

"Are you going to tell my dad that I didn't cooperate?"

"I threw too much at you at once. It's not your fault."

A few more sniffles. "Okay. I'll be right out. Just let me get out of this heinous cupcake."

Erica laughed, feeling better already.

They were seated at a table for two in the fairly nondescript little diner that locals knew was a hidden gem. Their butcher-block table was laden with thick burgers, baskets of steaming french fries and tall chocolate shakes before Erica even broached the subject of the *quinceañera*. She selected an extra-long fry, dunked it in their communal ketchup supply at the center of the table, then cleared her throat. "Can I ask you something, Hope? Woman to woman?"

Hope's cheeks grew rosy at the thought, it seemed. But she also looked pleased to be considered a woman. "Sure." She bit into her burger and waited, chewing thoughtfully.

"How do you feel about this *quinceañera?* I mean, really."

Hope swallowed her bite and set the burger carefully on her plate. She wiped her hands on her napkin, a worried little frown on her forehead. She peered up at Erica cautiously. "Do you promise not to tell my dad? I don't want to hurt his feelings."

Erica smiled. He'd raised such a thoughtful girl. He walked on eggshells around Hope's emotions, and she did the same for him. She wondered if Tomás knew this about his daughter. Erica pushed aside her food for the time being and concentrated fully on the young woman seated across from her. "I don't want to tell him anything that might hurt his feelings, either. But I want you to know that you can talk to me, as your party planner." But it was more than that, and she wanted Hope to know it. "Woman to woman. You can talk to me."

"Okay. Well, then…" Hope sighed, with the drama only a young girl can pull off. "I'm SO not into it, Erica. I mean, it's nice of my dad and everything, but no one has *quinceañeras* around here. None of my friends have them. Everyone just celebrates the regular American holidays, you know? Not the Mexican ones. I'm all weirded out about it."

"You know, a lot of cultures celebrate a young woman's coming of age, Hope. It's not just a Mexican tradition." Hope looked unconvinced. Erica flipped her hand. "Young Jewish girls have what's called a Bas Mitzvah at age twelve."

"Really?"

"Yes. And the Apaches celebrate the coming-of-age of

their young girls with the whole community dancing them into adulthood. The celebration is called the nai'es.''

Hope cringed. ''That sounds a little whacked.''

''I think it sounds beautiful. And let's not forget the debutante balls people have all over this country. It's the same thing. The *quinceañera* just honors your heritage.''

Hope stirred her thick milkshake with a straw. ''I just feel really uncomfortable, Erica. I don't even know any boys to be in my honor court. I don't know if I *want* boys in it.''

''But, why haven't you told your dad all this?'' Erica angled her head to the side quizzically. ''You really should.''

Hope's eyes bulged. ''Are you nuts? No offense. But my dad has been planning this thing since I was an infant, it seems. He's really into it. He'd be so disappointed.''

''He loves you. He would understand.''

Hope looked skeptical. ''I mean, I want to have it for him, I guess, but I wish...''

''What do you wish?''

''I don't know. That it could just be a regular old party without all the fancy parts.'' She slumped, absentmindedly dipping a fry into the ketchup cup with no apparent interest in eating it. Erica trusted her instincts and kept quiet. She knew Hope had more to say.

''Oh, but the fancy parts will be so much fun.''

''The thing is...no, never mind. It's really stupid.''

''I bet it's not stupid. Go ahead. I always find that things get easier if I don't keep them bottled up inside.'' HA. She was the queen of bottling her emotions—take this issue with Hope's gorgeous, unattainable father. But this was a *do as I say, not as I do* moment. She smirked at her own duplicity.

Hope twisted her mouth to the side, seeming to consider it. ''Okay. It's just—'' She broke off, and her face turned red.

Erica was astonished to see tears welling up in the girl's

eyes. She reached over and covered Hope's hand with her own, feeling alarmed. "What is it?"

"Oh, Erica," Hope cried. "You know the dress thing? The truth is, I just feel…stupid in them." Fat tears spilled over and rolled down Hope's cheeks. She sniffed loudly.

"What do you mean, stupid, honey?" She pulled a tissue from the pack in her purse with her free hand and passed it across the table to Hope.

Hope flipped the hand holding the tissue toward Erica, then wiped her eyes. "I mean, if I looked like you or something, maybe those dresses would look good. But I look terrible. I'm just so—" her voice dropped to a whisper "—ugly."

Erica's heart squeezed. She remembered being Hope's age and wanting desperately to fit in, to be cool. And it had been so difficult. At fourteen, very few girls had it together. But a person only knew this in hindsight. "Oh, Hope. Honey, you're not the least bit ugly. I can't believe you'd even think that."

Hope smeared her tears away. "Easy for you to say. You're beautiful. You always know how to dress. Your hair is perfect."

"I'm an adult. It takes a while to hit your stride, believe me. When I was your age, I had my problems, too. My hair was *stick* straight, and curly hair was in."

Hope touched her own messy hair. "I hate my hair."

"We all hate our hair, Hope. Welcome to being a woman."

A small smile touched the girl's lips, but faded away quickly. "I just… I don't know how to walk in high heels and I look…ugly." She leaned in and whispered. "I've never even shaved my legs yet because I don't know how and I don't want to ask my dad or Grandma Ruby." She squeezed her eyes shut and covered her face with both palms. "God, could you die?" she asked, the words muffled by her hands.

"Oh, honey."

Hope let her hands slide away, casting Erica a beseeching look. "It's the most humiliating thing ever, being me. And with the whole *quinceañera* thing. It's just…heinous. I SO don't want to be in front of a zillion people in some ridiculous cupcake dress and not knowing how to walk in heels, tripping over my dad's feet during the waltz while a whole bunch of boys who don't even like me stand around miserable. AND I'll look ugly. I'd rather DIE than that, Erica. I swear."

"Well, of course you would die if that happened. What self-respecting woman wouldn't?"

Hope's eyes bugged.

"But, point one, you don't *have* to include boys in your court if you don't want to. You don't even need to have a court at all, although it would be fun to have some of your soccer friends all dressed up with you, don't you think?"

A noncommittal, unenthusiastic sound came from Hope's side of the table as she sipped her shake.

"And, point two, you aren't going to look ugly."

"And the award for who's *high* at this table goes to…" Hope held a palm out toward Erica.

Erica couldn't help but laugh. "Silly girl. I'm not lying to you when I say you don't look ugly right now. And for the *quinceañera,* you'll be all dressed up like a princess."

A faint flicker of interest showed in Hope's eyes, but it was quickly doused by her insecurities. "You're just saying that because you're nice. I'll look more like one of Cinderella's ugly stepsisters."

"Hope, I'm not that nice. But maybe…maybe you don't have to have this party if you don't want to."

"I have to. This stupid *quinceañera* has been, like, my dad's dream for an eternity. I can't let him down, even though I'm SO totally dreading it." She paused, her chin quivering from the outburst. "I don't know what to do."

Erica hesitated. "Maybe we can talk to your dad together, work out some other kind of party."

Hope seemed to consider it. "I'm not sure. Maybe."

"You really should tell him."

"I'm afraid to."

Erica pondered Hope's admission, trying to come up with a solution, and an idea popped into her head. A *quinceañera was,* after all, a rite of passage from childhood to womanhood. Maybe it was time for Hope to grow up a bit, to gain some confidence that would help her through the event. At fourteen, Erica would've done anything to have a professional tell her how to do her hair and makeup.

She hadn't discussed anything like this with Tomás, but she felt sure he trusted her to do the right thing where Hope was concerned. For God's sake, he and Erica spent hours making love. Of course he trusted her judgment. And, it would be Erica's treat, a pleasant surprise for both Hope and her father, a way to show him that she cared.

"I have an idea," Erica said, in a conspiratorial tone, her excitement growing the more she thought about it. She retrieved her cell phone from her bag and held up a finger to Hope, then dialed. After a short conversation, she snapped the flip front closed and grinned.

"What is it?" Hope asked, clearly intrigued.

"Let's finish lunch quickly, okay? We have a full spa treatment and makeover appointment in thirty minutes."

Hope's eyes went round and bright. "Are you serious?"

"Absolutely. It will be fun." A thought gave her pause. "Wait. You're allowed to wear makeup, aren't you?"

"I'm allowed." She shrugged. "I usually don't because I don't know how, and the one time I did, some jerk in school called out, 'Who did your make-up, Garza? Sherwin-Williams?' I was so humiliated. I thought I would DIE right there."

"Well, after these women teach you how to use it, you'll be the hottest thing in the halls, I promise."

Hope, back to her eager, happy self, bounced in her seat. "Oh, Erica. This is the best weekend EVER." In a spontaneous move, she jumped up from the table and came around to give Erica a big hug. "You're the coolest."

Erica accepted the hug, feeling warm. "It's my pleasure. Won't your dad be surprised with your new grown-up look?"

Hope's face glowed until she was positively radiant. "I can't wait!" For the moment, all was right with the world.

Chapter Eleven

"Is it really okay?" Hope asked several hours later, but Erica could tell from the shine in her eyes that the girl loved it. The stylist had trimmed Hope's hair into a very updated shaggy bob with a light fringe of bangs. The feminine style framed her face and made her eyes look huge. As instructed, the aesthetician had gone light and natural with the makeup, and the result was a very polished, stunningly beautiful Hope.

"Okay? You're a total hottie."

Hope giggled, beside herself. "I can't believe it, Erica. I never thought I could look like this."

Erica slung an arm over Hope's shoulder and steered her toward the door. "On the other hand, I always knew you could. What do you say we splurge on a cute new dress to go with that look—" she leaned in and whispered "—and those newly waxed legs, and then we'll head to your house for the unveiling of the newest goddess on the planet?"

"Serious?"

"Dead."

"That totally rocks the most. This has been the best day of my whole life. Thanks to you."

Erica winked, thinking it had been a pretty fantastic day for herself, as well. Kids generally gave her the hives, but Hope was actually fun to hang out with. *"De nada."*

They started to leave, but Hope hesitated at the front of the salon, checking her image one last time in the large, gilt-framed mirror adjacent to the door. Her confidence faltered, and she bit her glossed bottom lip. "Do you think Dad will like it?"

Erica stood next to her and spoke to Hope's image in the mirror, her eyes smiling. "You're a vision. He's going to be the proudest papa around. How could he not love it?"

"What in the hell have you done?"

Well. Not quite the response Erica had imagined, not after two weeks of hardly any contact at all—and especially after the fun surprise she'd orchestrated to cheer up his glum daughter. And if his nostrils had to flare like that, she'd rather it was from passion than anger. This, however, was definitely anger, and a boatload of it. No smoldering looks, no affection, not even a simple hello. She hardly recognized the furious, posturing man looming before her.

"I asked you a damn question," he growled, his glower directed at Erica.

"Daddy, stop it," Hope cried, blanching beneath the artfully applied makeup, her bewildered gaze ping-ponging back and forth between him and Erica. "Don't be mad, I—"

"Quiet." He scissored out one hand, cutting off Hope's words with the efficiency of a machete, but his stony glare never left Erica's face.

Feeling off balance from Tomás's unexpected response, Erica flicked a sympathetic glance over at Hope, whose eyes brimmed with unshed tears, and her heart ached for the girl. She'd been so proud of her new polished, grown-up look, so eager to get back to Rociada and show her father. The makeover and the new little retro minidress that flattered her budding figure had given her a much-needed dose of confidence. All the way home, she'd repeated the words—*I can't wait to show Daddy.*

Now, here they stood in the middle of the kitchen, and *Daddy* was acting like a big, overbearing ogre, ruining everything. Erica felt a flare of anger on Hope's behalf. No matter what it meant for her, she had to try and salvage the poise and self-esteem that the makeover had given Hope.

"What do you mean, what did I do? I treated her to a special day." Her tone came out knife-edged, and she didn't care. She damn well hoped Tomás got the message that she thought he was acting like a controlling jerk. She'd never seen him like this, and she didn't much like it. They'd barely walked in the door before Tomás's eyes widened with surprise and then narrowed with accusation. Right after that, it was game on.

She stepped closer to Hope, taking her arm and thrusting her gently toward her father. "She wanted to surprise you with her new look. So, look at her, Tomás. She's beautiful."

He didn't. "She always *was* beautiful. She doesn't need that crap on her face."

"You never said I couldn't wear makeup, Dad!"

He flicked a dismissive hand toward his daughter. He didn't catch the hurt look in her eyes, though, nor did he see her flinch as if he'd hit her. He didn't sense the waves of shame that radiated from her, but Erica did and it infuriated her.

"It's not a matter of need." She frowned. "Why are you acting like this? It was a simple makeover."

"Yeah?" He loomed closer, arms crossed. "And what gave you the right to take my daughter out and dress her up like a twenty-one-year-old woman? You're supposed to be planning her *quinceañera,* not changing her appearance."

"Changing her appearance?" God, Erica had never

wanted to hit anyone quite so much. Her fists were clenched so tightly, she could feel her nails digging into her palms. "If you'll take a look, Tomás, your daughter is maturing—"

"You think I don't know that?"

"—into a very beautiful, sophisticated young lady," Erica persisted, ignoring his interruption. "Young ladies need guidance with looking their best, and that's all we did. She doesn't look like a twenty-one-year-old woman at all."

"She damn sure doesn't look like a fourteen-year-old girl."

"Daddy, please! Will you stop talking about me like I'm not even here?" Tears, black with mascara, had begun to streak down Hope's face, ruining the beautiful makeup job. Erica was glad Ruby wasn't here to witness this debacle. She ached for Hope and felt profound disappointment in Tomás.

"She does look fourteen." And then she forced an encouraging smile toward Hope. "You do, Hope. You look exactly like yourself, just a little polished up, and there is nothing wrong with that." She turned her attention back to Tomás. "If you'll step back from yourself for a moment and *look* at your daughter—"

"Don't you dare tell me how to raise my own—"

"Raise her?" Erica was so flabbergasted, she almost couldn't speak. "Tomás, for God's sake, would you be reasonable? She was feeling blue, so we—"

"Forget it!" Hope pleaded. "Forget it, Erica. I'm sorry. We never should've gone." Hope cast her a desperate look. "Just stop it. Both of you," she added, before running from the room.

Erica couldn't believe what had just happened. Where was the man who had looked at her as if he cared, who had touched her and made her feel safe? She released a small, enraged growl before starting after the girl. Tomás wrapped his hand around her forearm, stopping her. She whipped back to face him, livid, and yanked her arm out of his grasp.

Her chest rose and fell rapidly with the adrenaline coursing through her system. "What?"

"If anyone is going to go after *my* daughter, I am," he said, his tone deadly serious. He looked just as angry as she felt.

"Then go after her! Can't you see she's heartbroken?"

He clenched his jaw, stubborn enough for a good slap, Erica thought. "I'll see to my daughter when I'm done with you."

"Done with me? What—did I earn detention? A flogging? For God's sake, listen to yourself!" Her distaste for controlling men had just gotten one hell of a booster shot. Fine, she wouldn't go console Hope. She'd spent two hundred dollars on his daughter today because she cared for her, and she'd begun to imagine maybe she had a place in their lives. She'd wanted Hope to feel special—and isn't that what Tomás, himself, always touted? Two hundred bucks, down the drain. Hope was so traumatized over the whole thing, she'd probably never touch makeup again. Not only that, but Erica realized just where she stood with this family, and her heart shattered.

"I hope you're happy, Tomás," she rasped. "Hope and I had a wonderful, amazing day together. I finally got some insight into her personality, and you've destroyed it. You are unbelievable."

"Oh, now this is my fault?" He scowled.

"You're damn right it is." Erica jabbed a finger in the direction Hope had fled and spoke through clenched teeth. "Here's a news flash for you, Tomás. Ready? Are you listening? That gorgeous young daughter of yours doesn't even want to *have* a *quinceañera*." She realized, belatedly, that Hope hadn't wanted her father to know this. A needle of regret stabbed her, but he really did need to know.

"What?" His eyes widened with bafflement.

"And do you know why? Do you?"

He said nothing, but his expression softened from anger

to concern, although the stubborn set to his jaw remained. He gave a barely perceptible shake of his head.

"Because she felt clumsy in the high heels and awkward in the gowns. She didn't feel pretty enough," Erica snapped, throwing her arms out for emphasis. "And she was embarrassed to come to you about it. So, I'm sorry, but she came to me. And, I was honored to know she trusted me that much. I figured, with all you and I had been through together, that you'd be okay with that. That you trusted me enough to do right by her."

Tomás reached out a hand. "Erica—"

"Sure, you and I know she's not ugly, but our perceptions don't matter. She is fourteen years old." Arms clenched by her sides, she glared up at him. "She fled in tears from the dress shop, Tomás. In tears, because—"

"Listen, I'm—"

"No. *You* listen." Right now, she didn't care what he had to say. He'd mishandled her emotions. She had a full-out rant going and she planned on getting it all said before she left. "She burst into tears. That's how uncomfortable she felt. But, I guess you know all this, since you know exactly what it's like to be a fourteen-year-old girl, huh?" She tossed him a skeptical look. He had the decency to look chagrined.

Erica huffed. "Yeah, that's what I thought. I am not trying to horn in on your parenting, news flash number two. As you well know, I have no interest in being a parent. I wasn't *parenting* Hope, I was being a friend." She whipped two palms up to face him. "Excuse me for caring about your daughter, for assuming I knew how you'd want me to treat her. I figured you wouldn't mind if I took her under my wing. My fatal mistake, but believe me, I won't make it again. I see where the boundaries are now, Tomás, and—"

"Erica, I—"

"Oh, no." She poked a finger into his chest. "Don't you

dare chastise me like a child in front of Hope and then interrupt me before I'm done yelling about it.''

He inclined his head, a sign of surrender.

She took up a steady pacing from one end of the kitchen to the other, because the pain inside her could knock her to her knees if she stopped. She raked her fingers through her hair, realizing this wasn't just about Hope and the makeover. The ramifications ran way deeper than that, and she knew what she had to say. She was just having difficulty voicing it around the lump of pain in her throat. ''We made a mistake. We crossed that invisible line between business and personal when we both knew it could go nowhere, when we knew one or both of us would end up hurt.'' She cast him a miserable glance. ''And apparently, there's no going back, either. At least not for me.''

Tomás's eyes widened. ''What are you talking about?''

She gaped at him. Was she the only one who could see the forest for the trees? ''Me! You! The weekend at the wedding and this *quinceañera* your daughter doesn't even want.''

He glanced over his shoulder and then moved closer, lowering his tone. ''What does my daughter have to do with the night we spent together, Erica? These are two different issues.''

''Two different issues?'' she repeated, astounded. That statement was wrong on so many levels, she couldn't even begin to acknowledge it. Bottom line was Tomás Garza could share his body, but his world was completely off-limits, and Erica didn't think she could bear that. She cared too much. He might think they could have a nice little secret fling, but the threads of his family had already reached out and become entangled in the tapestry of her life. She was—

Oh, no. Erica's blood ran cold, and she stopped short.

She hadn't admitted it to herself, or to anyone—indeed, she'd been valiantly trying to repress the truth since the night they'd made love. But she couldn't deny it any longer.

Her heart was telling her the lie wouldn't work. She loved Tomás.

She was *in love* with Tomás Garza and headed for heartbreak.

Why? Because Hope was the most important person in his world, and yet clearly Erica was not allowed to care about her. That fact spoke volumes about where she stood with Tomás; tears stung her eyes, but she blinked them back.

Sadness swooped in and doused the heat of her anger. Her shoulders sagged. She clenched her temples with shaking fingers for a moment, then looked at him somberly. If she didn't leave now, leave *for good,* he would destroy her. "You know what, Tomás? You've been through a lot in your life, and you're a wonderful father, save this most recent hideous display, but no one's perfect. I'm sure she'll forgive you."

"Erica—"

"But, after all we shared—" her voice cracked, and she hated herself for it "—if you can't trust me to do right by your daughter, then I can't continue to plan this *quinceañera.* I cannot put myself in the position to be hurt by you, and that's exactly what will happen. We both know it."

He went very still. "What are you saying?"

She picked up her purse and hiked it onto one shoulder. What the hell—she might as well tell him the truth. "I'm telling you, Tomás, that our night together? It meant something to me. Obviously more than it meant to you. That's fine. I knew where you stood when I went to you. But, your *needs* will have to be met somewhere else, because I'm learning, quite surprisingly, that I can't be someone's ugly little secret. At least not yours." She reached up and tucked her hair behind her ears. "And I can't plan this party for Hope."

"You can. I…I do trust you."

She blew out a little humorless monosyllable. "No, Tomás. You don't. But don't worry—I'm not blaming you. It was completely my mistake. And I shouldn't have assumed that there was something between us, something that would make it okay for me to take Hope to the salon for a make-over.''

He reached out and cupped her elbows with his hands. ''Wait. Let's talk about this. Please. I—I overreacted.''

''Yes. You did. But I guess it's good it happened sooner rather than later.'' She eased out of his grasp, then backed toward the door. ''Goodbye, Tomás.'' She studied his face for one more long moment, then shook her head sadly and turned away.

''Erica,'' she heard him say, sounding hoarse with emotion.

She didn't turn back, though, opting to wave him away with her hand instead. If she had turned, he would have seen the tears in her eyes, and the last thing she wanted Tomás Garza to know was that she'd fallen in love with him...or that he had the power to make her cry.

He'd screwed up. In epic proportions.

In the silence that remained after the screen door slammed, Tomás stood his ground in the kitchen, clenching and opening his fists, replaying his knee-jerk reaction and feeling nothing but pure, undiluted shame. Dread settled like wet concrete in his gut, and all he could think of was how monumentally he'd ruined what had been a joyful, milestone event for his daughter.

God, he never thought he'd feel this kind of crushing regret again. Hadn't he carefully orchestrated his whole life around avoiding it? His so-called pain-resistant life plan? He'd been so damn smug about it, too. The image of Erica's sad eyes as she'd left kicked him in the gut, but he pushed it away for the time being. Right now, he needed to go to his daughter.

He replayed the whole ugly scenario in his head as he

moved through the house. It wasn't that Hope hadn't looked beautiful when she walked in the door. On the contrary. My God, she was so beautiful and grown-up looking, she'd knocked the air from his lungs. It was his damn pride that had tripped him up. If Hope needed a new haircut, some help with her wardrobe, it should have been him who noticed it. He should have caught on that she felt uncomfortable with herself, and then he should've done whatever he could have to remedy it.

But he hadn't caught on. Erica had.

And he simply hadn't been able to accept that someone else had perceived more about his daughter's needs than he had. He yanked the elastic out of his hair, so angry with himself for his actions. *Idiot. Control freak.*

What had it hurt for Erica to treat Hope to a special day? It hurt his pride, that's what, and he was a damn fool for letting that blind him to what was best for his daughter. He'd sworn he would never do that, and he'd failed.

His confidence faltered as he turned toward her bedroom. Her door was closed, and he hesitated in the hallway, hanging his head. His heart thumped like a gong in his chest, and he couldn't seem to slow down his breathing. *You're the adult, Tomás. The parent.* Setting aside his fear, he raised a fist and knocked softly. "Hope? Baby? Can I come in?"

A pause. Then, listlessly, "I don't care."

He pushed the door open with more than a little trepidation. His gaze moved around the room, from the new dress, wadded in a pile in the corner, to Hope's face, scrubbed so clean it was raw pink. Her eyes, too, were rimmed in red from crying, and her hair had been shoved into a ponytail. She wouldn't look at him.

Moving slowly, he sat on the edge of her bed and released a long sigh. After a moment, he scrubbed a hand over his face and started the only way he knew how. "Hope, I'm sorry."

"It's okay," she told him, her tone glum.

"No, it's not." He looked at her, but she refused to meet his eyes. He touched her chin gently. "Look at me. Please."

She did so, albeit reluctantly. Her eyes filled with tears once again and her lips quivered.

With a groan of self-disgust, Tomás pulled his daughter into a hug. She nestled her head onto his shoulder. "I don't know how to explain it. I…I just saw you standing there, looking so grown-up and beautiful. I guess I thought it should've been me taking you to the salon." Hope sobbed, then sniffed and wiped her nose on his shirt, which made him smile. "I overreacted."

"You were so mean to Erica."

He rubbed Hope's back slowly, her fleece pajamas soft beneath his palm. "I know I was. I didn't mean to be."

"Did you apologize? She's going to hate me now."

"No." A beat passed. "But I will apologize, I promise. And she won't hate you." *She'll hate me,* he thought, with a stab of pain in his chest that he couldn't bear to examine.

Hope pulled back from the embrace and studied his face, her eyes liquid with tears. "So, you don't think I look ugly?"

Tomás released a short, rough chuckle, then laid a hand over his chest. "Baby, you look so beautiful, it makes my heart hurt. I promise. My…stupid reaction had nothing to do with the way you look." He glanced into the corner. "You should hang up that new dress so it doesn't get ruined," he suggested gently.

"I'll never wear it again."

"Sure you will. To school." He made a few boxing jabs in the air, then winked at her. "I'm going to have to work on my boxing skills to keep away all the boys who will be after you."

Hope giggled wanly, then went somber again, pulling at a loose thread on her quilt. "She was only trying to be nice, Daddy. She likes me. And I like having a girl to talk to.

Woman to woman." Her eyes flicked up, then back down. "No offense. I like talking to you, too. But there's nothing wrong with me wanting to talk to a girl now and then. A woman."

"I know." He pulled the scrunchie out of her hair and ran his fingers gently through her new, soft hairdo. "I'm sorry. I should've realized that a girl your age needs...well, girl talk. I love you. You know that, right?"

She nodded again. "I love you, too."

"I'm your dad. But I'm not perfect."

"Yeah, no duh." She gave a mischievous little smirk, watery and vulnerable. "You were perfectly heinous in the kitchen."

He suffered a fresh wash of self-recrimination. "I know I was. Will you forgive me?"

She shrugged. "I guess. Of course. But you better apologize to Erica. I've never seen you be so mean to someone. I didn't even know you *could* be so mean."

He grimaced. "I regret that, *m'ija*. And I regret that you had to see it."

"You know, at school, when a boy is mean to a girl, the teachers say it's because he likes her."

He didn't want to get off on that tangent, no way. "Yeah, well I'm not a boy at your school. Hope...I've been thinking. Maybe we ought to hold off on plans for the *quinceañera* for a while. Think things through." It hurt him to see the barely disguised relief on her face, but he forced himself to remember that the *quinceañera* was for her, not him. If she didn't want it, what was the point?

"Really?"

"If that's what you want."

She slid her glance away. "What about Erica?"

He hesitated, avoiding the question by standing, walking around the bed, retrieving the minidress and hanging it up. Then he turned back to her. "Erica has other jobs. She doesn't need to help us plan the *quinceañera*."

"What?" Hope's eyes widened in horror. "Oh, no!" she wailed, then flounced back onto her pillows, pulling the covers over her head. "I didn't want her to go away, Daddy."

He swallowed, feeling like the biggest heel. "Do you want the *quinceañera,* Hope? Tell me the truth."

"Not if Erica doesn't plan it," was her muffled reply.

"And if she does?"

"If it will bring her back, then okay, I'll do it."

"But do you *want* the *quinceañera?*"

She uncovered slowly and pinned him with a pleading glance. "Who cares about the *quinceañera?* I want Erica. She was my friend, Dad, and you ruined it."

"I'm so sorry. A thousand times, I'm sorry."

Hope sniffled. "Maybe if I could have a more modern kind of thing. Do they ever have those? With…not so many stupid gowns. Don't you think that's sort of old-fashioned?"

He chuckled softly. He never imagined that he'd be considered old-fashioned at age thirty-one. "Okay, baby. We're going to work this out, I promise. Just go to sleep, okay?"

"But, will you make Erica come back?" She looked at him beseechingly. "Do you promise?"

He'd screwed up with Hope in more ways than one. He couldn't disappoint his daughter again. "I promise I'll try. But that's all I can promise. It has to be her choice."

"Make her come back, Daddy. I like her."

"I do, too." Way too much. And that, it seemed, was the least of his problems. Because his daughter liked her even more. Just what he'd been afraid of all along. "I'll do my best."

Erica cried all the way back to Santa Fe, and when she reached her house, all she wanted to do was sleep. She brewed a pot of green tea, changed into her most comfortable pajamas and sat down in front of her computer to catch up on e-mail. Since Tomás had come into her world, she'd dropped a lot of balls in this never-ending juggling act called life. Another clue that cutting off ties had been smart. Wasn't losing track of her own life just the first step toward losing her identity altogether?

She was initially surprised to see that her computer was on, but then she remembered Hope had been on it that morning, before they'd left the house. She rotated her track ball to bring the screen up, startled to see a dialog box with the message: RESULTS OF YOUR SEARCH. Studying the Web site header, Erica realized it was a service used to find lost family members. Her heart started to thump in her chest. Not this. Not now.

This wasn't her problem. It wasn't her business.

Tomás, as he'd displayed in spectacular fashion, didn't want her anywhere near Hope. She should just exit out of the Web site and go to her e-mail. Somehow, though, she just couldn't. She took a sip of her tea to moisten her dry throat, then clicked the dialog box. The Web site went to work loading the new page of results for the person for whom Hope had searched. Racquel Maria Silva. Her long-absent mother, not that it was a surprise.

Erica would bet money that Tomás had absolutely no idea. After all, they never spoke of Racquel. She rested her elbows on the edge of the desk, worked her fingers into the front of her hair and hung her head. Why her? She didn't want to know this. She didn't want to make the difficult decision, to tell or not to tell. She'd already violated one of Hope's confidences, telling Tomás about her lack of interest in the *quinceañera,* and she had a feeling that would pale in comparison to this bomb if she dropped it. He'd probably think Erica had a hand in the search.

Erica groaned. Tomás Garza and his complex family were a complication she just didn't need in her life. And they didn't want her in theirs. It should be simple. So why did everything feel so empty without them?

And what was she going to do about this Web search?

Deciding to table it for the time being, she printed out the search results and set them on top of her monitor, then she switched over to her e-mail program. She scanned the list of messages, and her heart jumped when she saw the message from ILUVDOGS@webfriends.net. Hope. It surprised her how glad she was to hear from the girl. She quickly opened it and read.

Hi Erica—
I'm sorry about what happened. I told Dad he was being mean, and he agreed. (We made up—I think he feels really bad.) He said he was going to apologize to you. He also said you weren't going to plan my party anymore. Are you mad at me? I don't want to plan the party without you. :-((((Even though things sorta sucked when we got home, thanks for taking me to the spa. It was the best day of my life. I miss u!!!

Love, Hope G.

Erica could barely see for the tears blurring her eyes. She had never expected to get so attached to a child, of all things. She smeared the wetness from her cheeks with the backs of her hands, then hit the reply button and wrote:

Dear Hope,

Of course I'm not mad at you, and I'm glad you had a wonderful day at the spa. I did, too. Let's take a little time and think about the *quinceañera*, okay? There is no reason for you to have it if you don't want to. I'm glad you and your dad made up. He really loves you, you know, despite what happened today.

I miss you, too, honey.

   Love, E :-)

Erica paused, torn, before adding the rest. She decided, though, that Hope could use a friend. Erica wouldn't go behind Tomás's back, and she wouldn't assist in the search for Racquel, but if Hope needed someone to talk to, she wouldn't deny her. Taking a deep breath, she added:

P.S. I have printed something from a search you did on the Web while you were here. I'll save it. You let me know if you want it, or if you want to talk about it.

There. She'd effectively put the ball in Hope's court. If she wanted to talk about her mother, Erica would allow it. As much as the girl's father had hurt her, Erica knew it was wrong to abandon Hope, especially after the way they'd bonded.

Erica smiled, ruefully. Her mother would be so proud. Erica Gonçalves, hanging with a child. She never would've predicted that one, not in a million years.

After sending the message, Erica signed off, deciding she didn't have the heart to read e-mail. She just wanted to curl into a ball and sleep for a week. And maybe, if she was lucky, when she woke up Tomás Garza and his amazing daughter would be long gone from her heart....

Chapter Twelve

It had been three days since his life had gone to hell, and Tomás was finding it difficult to work, to concentrate, to go on with business as usual. Oh, he went to his studio every morning, but that was mostly to wallow in his own self-pity and dodge the knowing glances from Ruby. He hadn't told her that things were off with Erica, and he didn't know whether or not Hope had expounded on their blowup. But he did know he didn't have the heart to get into it with his grandmother, who would pull no punches in her opinions. He knew he'd been wrong.

Bottom line, he didn't know how to handle this one.

Erica had taken a piece of him with her when she left, and the hollow void left behind continued to ache. He needed to go to her, to apologize. He knew that. He was just so ashamed of how he'd behaved, he dreaded the confrontation. He told himself he was giving her time. Ha. He was confused, scared—all those things a man wasn't supposed to be. Well, damn it, he was a man, and he unabashedly had feelings. Right now they were in tatters, and he didn't think he could survive her rejection again.

Tomás blew out a sigh, then scrubbed his hands over his face. The light coming in through his studio windows was perfect for detail work, but he had no motivation for it. When he couldn't even grasp the big picture in his own life, how was he supposed to concentrate on or care about details in his work? The door behind him squeaked open. He turned and realized, suddenly, that his wily grandmother was a welcome sight. "Hey, Rube. Come on in."

She held up her usual thermos container of coffee. Caffeine was an easy ticket into his world, she knew. "Care for a little jolt?" She eyed his worktable, which was pretty much clean. "It looks like you need something to get you going today."

"I'd love some," he said in a weary tone.

Ruby wheeled herself to sit adjacent to his table, then handed over the thermos. She eyed him knowingly. "As long as you don't report me, I'll let you in on the fact that I went ahead and added a few shots of Baileys Irish Cream."

"You know—" he smiled at her through the steam as he poured a cup "—you have an instinct for what a man needs. Thank you."

"Don't mention it." She clasped her hands together on her lap, drew in a deep breath through her nostrils, then blew it out through pursed lips. Watching and waiting.

He said nothing, avoiding her gaze. She said nothing, piercing him with her eyes. The standoff was unbearable. Finally, she broke it. "So. What's new, *m'ijo?*"

"Not much." He sipped.

"Getting a lot of work done?" She eyed both his worktable and the long drying table, a bit sardonically, truth be told.

His mouth twisted ruefully. "Not really."

"Had many insightful chats with your daughter recently?"

"Not...lately." A pause ensued, and Tomás braced himself.

"Things with the *quinceañera* proceeding as planned?"

He studied his grandmother, realizing he'd known all along that her rapid-fire questions weren't the stuff of idle conversation, not at all. She'd come out to ply him with laced coffee and get some straight answers. Things in the Garza household had been suspiciously quiet the past few days, and Ruby felt out of the loop. He had to hand it to her, her MO wasn't half-bad. "No, Rube. They aren't proceeding at all."

A beat passed, during which Ruby pressed her lips together and shook her head slowly. "You screwed things up, didn't you?"

Tomás groaned, furrowing his fingers through his hair. "You have no idea. I screwed things up astronomically this time."

"I figured as much," she said, her tone no-nonsense. "Pour me some of that coffee and then enlighten me. Problems never get solved if they're churning around in your gut."

"It's not pretty," he warned her as he poured.

"What do I look like, a lightweight?"

Half an hour later, he'd told her everything, except about the night he'd spent with Erica. He'd thought he could skirt that issue, because it wasn't really the *point*, after all, this thing with Erica. It had been a detour. The point was his daughter, and how he'd destroyed things for her by angering Erica into resigning the position. *Keep telling yourself that.*

Ruby pinned him with a wise, knowing stare. "You do know that your daughter is inconsolable, I assume?"

He nodded.

"And you know why?"

He didn't want to voice it, because it jacked him way up

on the who's-the-biggest-heel-in-the-universe? scale. Glumly, he muttered, "Because she misses her."

Ruby nodded, using a tone that pleaded with him to be reasonable. "She likes Erica, sonny. We all like her."

"I know that."

"Yes, but when are you going to accept that Hope having adult female role models is a positive thing? I try to stay out of your way with the parenting, God knows. But this time—"

"Listen, I want your advice, Rube. I always have."

Ruby sighed. "Okay, then. Here's my advice. Hope needs a female role model, especially at her age."

"She has you," he offered.

Ruby flicked an impatient hand. "I am six times her age, young man. Don't be ridiculous. I love her like my own child, and she returns that love, but I'm no role model. Don't play the obtuse male card with me. I know better."

He stood, pacing over to check a drying piñata. "You don't understand the whole situation."

"Then explain it."

"I agree, Hope needs female role models." He flashed her a grim glance. "I'm coming to terms with the fact that I can't be and do everything for her."

Ruby looked skeptical.

"I am. Trying at least." He turned back, braced the heels of his hands on the tall counter behind him and crossed his ankles. He stared at the toes of his boots, feeling morose. "But this thing with Erica is…more complicated than you know."

"Because you're falling in love with her." It wasn't a question. Ruby just flat out stated the words that had terrified him in the darkness since the night he'd slept by Erica's side.

And the world didn't come crashing down.

He had to admit, part of him was surprised. He studied his grandmother for a good long moment, chewing on the concept of being in love with Erica, and then shrugged. "I think I *could* fall in love with her, if the conditions were right. And that's the sum total of the problem, you see, because the conditions are completely wrong. Erica Gonçalves has no interest whatsoever in a long-term relationship."

"You learned this the night you spent together in Santa Fe, am I right?"

Heat suffused Tomás's skin. "Geez, Rube. For your information, I learned it long ago at that soccer practice she and I attended together. Do you have a tail on me, or what?"

"*M'ijo,* I've lived on this earth for seventy-nine years. Do you know how many people I've seen fall in and out of love in that time? I don't need to tail you. It was written all over her face when she came back to the apartment, and all over yours when we got home. Plain as day, *m'ijo.*" She waited, but he said nothing. "What are you going to do about it?"

He set his jaw. "There's nothing to be done about it. You know how I plan to live my life. And Erica—"

"Listen." She had his full attention, and he found, yet again, that he craved her guidance. "And, for once, I mean really *listen* when an old woman talks to you. I know you think I'm off base, missing the point, a couple of fries short of—"

"I'll listen, Rube. I promise."

She nodded. "*Bueno.* Let me tell you about a young woman I used to know." She held out her coffee mug and he topped it off with the thermos. "Rebellious? *Hijuela,* you have no idea how much. She was the only daughter in a family with six sons. Back in the day, you know. Long time ago."

Tomás nodded, then moved back over and took the stool facing his grandmother. He sipped his coffee, but did not interrupt.

"Good girls were supposed to learn from their mothers, obey their fathers and marry well." Ruby shook her head slowly, a faraway look in her eyes. "Not this one. She was smart, this one. Intelligent and so eager to learn, to be educated." She made a fist, palm facing up, and shook it. "She soaked knowledge up like a sponge. She begged her papa to go to school, broke him down until he let her." Ruby laughed, a thready sound.

"Those were blissful years, the school years. But, when she turned fourteen, her papa pulled her out."

Tomás made a sympathetic mutter, which earned him a sharp look from his grandmother.

"He wasn't cruel, you know. Resources were limited. They needed help on the farm. Only so many could go to school. The boys would have to support families eventually." She shrugged. "The girl only needed to marry well."

"Bet that went over with her like a stripper in church."

Ruby chuckled, then took a drink of her coffee. "Yes. Oh, she understood, you know. Things were different back then. Not so many choices. She should've been grateful for the time she *did* have in school."

"Was she?"

"No. She was resentful. She was smarter than a couple of her brothers by half, and they didn't even want to be in school. Couldn't care less—" Ruby cut herself off and sighed.

"What did she do?"

"What could she do? She followed her father's rules, learned from her mother, helped out on the farm while her brothers attended school." She held up a gnarled finger. "But, she vowed to herself that she would never marry, she wouldn't perpetuate the cycle that kept her from receiving the education she so yearned for, that destroyed her dreams. That much control, she did have." Ruby gave a thin, dry laugh. "She ignored or repelled the suitors her father paraded by until she became known as a spinster. Twenty-four she was, and unmarried.''

"Gee, what an unmarriageable hag," Tomás joked.

"Oh, no. At that age? Back then? Forget it. The hill was much shorter in the day, and, believe me, she was over it. The light in her papa's eyes dimmed. He stopped bringing suitors by, resigned to supporting this daughter forever. Which was fine with the girl. In her free time, she read books, newspapers, anything she could get her hands on. She would sneak and read her brother's books after the household was asleep and then stumble through her chores half-asleep the next morning. But that's what mattered to her.'' Ruby winked.

"So what happened to her?"

Ruby settled more comfortably in her chair. "One day, a young man came calling. Not for her, you understand, but she still lived in her father's house. The young man was a tutor to her youngest brother, who was sixteen and had zero interest in school. *Ay-yay-yay,* she was so bitter about that. What she wouldn't give for a private tutor, for the opportunity to study. And she took out her feelings on this poor, hapless tutor. He wore glasses, he was shy. He stuttered when she spoke to him and dropped his books whenever she was around." She flailed her hand, vaguely. "These days, they would call him a geek."

Tomás laughed.

Ruby stared down at her hands for a moment. "But, an occasion arose when this tutor came across the spinster girl reading, and he sat down and talked to her about the book. Oh, when they had those discussions, believe me, he wasn't so geeky anymore." She blushed. "He'd remove those glasses, and he spoke with such raw passion."

"Even stuttering?"

Ruby shook her head. "He didn't stutter when they spoke of their shared love of books. Of reading. He respected the fact that she yearned for knowledge, and he didn't care that she was so old or that she wasn't interested in finding a husband. This young man, he yearned to give her exactly what she wanted in her life, what she thought she'd never have." Ruby drifted off.

"And?"

She smiled, looking a little misty. "And I married him."

"Grandpa?"

"Yes. He convinced me to marry him by promising to help me learn, to give me time to read and grow into the person I wanted to be. He did it, too. He helped me with the children while I finished high school—" she looked at him sharply "—something that wasn't done back then, *m'ijo.* A man helping with babies? Never. He helped me realize all my dreams and then some, your grandpa, God rest his soul." She crossed herself, then kissed her knuckles. "And he gave me love, too. And a family."

When she finished speaking, she had tears in her eyes and Tomás had a lump in his throat. "It's a beautiful story, Rube. But, with all due respect, what does it have to do with me?"

She sighed. "Sometimes, Tomás, we truly believe we know what we want out of life. We have this image in our mind, and we're stubborn about it. Believe me, I know. I wanted knowledge, and I was certain marriage would stand in the way of that. But then Grandpa came along and showed me options I'd never imagined. It wasn't that I didn't want family, but I didn't want the sacrifices that I believed went along with family. The two don't have to be mutually exclusive if we're willing to bend, to entertain possibilities. To let go of our fear." She reached out and patted his knee. "Erica reminds me so much of myself at that age, it hurts sometimes to look at her. She believes a man will strip her of herself."

He spread his arms. "Right. So, what's the point?"

"Perhaps she just needs a man who respects her enough to love her…and let her be Erica."

He mulled this. "You're forgetting the fact that I don't want a woman in Hope's life. I don't want her hurt."

Fire flashed over his grandmother's expression. "Look me in the eyes, sonny, and tell me that you believe Erica Gonçalves would ever hurt our girl."

A long moment passed. Neither spoke.

"How long are you going to punish yourself for one mistake you made as a boy, *m'ijo?* Don't you think you've more than atoned for your sins? You've raised a beautiful daughter, kept the family business going. You take care of me." She smiled at him. "You may have made your mistakes as a boy, but you've grown into an amazing man. You deserve love."

"I don't...feel like I deserve it."

"Go to her, Tomás. Make it right."

He rolled his shoulders and stretched the tension from his neck. "I want to believe what you say, but I've lived one way for so long. I don't know if I'm ready, *Abue.*"

Ruby leaned forward. "Then go to her and ask her back for Hope's sake. Just ask her to plan the *quinceañera,* like the whole thing started. This connection between the two of you can stand to steep a while longer."

"Hope's not even sure she wants a *quinceañera.*" He slid Ruby a sidelong glance. "Thinks the tradition is antiquated."

"Then find out what Hope *does* want." She drained her Baileys-laced coffee and set the mug on his worktable. "Details can be updated, traditions changed, what does it matter? Ask her questions and really listen. And when you're done?"

"Yes?"

"Go make your peace with Erica Gonçalves. Ask questions, and really listen to her, too." She smiled sadly. "It's all a woman wants, to be listened to. Validated. She's a good woman, Tomás. I know. I've met her mother, and you can tell a lot about a woman from her mother."

"And a lot about a man from his grandmother."

She half nodded. "One would hope."

He swallowed thickly, marveling at the ease with which Ruby could whittle a problem down to its simple core. What would he ever do without her? "I love you, Rube."

She looked pleased, but she brushed away his affection, glancing away. "Oh, go on. Save your 'I love you' for Erica."

"I never said I loved her."

"I know, *m'ijo*." She gazed at him with such raw emotion, his heart squeezed. "You didn't have to."

Erica set down the note card with a dejected sigh. Tomás had been calling her at her firm, sending notes, flowers, cards and e-mails for three weeks. Initially, she avoided contact because she was angry. Then, because she was too charmed by his efforts to trust herself with him face-to-face when she knew nothing could come of it except further pain. Now, after numerous back-and-forth e-mail conversations with Hope, Erica was avoiding Tomás because she knew something about his daughter that could hurtle them back to square one.

Hope was searching for her birth mother.

Erica knew. Tomás didn't.

Been there, done that, had the bruises on her heart to prove it. No thanks. Oh, she'd urged Hope to speak to her father about it on numerous occasions, but just as Erica had known she would, Hope demurred. She didn't want to "hurt her father's feelings." But she had questions about her mother, which Erica thought was absolutely normal. In a perfect world, Tomás would understand and honor his daughter's desire. In a perfect world, come to think of it, Erica would be by his side supporting him through this very difficult conversation with his daughter. But, he'd made it ultraclear he had no desire for that, either.

And it still hurt so much.

How had she fallen in love with an unattainable man?

Didn't she know better? "Ugh, I'm an idiot." She clonked her forehead down on her desk and left it there. God knows, she wasn't getting any work done anyway.

Something made her think of that scene in *The Wizard of Oz*, when Dorothy enters Oz and suddenly the previously black-and-white film bursts with color. The world, as Dorothy had known it, had completely transformed into something brilliant and exciting. That was exactly how it had been for Erica, the weeks she'd spent getting to know Tomás and his family. Her heart had, effectively, dropped into his technicolor world. Now she'd been thrust back into her boring black-and-white life, and she was as miserable as summer in a Midwest dust bowl. The only color in her office came courtesy of the flowers, and Tomás had sent those.

And yet, she still loved the man after all that pain.

She ached for him, would throw it all away for him. That should be a warning sign. Still, so much unresolved nonsense hung between them, and she didn't feel able to move on. Erica lifted her face, then rested her chin on her crossed arms atop her desk and considered her dilemma. She was disconsolate. He sounded forlorn. From all reports, Hope wasn't so hot herself. Fine. You know what? He wanted to talk to her, to see her, to apologize. What could it hurt to talk to the man, to hear him out? She could use a little splash of color in her day, and it would give her the opportunity to tell him some things she needed to get off her chest, too. Namely, that what they'd shared was history, and they both needed to move on.

Brimming with anticipation now that she'd made up her mind, Erica reached for the phone and began dialing Tomás's cell-phone number when her assistant, Gina, popped her head inside the doorway. Erica raised her eyebrows.

"You busy?" Gina whispered.

Erica reluctantly set the receiver back in its cradle and shook her head. She bestowed a tight-lipped, no-teeth version of a smile on Gina. "Nothing that can't wait. What's up?"

"Client here to see you. Shall I send him in?"

Him? Great. Another groom, coming to pour out his woes about his bride turning psycho the closer they got to the wedding. She was used to this. Business as usual. Erica sat up straighter and smoothed out her suit jacket. "Yes, that's fine."

Gina disappeared, and, moments later, Tomás Garza filled her doorway. He'd lost a couple pounds, and his jaw was dark with whiskers. Circles under his eyes told her he wasn't sleeping so well these days. Join the club, she thought. Still, his mere presence seemed to siphon all the air out of the room, and Erica felt breathless, wary and, at the same time, tearfully glad to see him. Bad sign.

She shot to her feet. "Tomás."

One corner of his mouth lifted in a wry, tired smile. "I was planning on camping out on the hood of your Honda like a passive protestor until you spoke to me. I'm glad you decided to see me this way."

"I—I didn't know it was you. Actually."

His face fell a little. "Oh."

Erica came around her desk to greet him properly. "But come on in. I was just…trying to call you."

That hopeful quality in his expression returned. His whole face seemed to brighten, albeit cautiously. "You were?"

"Yes. Have a seat."

"Thank you."

Okay, what now? He was on her turf; she should feel more at ease. Instead, her palms were sweaty and her heart pounded in her chest. "Can I…get you a drink?"

His gaze locked with hers, in a place warm and welcome…and so familiar. "I didn't come here for a drink, Erica."

She recognized his words, *her* words, actually, from the night she'd stolen through the hotel corridors to his room, and desire struck her in the gut. "What did you come here for, then?" she said, her voice not much more than a whisper.

His lips quivered with mirth, but his eyes were sincere. "Something that probably indicates I've gone around the bend."

"Oh, Tomás." She didn't know how he could do that to her, how he could…reduce her with a few simple words. Her shoulders relaxed, and she shook her head at him gravely. "You went around the bend a long time ago."

He chuckled, both of them knowing the ice had been broken, then sat and glanced around. "So, you got all the flowers."

"They're lovely. And unnecessary."

He spread his arms, and his expression softened into something needy and sincere. "I was groveling. Hell, Erica, I'm still groveling. I've been so ashamed of the way I acted the last time I saw you… I didn't know how to make it up to you."

She took her seat behind the desk and inclined her head. She knew she owed him something in return. "I shouldn't have taken Hope for a makeover without your consent. I'm sorry."

"No." He scooted forward on the chair, his manner urgent and unrestrained. "It was wonderful what you did. The ugly truth is, I was…jealous that she'd confided in you and not me."

She blinked at him, startled.

He quirked his mouth to the side, a self-deprecating not-quite smile. "You have to understand…or maybe you don't, but I have to explain. Please. And you know so much of this already."

"I'm listening."

Erica watched as he garnered courage with one deep breath. "It's always been just Hope and me. And Ruby, of course, but she doesn't butt in on my parenting." He held up a hand. "Wait. I didn't mean that the way it came out."

She smiled. "I know you didn't. Please go on."

He smoothed his palms together slowly. "When you brought her in, so beautiful, and so obviously happy, I was jealous that you'd been the one to make her feel that way. It's been months since Hope and I have truly connected. She's so…secretive around me. I felt like it should've been my job, my honor, actually, to get to the bottom of things. And…I took it out on you." He shrugged, looking so contrite. "What can I say? I'm not proud of it, but it's the truth. I'm truly sorry."

Her heart thumped with sympathy and something more. "Tomás, I would never come between you and your daughter. I was merely trying to treat her as special as I knew you would have."

"I know that now."

"I care about her so much." She pressed her lips together for a moment, weighing the wisdom of her next words. At last, she cast him an appraising sidelong glance. "We've been e-mailing. Initiated by her, of course. And if she wants to confide in me because I'm a woman, I'm going to let her."

"I don't mind."

"No?"

"How could I? She's not opening up to me. I'm just grateful she has someone to talk to." His Adam's apple raised and lowered slowly with a swallow. "I never thought these words would come out of my mouth, but…any suggestions for me in the dad department? God knows I could use the help these days."

She cleared her throat and straightened a few items on her desk blotter before meeting his gaze. "Sit down and ask her what's bothering her. And really listen to what she says."

"Is something bothering her?"

"Ask her. And *listen* to what she says."

Tomás recognized the irony that the advice Erica gave mirrored Ruby's wisdom. He nodded. "I appreciate that you're talking with her. I...want her to have a friend. A role model."

Erica laughed. "I'm hardly the role-model type, Tomás."

"You'd be surprised." A long moment stretched between them, stuffed full of all that was left unsaid. "Erica...Hope has decided she wants to have the *quinceañera.* Sort of."

Erica rolled her eyes, glad they'd moved on to a subject a little less charged. "*Hijuela,* fickle women."

"Tell me about it. I'll be gray by the time I'm thirty-five." His eyes sparkled with amusement, but he sobered again, by degrees. "The caveat is, she won't have it unless you plan it."

Erica ruminated on this, not wanting to throw herself into the ring again if it would result in another knockout punch to her heart. But she had to think of Hope. "I won't plan it unless you trust that I have only the best intentions where your daughter is concerned." Her look hardened. "I mean it, Tomás. No matter what comes up in the future, no matter what Hope tells me, or what I share with you—" she thought of the secret she held right now with a pinprick of guilt "—you have to swear that you'll handle it honestly. And fairly. To all three of us."

"I will, Erica. I've learned my lesson, believe me."

Now, for the uncomfortable part. She shifted in her seat, making busy work of uncrossing and then recrossing her legs. "And...as far as you and I are concerned..." The raw hopefulness on his face almost undid her. Beneath her desk, she clamped her fingers together in a painful knot, because this would be the most difficult thing she ever did.

"Anything, Erica. However you want it."

However she wanted it? She wanted to love him and be loved back unconditionally. She wanted to maintain her independence and yet share in the lives of Tomás and his family. She wanted to have her cake and eat it, too, but she knew that wasn't possible. So, the pendulum had to swing the other way. "Things between you and me need to remain strictly professional. I don't regret the night we spent together, but I can't handle more than that right now. I'm sorry."

His expression dropped, but he made a valiant effort to mask his disappointment. "I understand. Strictly professional." He held out his hand, eyes warm as they beheld her. "Deal?"

She stood, came around the desk, then slid her hand into his, stunned by the unbidden visceral response to his touch. One touch, and she was back in his arms, feeling his body filling hers, entertaining wispy dreams of something more, something impossible. Somehow, she managed to keep the shakiness out of her voice and smile. "Deal. And thank you for the apology."

That should have been it. But it wasn't.

He held her hand when he should have let it go, her gaze when they both knew it was dangerous. Gradually, he pulled her closer until she was in his arms. She accepted the embrace, sank into it, really, resting her cheek against his chest and closing her eyes. She felt him kiss the top of her head, then heard him whisper, "I'm so sorry. For everything."

"Me, too," she whispered back. In more ways than one, and more than he'd ever know. Because she'd glimpsed perfection with Tomás Garza, and the absence of it would haunt her forever, no matter how successful and independent a life she led, no matter how quickly she reached her goals.

Just as she'd always suspected, love destroyed everything.

Chapter Thirteen

Life did go on, just like the old, annoying adage promised.
A semblance of life, anyway. A few weeks after Tomás's
apology in her office, the two of them had settled into an
uncomfortably polite truce, and plans for the more "modern" *quinceañera* were full-steam ahead. Erica did her best
to forget Tomás by focusing on his daughter. It didn't work.
The closer she grew with Hope, the more she fell in love
with the girl's father. Only a good man, an outstanding man,
could've raised a daughter like this, and Erica felt an ache
for him all the way down to her soul. The more her feelings
intensified, the more she pushed them away. Tomás didn't
want permanence, and, with him, she'd come to realize, she
could accept nothing less. He'd always been up-front about
it. He was blameless. She was the fool, so what was the
point? For now, she'd take what she could get, and what
she could get was a lot of quality time spent with his daughter.

At Hope's request, her court would consist of her four

best soccer friends—no boys. The spiritual part of the ceremony would take place in their backyard rather than a church, and the subsequent party would continue at home, as well. These choices would save Tomás a lot in rental fees, but Erica planned to funnel a good portion of the saved money into decorating the yard, fairy-princess style. The *quinceañera* was set for the third weekend in August, and they still had a lot to do.

On the first Saturday in July, Erica and Hope sat at Erica's kitchen table in Santa Fe, eating the take-out Chinese they'd picked up on their way back from the dressmaker's shop. A gorgeous, tea-length formal, the antithesis of all the rejects, hung on a hook outside Erica's bedroom door, sheathed in plastic. They'd even managed to choose gowns for Hope's small court which Hope thankfully claimed "did not make her want to hurl."

Hurl, indeed. The girls would look adorable.

Hope sat cross-legged in her chair, and Erica had both legs stretched out, feet propped on a third chair beneath the table. They both kept stealing peeks at the dress as they ate.

"I love it, Erica. It's SO not cupcakeish."

"I know. It's lovely."

"Lovely is too adult of a word to describe it. It's boss."

"Boss, it is, then." Erica gave a decisive nod. "It's the most boss, least cupcakeish dress I've ever seen."

Hope giggled, gazing adoringly at Erica. Tired from their shopping day, they ate for a few more minutes in silence, and then Hope blinked up with a feigned innocent look that Erica had begun to recognize…and dread.

"Um, may I use your computer after dinner?"

"Actually…no."

"Huh?" Hope asked, incredulous.

A pause ensued. They didn't even pretend anymore that Erica was unaware of how Hope spent her time on the Web. She wasn't surfing porn or visiting dangerous chat rooms, but from Tomás's point of view, the search for Racquel might seem even worse. And, as much as Erica empathized with Hope's thirst for knowledge about her maternal heritage, she couldn't let it go any further without his consent. She owed him that much, loved him enough to respect his pain. "You have to tell him before I'll let you use it," Erica said, forking into a piece of sesame chicken.

"I can't!"

"Hope. He's your dad, he loves you. You have every right to be curious about your mother. But you have to tell him."

"Easy for *you* to say. He'll freak."

"It's not easy for me. I know firsthand how your father can react when he doesn't agree with something, believe me. Look, everything worked out after he—" she made quotes with her fingers "—freaked on me." Well, that was a lie. Not *everything* had worked out, but Hope didn't need to know Erica was desperately in love with her father and he didn't return the feeling. "You have to trust me. Your dad wants what's best for you, he wants you to be happy. If meeting your mother will make you happy…"

"I don't know." Hope sighed, poking mulishly at her cashew beef. "I'm not sure if I can do it."

Erica set down her fork and leaned her forearms on the table. "Hope Genavieve Garza—"

"Great." Hope rolled her eyes. "Sounds like a lecture."

Erica laughed, despite herself. "You have some tough decisions to make, but you need to make them. You're not a child anymore. You have a *quinceañera* coming up in six weeks, which means you'll officially be considered an adult." She paused, searching the young girl's face. "I'm sorry. If you want to use my computer to keep looking for her—" she gave what she hoped was a sympathetic smile "—then you have to tell him. I won't be a party to a lie of omission."

"But the thing is—" Hope cast her a quick, furtive peek, her face flushing.

"Oh, there's a *thing?*" Erica teased.

"Yes. A bad thing. I think he hates her."

Erica blinked back her surprise. "What?"

"I think Dad hates my mom. Racquel. That's why he never talks about her to me." The turmoil showed in the pensive expression on Hope's face. "I mean, what if he really big-time hates her, and then I ask to meet her? He'll be *so* hurt."

Erica carefully sat back, realizing she was way out of her depth. Hope and Tomás needed to talk this out. Erica wouldn't lie—she loved them both. If she could leave them with anything after her time working with them—other than her heart, of course, which they both possessed despite her attempts to protect it—it would be the gift of open communication. Of course, *she* knew Tomás didn't hate Racquel. But how could Hope possibly know anything about it when the only thing she'd heard regarding her mother was silence?

Racquel had hurt Tomás, true enough. And he didn't want her hurting Hope any more than her abandonment already had. But, it wasn't Erica's place to discuss or explain this. She trusted that Tomás would step up. "If you think he hates her, ask him."

"No freakin' way." Hope paled. "You and I can talk, but we just don't spill our guts about that stuff in our family."

"Well, it's high time you started."

Hope, looking uncertain, seemed to ponder this. Finally, she darted a furtive glance at Erica. "Okay, but what if *I* hate her, Erica?" Hope whispered, her voice full of shame. "What if I find her and just…hate her?"

Erica smiled, then reached out and covered Hope's hand with her own. "You don't have it in you to hate, honey."

"But she left me."

"I know. It might take some time, but you're going to have to forgive her for that. She was a young girl, not much older than you, as a matter of fact. Children make mistakes. Come to think of it, so do adults.'' She paused for a moment, wondering about the wisdom of asking the question that had popped into her head. ''Do you feel...hate for her?''

Hope pondered it, then shrugged. ''To be honest, I don't feel anything for her. That's bad, too. But I've never even seen a picture of her. It's like she's a made-up story.''

''Miz Hope?''

The girl managed to grin. ''Yes, Miz Erica?''

Erica reached across the table and squashed Hope's cheeks between her hands. ''Talk to your father!''

Hope groaned, covering her face with her palms. After a moment, the hands slid off slowly. ''Okay, fine. But, will you help me? Go with me and maybe...bring it up. I mean it's not like I'm having any luck finding her anyway.''

Erica studied her for a long, worry-laced moment, then sighed. Hell, why not? Tomás had already come unglued with her once, and she'd survived. What did she have to lose? This was her chance to do something meaningful for Hope, a chance to feel included in their tight family circle. ''Okay.''

Hope looked genuinely startled. ''Really?''

Erica held up a finger. ''Yes. But, after I bring up the topic, it is up to *you* to ask the questions you want answered. I'm not going to do this for you. It's not my place.''

Hope bounded up from her seat and folded Erica in a hug. ''You're the best. I...I love you,'' she finished shyly.

Erica felt as if her heart tripled in size, taking up all the room in her chest and squeezing the air from her lungs. The honest emotion in Hope's words wrapped around her like the warmest embrace. They'd grown so close since the makeover debacle, closer than Erica ever imagined possible. She only wished Hope's father shared her feelings. How she craved hearing those three, small words from Tomás. ''I love you, too, Hope. I know you can do this. And who knows? Maybe it will lead to your mother. Mystery solved.''

Instead of letting go, Hope laid her head on Erica's shoulder. ''Know what I wish for real?''

''What's that?''

''I wish you were my mom.''

For a moment, Erica couldn't speak. All the air had been sucked from her lungs as the powerful emotions hit. ''Aw, honey.'' She held Hope away from her and laid a palm against the girl's cheek. When the lump in her throat cleared enough for her to speak, she said, ''I'm not anyone's mom.''

''I know,'' Hope whispered. ''But…you should be.''

Tomás stood over a bubbling pot of homemade spaghetti sauce in the kitchen that Sunday evening, listening to Keb' Mo' on the stereo and ticking away the minutes until Hope would be home. Until Erica would *bring* her home, more precisely, and he planned on doing all he could to keep the woman in his home for as long as possible. He missed her so much, craved her nearness. He'd already decided on a plan, and it wouldn't seem anything but innocent. His weekend had been productive; all the piñatas for the arts festival were complete, the last two drying. Surely Erica would want to see them.

And he also wanted to see his daughter. He knew she enjoyed these weekends with Erica and he appreciated how much she'd blossomed since he and Erica had worked things out, such as it was, but he missed his little girl so much when she wasn't home.

He'd just added a little extra garlic and oregano, then closed the lid on the steaming pot when the phone rang. He snagged it on the first ring. ''Hello?''

''Tomás, it's Erica.'' Something in her voice sounded rushed.

His heart leaped, partially with worry, but mostly with pleasure at hearing her voice. ''What's wrong?''

"Nothing. I promise. Hope's in the shower, and when she's done we're heading your way." She cleared her throat. "We got the *vestido,* finally. It's absolutely gorgeous."

"That's wonderful." He leaned back against the counter, smiling as the sound of her voice wrapped him in warmth. "She doesn't look like a cupcake?"

"No, and you'll be thrilled to know she doesn't look like a tart, either." Erica laughed, but sounded nervous.

"That's what a father wants to hear," he said. But instinct told him this wasn't about the dress. His nerves suddenly went on full alert. "So, what's really up?"

"You and your blasted intuition."

Something was wrong. Tomás braced himself.

"I wanted to catch you while Hope was out of earshot, give you a heads-up." She paused, and, again, Tomás experienced a sickening wave of foreboding. "Will you have time for a bit of conversation this evening when we get there?"

His throat squeezed. He and Erica had walked on eggshells around each other ever since that awful argument. They hadn't had many sit-down-and-relate conversations. The fact that she was requesting one was huge. He swallowed, hoping to pull off a semblance of steady nonchalance. "Sure. Ruby's down the road playing poker with some of her friends. I'll have dinner ready." He paused, then took a risk. "You can stay if you'd like and we can talk afterward."

She paused, too. "That sounds…perfect."

"Are you sure everything's okay? This is my daughter we're talking about. I want you to tell me if anything's wrong."

He heard her slight hesitation, keyed in on the quiet urgency when she finally spoke. "You have to believe me, Tomás. I wouldn't lie to you. Everything is *really* okay. But we need to talk to you. Well, Hope needs to talk to you, and she's asked me to be present, if that's okay with you."

It didn't comfort him. "Uh-oh. That sounds ominous."

"It isn't," she insisted. "I promise you. She's just nervous and hyperconscious of your feelings."

"My feelings? Don't tell me she's changed her mind about the *quinceañera* again?" He groaned.

Erica laughed. "It's not that. But please, try and remember what we agreed to in my office, okay? Your daughter wants to talk to you. To confide in you." She let that sink in. "That's a good thing, right? It's what you want."

"Yes," he said quietly.

"Please, just promise me you won't make her regret opening up to you. Or the fact that she confided in me first. I've worked on her so hard to get her to this point."

Needles of jealousy pierced him, and he struggled against the acrid emotional pain seeping from the wounds. Since when did an outsider have to coach his daughter to be able to talk to him? With considerable effort, he kept the destructive feelings at bay. Erica, he knew, was on his side. And was she really an outsider anymore anyway? God knew, she'd made her way into his heart and taken up permanent residence. She cared about his daughter, and him. He needed to give her credit for being a woman of integrity. *A woman he loved enough to leave her alone.* "I won't. I give you my word."

"You're an amazing father, Tomás."

And you'd make an amazing mother, he wanted to reply. But of course, he didn't. Those weren't words Erica Gonçalves wanted to hear, not from him or anyone. The pain of that pierced him through the chest.

By the time Erica and Hope showed up almost two hours later, Tomás was completely rattled. He'd created the worst-case scenarios in his mind and had convinced himself that he couldn't bear to hear any of them this evening.

Hope was dying.

Hope was pregnant.

Hope was on drugs.

Hope had an STD.

The thing was, he couldn't make himself believe any of those outlandish ideas. No parent could be one hundred percent certain, but he truly didn't think his daughter was sexually active. She was immature for her age, more interested in sports and her friends than in boys—thank God. That knocked off the pregnancy and STD possibilities. He hadn't noticed a dramatic change in her behavior, and her grades remained high. Unlikely she was on drugs. She didn't seem the least bit ill, and, if she was, he didn't think she would go to Erica instead of him. But if not those dreadful possibilities, what could she possibly have to tell him? What on earth could cause her so much fear that she'd call in Erica as backup while she broke the news?

He managed to push it away while they dined on spaghetti and garlic bread, green salad and Sara Lee cheesecake, and, frankly, he was just happy to have Erica at the table with them. He could get used to that, way too easily. As it was, he simply basked in her presence while doing his best to maintain the illusion of *not* being in love with her.

He listened as Hope regaled him with the events of the weekend without really hearing a word, but judging by his daughter's face, he'd responded appropriately and at all the correct moments. After their meal, he poured himself and Erica a healthy brandy and made Hope a mug of mint hot cocoa, and then he sat down across the table from the two females who'd stolen his heart in different ways and faced his fears directly. "Okay, give me a break, here. We've made small talk. We've eaten." He looked from Erica to Hope. "I'm ready to hear whatever it is you have to tell me."

Hope went pale and blinked uncertainly at Erica, who took her hand. After a sip of brandy followed by a drink of water, Erica cleared her throat and faced him head-on. "The day we had our…disagreement over the makeover, I found something on my computer when I returned home. Something of Hope's."

He flashed a glance at Hope, who looked terrified.

"Initially, I didn't know what to do. Finally, I opened up the door for Hope to talk to me about the situation, and eventually she did." Erica held up a finger. "From the first, I want you to know, I've encouraged her to come to you about it."

"She did, Daddy."

He nodded, a barrage of chat-room nightmares racing through his brain like a runaway train. "I understand. It's okay." But he didn't, really, and it wasn't okay. He was more overwhelmed with trepidation by the second. "Go ahead."

Erica reached over and covered Hope's knotted hands with her own. "I also want to be very clear about the fact that I haven't assisted Hope in any way. I've simply been there for her, just to listen, until she felt she was ready to talk to you."

His jaw clenched. He worked to relax it and kept his tone even, nonthreatening. Fearing he would shatter his brandy snifter, he released the glass and clenched his hands together beneath the table. Apparently, Hope had been doing something behind his back, something to which Erica had been privy. He tried not to be angered by that. Or hurt. It was probably all his fault anyway, the way he held on to Hope so tightly, the way he'd come unglued with Erica after the makeover. "What exactly did you find on your computer, Erica?"

She exchanged a quick, supportive glance with Hope before answering. "I found the results of a Web search that Hope had begun while at my house, unbeknownst to me."

Something heavy pressed on his chest, and the room seemed to waver before his eyes. He recognized the surreal state as abject fear. He'd experienced the same feeling the moment Racquel had told him she was pregnant all those years ago. But this situation concerned his child, not his high school girlfriend. And he'd sworn to Erica that he would take it like a man. "A search for what?" he asked finally, his voice hoarse and unfamiliar to his own ears.

"For my mother," Hope said, in a tiny, quavery voice. "I just...want to meet my mother. I'm sorry, Daddy."

It took several moments of silence for Tomás to absorb what he'd heard, and, the whole time, he stared at his daughter. Relief came to him in stages, as he realized all his worst nightmares weren't coming true. Just this. "You're looking for Racquel?" But of course. It all fell into place now. He remembered all the secretive time Hope spent behind the computer, the non-sequiturs... *What's my mother's middle name? Do we have any pictures of her?*

Hope bit her bottom lip, then nodded. Big fat tears welled in her eyes, and her chin began to quiver. "I love you, Daddy. It doesn't have anything to do with that. But we've never even talked about her and I'm curious."

It shocked him to realize that what he felt right now was happiness. It could have been so much worse than this. And guilt, he felt a boatload of that, too. He'd thought he was doing the right thing, not talking about Racquel. But, no. He'd only managed to distance himself from Hope once again. He'd never realized parenthood would be such a humbling affair. A gush of love washed over him, for both of the women who sat before him. He suddenly realized that Erica couldn't be more different from Racquel if she tried. He found that soothing. "O-of course you are, baby. Don't cry."

With his easy acceptance, her tears intensified. "I'm going to be f-f-fifteen, and I'm supposed to be making this big transformation from a girl to a woman. But I don't even know the woman who gave birth to me. It just seems so weird to me."

Tomás glanced at Erica for cues, and she kind of jerked

exited his life, consequences be damned. She'd regret it forever if she didn't make it clear to Tomás that she loved him,
no strings attached. But she had to wait until the time was
right.

Hope went on. "Maybe she has a new name, or…I don't
know. All of the name matches have been for people too
old." She blinked up at him, looking sad. "Do you think
she has new kids? Kids she didn't leave?"

Erica closed her eyes, aching for Hope.

Tomás rocked her for a moment, contemplating how best
to answer the difficult question, Erica could see. She had no
idea how he'd handle it and found herself holding her
breath.

"She might have other children. I don't know. But
whether she does or doesn't, you have to remember that she
didn't leave you because you weren't worthy, or she didn't
love you."

Hope's lip quivered, and she nestled into her father's
neck.

He rubbed her back. "I will help you get all your questions answered, okay? What can I tell you about your
mother? What do you want to know?"

"Why did she leave?"

Erica saw the pain in his eyes, knowing Hope's question
hurled him back to those frightening days. She bit her lip.

"She was very young." He pressed his mouth into a flat
line. "She wasn't ready to be a mother, *m'ija.*"

"But she *was* a mother. I was already here. It's not like
you can just decide you are or aren't."

"I know that. I'm not saying what she did was right."

Hope swallowed, studying his face. "You were young,
too. And you didn't leave."

He kissed the top of her head. "I would never leave you.
The moment I looked in your eyes, I fell in love. But, I was
two years older than your mother, and when you're fifteen
and seventeen, two years makes a big difference."

Hope absorbed this for a moment. "Did she...even love me?"

"Oh, Hope." Tomás held her closer, tucking her head beneath his chin. His eyes shone bright with unshed tears. "Of course she loved you. I promise you she did. She loved you enough to know that she wasn't able to take care of you. She loved you enough to bring you to me. And we've done okay, haven't we?"

She nodded against his chest. "Hope and Daddy against the world," she whispered.

With those words, Erica became profoundly aware of how little space there was in this family for someone like her, and the pain was racking. Despite her best efforts to remain detached, a traitorous tear ran down her cheek. She sniffed and held her head back, to discourage any followers.

Tomás met her eyes over his daughter's head, and a slow, sad smile spread his lips. She tried to smile back, but her lips wouldn't cooperate. Tomás winked, and Erica felt his pull, so strong, so completely right...even though it wasn't.

"Your mom played sports in school, baby," he told Hope. "She was almost as good as you are."

"Do I look like her?"

"You have her figure. My eyes and chin. Her temper."

Hope laughed, a weak sound.

"I won't lie to you, babe. When your mother left you in my arms, I was so scared, and so hurt."

Hope lifted her face and studied him. "Why scared?"

"You were the smallest, scariest thing I'd ever seen. I didn't know how to feed you or change your diapers. I was afraid I'd break you, or worse, that you'd grow up and wish she'd taken you with her instead of leaving you with me."

"Never." She hugged him tightly.

He smiled, with one half of his mouth. "And a few months after she'd left, you were really sick with something babies get called the croup. I swear, you cried for three days straight. Nothing I tried could make you stop, and I felt like such a failure." He paused, and Erica watched his Adam's apple rise and fall a few times. "No more lies, Hope. I'm going to tell you something that doesn't make me proud, okay?"

"Okay."

"I was so…angry with your mother for leaving at that time. I was seventeen, with a sick infant. I felt overwhelmed, inadequate, guilty." His lips thinned in regret. "When I finally got you to sleep, I took every picture I had of her and I burned them in the kitchen sink with a lighter."

Hope's eyes widened. "Wow, Daddy. Harsh-o-rama."

"I know." He shook his head. "And I'm sorry now that I did it, because I deprived you of seeing her."

"It's okay. I understand. I probably would've done the same thing if I were you."

"Maybe you have more of my temper than I thought." Father and daughter smiled at each other for a moment. He reached up and wicked a tear off her cheek. She reciprocated the gesture.

"Hope, you can talk to me about Racquel. I promise I won't get angry with you or keep anything from you. Not anymore." He glanced at Erica, warm and appreciative. "I'm glad Erica was there for you and you can talk to her as much as you want, but you can talk to me, too."

"Can I still look for…Racquel?"

"Is that what you want to do?"

She bit her bottom lip, tucked her chin and nodded.

"Then that's what we'll do. We'll look for your mother."

"You'll help me?"

"Of course I will. I just want you to be happy."

Hope wrapped herself tightly around her father and squeezed her eyes shut. "I love you, Daddy. So much."

He answered her, but his eyes locked with Erica's over the top of Hope's head. "I love you, too, baby girl. More than you'll ever know."

Erica held his gaze until she couldn't bear to any longer,

and then she looked away. She felt shaky with emotional release, off-kilter and keening with need for this man. She had wanted a lot of things in her life. A ten-speed when she was twelve. A Corvette when she was sixteen. And her independence for as long as she could remember. But, sitting in Tomás's warm kitchen that night, caught up in the spell cast by their love, Erica knew she'd never wanted anything as much as she wanted Tomás Garza's love right now. And forever.

No regrets. It had always been her motto and always would be. But suddenly, she didn't know which she would regret more...loving Tomás and Hope, or pushing them away in the almighty pursuit of her goals.

Chapter Fourteen

"If you'll stay a few minutes," Tomás said to Erica, as he stood to accompany Hope to her bedroom for a tuck in. "I'll show you the piñatas for the festival."

She raised her eyebrows. Was it her imagination, or was Tomás looking for ways to keep her around longer? The thought flattered her. "You're done?"

He grinned. "I am. Can you wait?"

"Sure. I'm not driving back to Santa Fe tonight. I'll just stay at the apartment in Vegas."

It was early for bedtime, only eight o'clock, but Hope's difficult confession had clearly exhausted her. She'd begun yawning fifteen minutes earlier, and finally told her dad she wanted to hit the sack. "Let me just tuck this one in, and I'll take you to them."

"I want a tuck in from Erica, too."

Erica's heart lurched, thinking maybe Hope had crossed the line with that one. She knew how fiercely Tomás guarded special moments with his daughter. Now that they'd reached a tenuous safe spot, she didn't want anything to screw it up. To her surprise, Tomás didn't appear threatened by the request.

"Absolutely. Erica?" He tossed her a mischievous grin. "It won't throw you into a panic to tuck a child in, will it?"

"She always tucks me in at her house," Hope informed him, her tone matter-of-fact. Of course, she didn't know all the emotional subtext beneath her father's words.

"Well. Then, Erica?" Tomás stood to the side and twirled his hand in the direction of the hallway, indicating she should precede them. "Let's go to it."

Flushed with pleasure at the inclusion, Erica ducked her head and made her way down the hall. The hardwood floors creaked beneath their feet, a sound so homey and comforting, a fresh lump rose to her throat. What would it be like to walk these boards every night? To kiss Hope on the cheek and then walk hand in hand with Tomás from Hope's room to their own? She'd always thought such routine would be stifling, a burden. Right now, it felt like a gift. Instead of reading too much into it, she chose to live in the moment, to take this experience and emblazon it on her memory for all those times on the road, all those empty hotel rooms, all those nights when she would live the life she'd chosen.

Which now seemed rather...empty. Hollow.

But what was the alternative? Giving it all up for evenings like this? She didn't think she could do that, either. She was an ambitious woman, and her work gave her pleasure, a sense of vitality. She blinked back the frustration, the impossible choices she felt unable to make. There was no easy answer. If *only* she could have it all.

Half an hour later, Tomás led Erica across the moonlit path toward the wooden building that loomed behind Tomás's adobe home. When they moved within range, a motion-detector light flashed on. "Oh," she exclaimed. "I always thought this was a barn."

He smiled, working the key into the dead bolt. "Let's get one thing straight, Erica. My jack-of-all-trades designation does not include ranching or animal husbandry."

She smirked. "Good to know you have limits. I suppose that's why Hope's puppy requests are continually denied?"

"Yeah." Tomás sighed. "Like I have room in my life for one more responsibility."

"Poor Hope, deprived of man—and girl's—best friend." She was making small talk. She knew that. But it was that or throw herself at the man's chest and profess her love, and he'd had enough confessions for one night.

He stood aside and let her cross the threshold into the darkened room ahead of him. "As for the studio, it's built like a barn, to be sure, but this is where I ply my craft."

Once inside, he flicked on the overhead lights, and Erica gasped. Thin strips of tissue in every color of the rainbow hung from what looked like a clothesline adhered to one wall with metal eye hooks. Overhead, more anchored lines held piñatas in every shape and color. Traditional star piñatas, multicolored and festive with their conelike protrusions tipped with pom-poms of color, piñatas designed to resemble animals, planets and flowers. A cache of Mexican red-clay pots were stacked beneath the windows, and large worktables held other tools and supplies. The room, with its painted concrete floors and plank-and-sawhorse tables, was utilitarian, no doubt about that, but the unexpected bursts of color transformed it into a technicolor dream world.

"Oh!" Erica said, awed. Her head tilted back as she twirled and soaked it all in. "I had no idea what to expect. It's wonderful." She pointed to a dalmation piñata hanging next to one shaped like a red fire hydrant and laughed with glee.

He smiled. "For the local fireman's ball."

She spun to face him, feeling filled with life, her hands clasped at her chest. "You're amazing."

His face colored slightly from the compliment, but he made light of it. "No, I'm a craftsman who is simply lucky enough to make a living doing what I love. You, Erica Gonçalves, are amazing." Suddenly, alone in his workshop, the air between them changed. Everything seemed electrically charged. His voice sounded husky, brutally sincere and more than a little aroused. "Thank you so much for how you dealt with Hope over this Racquel thing. I don't know what to say."

Her attention leaped immediately from his work to the man himself. She felt unsteady with desire and reached out to rest the fingertips of one hand on a worktable to her left. Brushing aside his compliment as he had hers, she moistened her lips. "Who are you, and what have you done with Tomás Garza?"

"I mean it, Erica. I know I've handled things in the past…badly. I'm learning from my mistakes."

She inclined her head. "If I may say, without sounding too patronizing, you handled everything so perfectly tonight, Tomás. And thank you. For including me. You didn't have to do that."

He advanced on her in two slow strides. Their bodies weren't touching, but he stood so close, she could feel the energy vibrating from him, could feel his heat. His golden-eyed gaze caressed her, and he reached up tentatively and threaded one hand into the side of her hair, cupping her head. "What you've done for my daughter…for me—"

"It was nothing," she rushed to say. Nothing any woman wouldn't do for a man and child she loved, she almost added. But she couldn't say the words.

"It was something, all right. Something beautiful. Such a gift." His gaze dropped to her lips, and her physical response was instantaneous. Blood pounded through her veins, and her mouth tingled. Low and deep, something ancient and wanting swirled. "You're so good with her, Erica."

"Thank you. I...I love her. She's so special. I just...appreciate the time you let her spend with me."

He moved closer by degrees, and now their bodies were touching, just barely. She felt him, hard against her, saw his chest begin to rise and fall raggedly. "I never expected someone like you to come along in my life. Into our lives."

Erica's heart started to pound. This was no simple walk to the studio, and she didn't know how she should handle it if things got heavy. She was still trying so hard to protect her heart from him. "You have to be careful who you hire," she quipped, in an attempt to lighten the atmosphere of crackling awareness between them, but the joke fell flat. He was in no mood for jokes, that much was certain.

He dipped his head, not kissing her but brushing his warm, firm lips ever so gently side to side over hers. Without moving away, he whispered against her mouth, "I made you a promise."

"What?" she whispered back, her pulse rapid.

"To keep things strictly business." His lips caressed hers once again, and he pulled her bottom lip just barely between his teeth, then released it.

"Right. Strictly business."

"I want to break that promise, Erica Gonçalves. You have no idea how much I want to break it. Right now."

She heard a sound and realized it had come from her. Had she actually whimpered? *Yes,* she thought. *Please, break that promise.* But she knew the time wasn't right, that she wasn't strong enough to start up their affair where they'd left off. He might be attracted to her, he might appreciate how she dealt with his daughter, but she *loved* him. Big difference. She gripped more tightly to the table beside her, for fear her shaky legs wouldn't hold her. "We can't."

"I know," he said with regret.

Erica blinked in surprise. He knew?

He smoothed one beard-roughened cheek against hers, then nestled his face into her neck and inhaled. Tingles shot down her spine, settling at the throbbing center between her legs. His lips grazed her neck as he pulled away. He caressed her cheek with the back of one hand. "I've broken enough promises to the women in my life, and I don't want to add another one to the list. Especially not to you."

She felt both relieved and disappointed. Fickle Erica.

"So here's the plan." His hand continued to caress her face. "I'm going to show you the art festival piñatas, and you're going to finish planning the *quinceañera* for my daughter."

She nodded, not quite understanding. "O-okay."

He slid his hands around her waist and pulled her gently against his arousal. Not in a threatening way, but just so there was no mistaking how he felt. "But, I'm telling you, this thing isn't over between us. Unless you want it to be. Do you?"

She took a deep, shaky breath, fighting not to rub against him as her body's instincts were urging her to do. She stared into his eyes for moment, then closed hers, knowing she couldn't lie to herself. If an affair was all that she could have with this man, she'd settle for it. Oh, sure, she'd probably despise herself down the road, but anything was better than losing him altogether. A lump rose in her throat. She swallowed. "No."

"Good. Neither do I. Not by a long shot." His hands slid up her back and into her hair, and he tilted her head until their eyes met. "We're going to finish this business arrangement like we've promised we would. Strictly—" he brushed her lips again "—business. But when the *quinceañera's* finished and the festival is done?"

She shivered, so wet for him, wondering if he could somehow sense the waves of desire coming from her. "Yes?"

"You and I, Erica Gonçalves, we're going to talk."

"Talk?"

"Yes, talk. No promises. No pressure. Deal?" He stared down at her, his desire plain.

No promises and no pressure spelled affair, with a capital *T* for temporary. But she didn't care, she wanted him so badly. He weakened her resolve, blurred formerly diamond-sharp lines around her life. Was that what had happened with her mother when she'd met her father? "Deal."

"See? I'm sticking to my guns and keeping my promises." He tucked his chin, and one hand came up to gently hold hers and tilt her face. "I am, however, going to kiss you. Consider it a thank-you for tonight if you have to. Rationalize it however you need to, Erica, but I'm going to—"

"Just do it," she whispered.

And then his lips touched hers, once tentatively and then with more passion. Finally, his tongue met hers, and just like magic, all her worries disappeared…temporarily.

"Mama?" Erica asked her mother three weeks later, on a particularly needy evening. Tomás had flown to San Antonio without warning for the weekend—something about a business opportunity that had just come up. Erica had eagerly offered to stay with Hope and Ruby, but Tomás said they were fine on their own. He didn't want to "inconvenience" her.

Translation? They didn't need her.

More to the point, *he* didn't need her.

Tomás Garza's family was complete, and she'd do herself a favor to remember that in the future. But she was feeling lonely and vulnerable, and she needed to talk. Who else would a woman call besides her mother? "Can you come over?"

Erica could hear Susana Gonçalves's confusion across the phone lines. "Sure, *m'ija.* Is anything wrong?"

Her lips trembled, but she steadied her voice. "Does

something have to be wrong for a woman to want to spend time with her mother?''

A slight pause. ''Of course not. I'll be right there.''

''Mama?''

''Yes?''

''Could you…bring a bottle of wine? I'm out and I could really use a glass about now.''

''I'll bring two,'' Susana replied, her voice soft and knowing. ''And an overnight bag.''

Tears of gratitude blurred Erica's vision. ''I'd like that.''

They'd just cracked open their second bottle of Sangiovese two hours later when Erica felt brave enough to broach the topic. During bottle number one, she'd regaled her mother with every last detail about Hope's very nontraditional *quinceañera* and the Cultural Arts Festival. She finally felt strong enough to talk about the real reason she'd asked her mother over that evening. She twirled her wineglass stem between her fingers, not quite meeting her mother's eyes. ''Can I ask you a question?''

''Of course.'' Susana Gonçalves was reclined on the love seat, wearing plum-colored silk pajamas, her head supported by a velvet throw pillow. Erica studied her through a veil of lashes and realized, as if looking at Susana for the first time, that her mother didn't look resentful. Regrets, anger and resentment tended to etch vertical lines between a woman's eyebrows, to pull the visage into a permanent, unpleasant mask. On the contrary, Susana's face, while aged, showed the lines and wrinkles of happiness. Crinkles around her eyes, smile grooves from nose to mouth. She looked like a woman who'd lived a rich and satisfying life and had enjoyed every moment, every experience.

Why had Erica never noticed this before?

Had she never really looked at her mother? The thought shamed her, and she forged ahead, needing answers. ''Why did you stop playing the guitar?''

''Oh, that.'' Susana flicked a hand, her tone unconcerned.

"Frankly, I wasn't very good. Hobbies come and hobbies go."

Erica blinked, feeling disoriented, trapped in the gauzy web that was her own version of the past. "But that's not true. You were as good as Joan Baez. You could've had an amazing career."

Susana laughed. "Oh, who told you that? Your father?"

Erica thought back, startled to realize it *had* been her father talking up her mother all those years. Why hadn't she remembered that? "I...I guess he did. I'd forgotten."

Susana sipped her wine, shaking her head as she swallowed. "That man. He always made more of my talent than was there. He was always so proud of me. Still is."

"But I thought you were a music major in college?"

"I was. I'd planned to teach. But the fact remains, guitar playing was a hobby, *m'ija*. Sure, I enjoyed it, but I was never cut out for the big lights. I never even wanted that."

Erica couldn't quite believe time had edited her memories in such a distorted way. "Are you sure?"

"Completely sure." Susana crossed her feet at the ankles. "I'm a small-town girl at heart, Erica. You, of all people, know this about me. Why all these off-the-wall questions anyway?"

Erica heard a loud rushing in her ears and felt disconnected from herself. This couldn't be happening. She had based her whole life around the fact that her mother had been forced to abandon a creative dream and live her life surrounded by "what ifs," and it turned out music hadn't been her dream at all. "If not that, then what did you want to do with your life?"

Susana frowned, studying her daughter as if she'd gone around the bend. "Why, I wanted to raise a family, of course."

It couldn't be true. Her mother was just protecting her with a polished version of the past. "But there's just me."

Susana shrugged. "There were complications during the

delivery and, frankly, it scared me. You were enough, Erica. You've always been enough.''

Erica had to get a grasp on this. She set down her wineglass and ran her fingers slowly through her hair. "So, it was Daddy's dream all along, the Joan Baez thing?"

"Absolutely. But he supported me in my decision to give it up. He's supported me in every decision I've ever made, including having only the one baby. Even though, after a few years and some medical tests, the doctors pronounced me fit to try again. I didn't want to. I had you and Daddy." She grinned. "It's called love, Erica. And it's amazing."

Erica looked down at her knees and thought of Tomás and Hope. She thought of how alive she'd felt since they'd come into her world, how she didn't quite know how it had happened, but she couldn't imagine life without them. "I know it is."

A beat passed. Susana readjusted her position. "Is it Tomás, honey?"

"Yes," Erica whispered, and then she began to cry. "And Hope and Ruby, too. But it's too late. I told him it would never work between us and sent him away. He said we're going to talk when the *quinceañera* is over, but I know I've ruined everything before I even gave it a chance."

Susana set her glass on the side table and moved across Erica's living room. She knelt on the floor before her daughter and took hold of her hands. "It's never too late. If he loves you, and you love him, it's never going to be too late. I promise you." She kissed one of Erica's hands, then the other. "That's the thing about true love, Erica. It's forgiving, and it can weather just about any storm."

Erica sniffed. "Yeah? What do I know about being with a man long-term? A man with a daughter?"

Susana stood, then took the seat next to Erica, wrapping her arm around Erica's shoulders. "Tell me everything. We'll work this out, you and I."

"I'm afraid, Mama."

"It's okay, honey. Fear means you've got something worth fighting for. But, if you want to fly, there comes a point when you must simply close your eyes and jump."

Hope had chosen to have a candlelight service at dusk, and on the evening of the *quinceañera,* nearly everything was perfect. All the details Erica could control were in place, naturally, but she did have a few regrets. Hope hadn't been able to find Racquel, despite almost constant searching since she'd told her father. Erica could see the slight shadows in Hope's otherwise excited face because of it.

Erica herself was feeling a bit melancholy, knowing her days spending time with this amazing family were numbered. She'd decided, with her mother's help, to try and take things as they came, to let things build. Sure, Tomás said they'd talk about their so-called relationship, but she'd come to realize that, as much as she would like to, she couldn't settle for a secret affair with Tomás, which is certainly what he had in mind.

She loved him. All or nothing.

Melancholy cast a pall on the day, but Erica was determined not to let it show. It was Hope's day, and Tomás wanted it to be perfect. It was up to Erica to make that happen.

And, Tomás…well, Tomás was a mess. She'd never seen a man so green around the gills with nerves. She found him standing at the front-hall mirror, looking like a rock star in a *GQ* ad. He made her legs feel wobbly, he was so gorgeous. His tuxedo fit like a dream, his long hair hung loose and shiny at Hope's insistence, but he couldn't seem to get the hang of his tie.

Erica rounded the corner, then leaned one shoulder against the wall, crossed her arms and smirked, ignoring the poignant pull in her middle at the sight of him.

He flickered a glance at her. "What's so funny?"

"You mean, other than you?"

"It's this damn tie. I just can't make it look right, and it feels like a noose anyway. I despise ties."

"Oh, you artists. So anticonvention."

"It's a perk of the job. One I enjoy, thank you very much."

Chuckling softly, Erica pushed off the wall and walked up behind him. "Squat down a little." He complied. "My father taught me how to properly fix his ties, but I can only do it from behind." She fiddled with the bit of silk for a moment, then patted his shoulders. "There you go."

He checked her work in the mirror, then turned to smile down at her, so close he made Erica's stomach flutter. "What would I do without you?" he asked softly.

I guess we'll find out soon.

In just a few hours, she'd hand him her final bill, he'd pass her a check, and their obligation to each other would end. Next month, they'd see one another at the Cultural Arts Festival, and after that…nothing. She couldn't bear the thought of any of it. Biting back a rush of grief, she turned to leave him in a cloud of perfume and unanswered questions.

"Go on and deal with the guests, Tomás. And relax. Everything's in place. The cake was just delivered, along with my surprise." She grinned, in spite of herself. In honor of Hope's aversion to looking like a cupcake, she'd had the baker design little cupcake women, one for Hope and each of the girls in her court. The little cupcake ladies would take their place of honor in front of the five-tier cake. "The yard looks spectacular. A few guests are arriving already."

"Is Hope—?"

She flicked her hand at him. "I mean it. Shoo. I'll deal with the ladies. Do yourself a favor and mingle. I'll bring Hope and the girls down when they're ready. They need time to primp, giggle and squeal. It's a girl thing."

"Erica," he said, his voice rough and soft at once.

She turned, cocking her head in question.

He seemed to struggle for words for a moment, before pressing his lips together in a flat line. "Never mind. I'll talk to you about it later."

"Tell me now. I'm going to be busy later."

He swallowed once, then smoothed his palms together. "You know the part of the ceremony where I place the *corona,* the little crown, on Hope's head?"

"The tiara? Yes?"

He swallowed once, but his words came out strong and steady. "I want you by my side."

Her stomach plunged, and she splayed a hand on her torso, blown away by the request. How could she bear this, and then hand the man a bill like some contractor? "Tomás, you don't have to do that." That honor was usually left to the father alone.

"I want to. And Hope wants you there, too." He smiled. "Actually, it was her suggestion. But I agree with it."

A hot lump of emotion clogged her throat. She'd come into this thing as hired help, the party planner. But over the months, she'd become so close to Tomás and Hope, she almost felt guilty charging her fee. She didn't *want* to be the "party planner" tonight. She yearned to be so much more. She yearned to be the special woman in his life…and in Hope's. This request gave her a little taste of what it would be like.

Tomás had always been an exemplary father, faults and all, but she'd watched him wrestle more than a few demons in order to grow into an open, communicative man. A man less afraid of losing his daughter to the outside world. This gesture, inviting her to share in the *corona* ceremony meant more to her than she could ever express. "I would love to stand by your side, Tomás."

She saw him release a breath, and then he grinned, pure relief showing on his face. "Thank you. It means so much to both of us." He strode quickly to her, cupped her face in his hands and leaned in and bestowed the most tender of kisses, a magical caress of his mouth against hers. Quick, but lingering, too. "Thank you."

"*De nada,*" she whispered. But it wasn't nothing. It was something, indeed. Something that would both buoy her and haunt her in the days that followed. She pulled away, regretfully, and headed toward Hope's room.

The ceremony went off without a hitch. After all the initial struggle, Hope had really gotten enthused about planning the perfect *quinceañera*—Hope Garza style. Intrigued by what Erica had told her in Santa Fe, she had researched the Apache nai'es ceremony, the Bas Mitzvah and the various debutante rituals, and Erica had helped her incorporate a little of all of them into the ceremony. The research into all the various customs had been a joy for both of them.

In a short speech after the spiritual blessing, Hope had described working with the MS patients' hippotherapy at the ranch and all that it had taught her. Her poignant, heartfelt speech left the huge group of guests sniffling into their handkerchiefs, even Ruby, who was one of the toughest women Erica had ever met. Her eyes shone with pride at her great-grandaughter's blossoming. She really had changed *so* much over the past several months.

When she and Tomás presented Hope with her dainty little tiara, Erica couldn't keep the tears from running down her cheeks and didn't even try. She was busting with pride for Hope, so grateful to have been included in this occasion in this meaningful way. It would make the walking away part easier....

As the serious portion of the *quinceañera* came to a close, darkness settled over Northern New Mexico, and the yard glowed with fairy light. Erica's crew had draped white gauze swags and white light strings over every possible tree, bush, building. A grid of high, overhead lines had been erected, and from them hung twenty small white star piñatas

Tomás had created, filled with gifts and cards for Hope. Round, rented tables draped in white linen surrounded a rented dance floor and dais that the guests had helped lay out after the service—it was truly a community effort, welcoming Hope into adulthood.

Soul Searchers, with a stand-in lead singer, of course, was set up at one corner of the stage, playing soft music in the background, a preamble of the celebration to come. But before the eating, cake cutting and dancing commenced, Hope stood, flanked by her court, in a receiving line, accepting congratulations and kisses like the graceful lady she'd become.

Erica looked around nervously. Where was Tomás? He really should be standing by Hope's side. She didn't see him, though, and didn't have time to hunt him down. They had decided to have the event catered by women from town, and Erica needed to make sure they were on schedule with the food before everyone started swarming the buffet tables. The gracious ladies weren't professional caterers, and she didn't want them to become overwhelmed by the crush.

She started toward the kitchen, but just then caught a glimpse of Tomás rounding the corner of the house. He wasn't alone. The woman at his side was tiny, five foot four and a hundred pounds, soaking wet, probably. She wore a simple, red calf-length sheath and flats, and she looked vaguely familiar. But the single distinctive quality Erica recognized about the woman was fear.

And then it hit her. This was Racquel.

Tomás had somehow located Hope's mother and brought her to join in this very special day. It was a huge concession on his part, but the one surprise that would make the event perfect for Hope. Knowing how vulnerable he felt about Racquel, how much she'd damaged him emotionally when she left, this gesture struck Erica as so profoundly selfless, it left her weak. She sank into the nearest chair and simply watched the surprise unfold.

The guests at the *quinceañera,* for the most part, had lived in this part of New Mexico for decades, and as they caught sight of Tomás and Racquel crossing the yard, the crowd hushed and parted. Most people recognized Racquel, and, as it dawned on them slowly what was happening, from what Erica could see, everyone was as stunned as she. Finally, Tomás and Racquel stood before a confused-looking Hope, surrounded by complete silence. Even Soul Searchers seemed frozen, their instruments idle.

Tomás reached out with a shaking hand and touched his daughter's cheek. "Baby?" He paused, composing himself. "I have a surprise for you." He touched the woman at his side on the small of her back. "This is your mother, Racquel."

Hope's jaw dropped, and for a moment Erica could almost feel the girl soaking in the sight of the woman she never thought she'd see. Racquel was visibly shaking, and Hope looked poleaxed by the whole moment. "W-where did you find her, Daddy?"

"In San Antonio."

Hope gaped at him, then grinned. "You tricked me. I thought that trip was some piñata thing."

He chuckled. "I wanted to surprise you."

Hope studied the woman before her again, swallowing carefully. She reached out and touched her mother's arm gently, then said, "You look so young."

Racquel blurted a nervous laugh. "I am young. And you're so absolutely beautiful."

Hope smiled. "Daddy was right. I do have your figure."

With that, Racquel broke into ragged sobs and opened her arms. Hope looked to Tomás for confirmation, and he nodded his encouragement. It was all Hope needed. She went softly into her mother's arms, the two of them rocking, a mixture of tears and laughter.

"I'm so sorry I hurt you, Hope. I never, ever meant to."

Hope pulled away, still holding her mother's arms, a big

smile on her face. Suddenly, it seemed as if Hope was the adult and Racquel the child who needed comforting. "It's okay. You didn't. I wanted to meet you, but my dad is the best parent in the world. We have a good life together."

Erica flicked a glance his way and noted that Tomás's jaw worked around emotion he fought valiantly to keep in. It appeared he was the only person there attempting to keep his emotions in check. The majority of the guests dabbed at their eyes. But, aside from the emotion on his face, Tomás looked more settled, more open and freer than she'd ever seen him. That constant air of watchfulness she'd first noticed in him was gone, replaced by a soft white aura of profound peace. As though sensing her gaze, he glanced over, and his smile widened.

Filled with admiration, she lifted a hand to her lips and blew him a kiss. He winked, and then blew one back.

"Come here. I want you to meet someone," Erica heard Hope say. She glanced over to see that Hope had taken Racquel's hand and they were coming her way. Oh, gosh! Heart suddenly pounding, Erica jolted to her feet, swiping at her face. A rush of uncertainty flooded her. She felt so unprepared for facing the woman who'd broken Tomás's heart and weakened his spirit, and yet, the fact that Hope wanted Racquel to meet her was huge.

Finally, they stood face to face. The woman who'd left Tomás and the woman who loved him with her whole soul. Erica studied Racquel and noted, with a pang of compassion, that she looked older than she was. She was attractive, but her face held the lines of a woman who'd lived a life of regrets. Erica never wanted to be in that place.

Hope cleared her throat. "I want you to meet the person I think of as…my spiritual mom."

Erica's throat closed. She smiled reassuringly at Hope.

"And friend," Hope added quickly. "She planned the whole *quinceañera.*" She reached out and took Erica's hand, squeezing it. "Erica. I want you to meet Racquel, the mom who...had me and gave me to my father."

Erica and Racquel stood watching each other through their tears. Racquel's hands were knotted in front of her. "Thank you for loving her," Racquel whispered, her voice timid and quavery. "It means the world to me knowing she had you."

Touched, Erica embraced the small, humbled woman. Racquel seemed to stiffen in surprise, but then her arms went tentatively around Erica's back, and Erica sighed. Racquel wasn't a selfish, uncaring monster or an evil person. She was a young woman who'd made difficult choices and paid dearly for them. That much was obvious. And, right at that moment, Erica knew she wouldn't want to change places with Racquel Silva for the world. "Believe me, Racquel. Loving your daughter was the easiest thing I've ever done. Thank you for bringing her into the world to be loved."

The party was in full swing when Tomás commandeered Erica, whispering something about a surprise that just couldn't wait, and dragged her through the darkness toward the studio. "Come on. I don't want anyone to see us."

She laughed, and stumbled along. "Tomás, I'm wearing heels. Give me a break here. What's the big surprise anyway?"

"I wanted you to be the first to see." He grinned with childlike abandon, then turned to work the key into the lock. He opened the door to the dark studio, and before he'd even flicked on a light, Erica heard a sound she both recognized and loved.

The thump of a dog's tail...and some puppy whimpers.

"Oh, you didn't!"

The lights went on, and Erica glanced across the room to a small, makeshift pen piled with blankets. Inside sat the most adorable little scruffy terrier pup she'd ever seen. His golden ears perked—well, at least one of them—and he shivered with delight at having visitors. Erica quickly moved toward him. "Oh, Tomás. She's going to absolutely lose her mind."

He stood, hands on hips, tie loosened, looking down at the puppy with a mixture of exasperation and adoration. "Yeah, and *I'm* going to lose my mind if this little beast doesn't get housebroken, and soon."

"How long have you had him?" Erica bent over and lifted the puppy out of the pen, holding him against her chest.

"I picked him up yesterday."

Erica rubbed her face in his soft fur. "You're not going to regret this."

He snorted. "Believe me. I already regret it. I'm thinking of naming him Annoyance." He sighed. "But you're right. Everyone needs a puppy."

"You know, I never actually said that to Hope."

"No?" He shook his head. "That little trickster."

Erica laughed, then kissed the puppy's head. "But he's perfect and adorable. Come on. Let's go give him to her."

"Not just yet," he said. "First, there is something I have to say." And then he shut the studio door behind him, locked it and turned back toward her.

Tomás knew he'd agreed to wait until after the Cultural Arts Festival to "renegotiate" this thing with Erica, but he couldn't wait. This had been a day of high emotions, the culmination of several months of change and growth for all of them. He couldn't lie to himself anymore, or deny what he knew to be destiny. Because, the one emotion he'd felt consistently throughout the past several weeks was a deep love and desire to spend his life with Erica.

He loved her. Risks be damned, there was no going back. He'd never forgive himself if he didn't tell her.

Part of him wanted to simply pull out the ring he'd bought

and beg her to marry him, to come and live with him and Hope and Ruby in Rociada. But that wasn't the right approach with her, and he knew it. As Ruby had told him, he needed to show Erica that he appreciated her for the woman she was. And he did. Still, his need to come clean with her about his feelings was overwhelming, and he couldn't think of a more perfect night on which to do so.

A wash of nerves struck, and he ran both hands through his hair. "Erica, I need to tell you a few things."

"Okay, you've said that. Twice." Her expression went serious, and she kissed the puppy once more and placed him gently back into his pen. She turned back to face him, wiping her palms down the sides of her skirt. "Is something wrong, Tomás?"

He shook his head, moving closer to her. "Nothing's wrong. Everything's right. Bear with me. I'm not so good at this."

Erica spied a stool and sat down. "Okay."

"And don't interrupt until I've gotten it out," he said, then realizing that it sounded a bit harsh, he added, "Please."

She nodded.

He reached inside his tuxedo jacket pocket and retrieved the cobalt-blue velvet box. Her eyes widened when she saw it. He snapped the box open, turning it so she could see the platinum-and-diamond ring. "I bought this for you in Taos on a whim, because I thought it would look beautiful on your hand. And because I…" He took a deep breath, and his eyes begged for acceptance. "Because I love you, Erica. With my whole heart. I love you like I never thought it was possible to love anyone. You've shown me how much you love my daughter, and you've proven to me that I don't need to hold on so tightly to her." He smoothed a hand down her cheek. "That's priceless. I can't ever repay you for what you've done. And I want you to share your life with us." His gaze was level and sincere. "I won't apologize for that."

"Oh, Tomás—"

He held up a hand. "Wait, let me finish."

She closed her mouth obediently, folding her hands in her lap. Her focus remained completely on his face.

"The thing is," he continued, "the ring idea was my first, most natural instinct. You know, buy the ring, give you the ring, beg you to consider marrying me." He paused, holding his breath. She looked to be doing the same. "But then I realized that would be the worst thing I could possibly do."

Her expression faltered. "It would be?" He watched her go pale, her eyes straying to the ring, and he knew he had to convince her now, once and for all, that he respected her, that he supported her dreams. He loved the businesslike Erica. He loved the antiparenting Erica. He loved her as he'd never loved another woman his whole life, and he needed her to know.

"Yes," he said, urgently. "Because I fell in love with *you*, with the Erica Gonçalves you are. And I don't want to change you, not one bit. I know you don't want to be saddled to a man, and I respect that."

"But, Tomás, things have changed so much—"

Again, he held up a hand. "Not yet. Please, I have to get this out." He paused, and she remained quiet. "The thing is, I don't want you to change for me. So, I have a proposition for you instead. A business proposition," he quickly added.

"Business, huh?" She smiled softly, crossing her legs. "Before you say anything further," she added, her voice a teasing purr. "I'd like to make it perfectly clear that I don't date business associates. Ever."

He caught on immediately, realizing how far they'd come from the day they first met. His eyes crinkled with amusement to match her own, and he held up his palms. "You think I'm hitting on you?" he asked playfully, then added,

"Of course you do. Why wouldn't you, the way I phrased it. Not to mention the fact that I *am* hitting on you."

She laughed, a warm, bubbly sound.

He joined, her, but sobered again soon. His unapologetic gaze met hers. "Let me assure you, this proposition isn't a ruse. It's something I've been thinking about for a while. Watching you work with Hope gave me some ideas."

He could see her interest pique. "Yeah? I'm all ears."

"You're trying to find your niche in the wedding-planning business, find a way out from under working for the man, right?"

She nodded.

"I think you need an angle, and it just so happens I've come up with one." He smoothed his palms together slowly. "Use the Cultural Arts Festival and this *quinceañera* as a starting ground. Advertise yourself as a planner who will create weddings, *quinceañeras,* and other events with cultural themes. I don't just mean our culture, but all cultures. Look at how you and Hope have transformed the *quinceañera* into something updated and fresh." He felt the surge of excitement inside him. This was a great idea, and he knew it. If only he could convince her. "You incorporated Jewish, Apache and other traditions, and Hope told me you both loved the research. You could do this, Erica."

She leaned forward slightly, taking this all in, looking suddenly energized. "Tomás, this is a fantastic idea."

He shrugged, but felt pleased. "Like I've told you before, I'm a right-brain guy. Creative…delusional."

"Delusional?" She looked at him quizzically. "How so?"

He cut his gaze to the far corner of the room for a moment before looking at her directly again. It had to be said. He'd regret it if he held it in. "Well, I had this crazy idea about you selling your place and moving in here. You can use the money from the sale of your place and the fee from Hope's *quinceañera* to launch your business."

"Oh, Tomás."

He held up a hand, and his tone softened. "And then, maybe someday when you're ready, I can give you that ring."

A long, tension-wrought pause ensued.

"It won't work," she told him finally.

His face fell. "Why not?"

"Because—" she stood and crossed over to him, wrapping her arms around his waist "—I want that ring now."

Her answer stunned him. "You do?"

"Yes. Because I love you, too, Tomás. And I love Hope. I can't even tell you how much. And what I've always sworn by is true—I don't want to have regrets. If I go back to living the way I always have, if I don't have you and Hope in my life, that will be my biggest regret, one I simply can't live with."

"Erica," he whispered, so moved by her admission, so imbued with hope and love, but she cut him off.

"First, though. About this business proposition."

He cocked an eyebrow.

She smiled, wryly. "I wish I'd thought of it myself. But I think we're going to make a fantastic team."

"Does that mean you'll give it a try? The business?"

She held up a finger. "On one condition."

"What's that?"

"That you slip that ring on my finger right now, and the first wedding I plan…is ours."

It was more than Tomás had ever hoped for, and, for a moment, he just stared into Erica's eyes, his heart pounding. Finally, he reached out and lifted the box, taking the ring from within it. Feeling shaky, he went down on one knee.

"Erica?"

"Yes, Tomás?"

"Will you complete my life? Will you accept me as I am, faults and all, as I will accept you? Will you promise to love me and my daughter with your whole heart? And will you never, ever change from the woman I fell in love with?''

"Yes."

He swallowed past the sudden need to yell out with joy. ''Does that mean you'll marry me, too?''

"I thought you'd never ask.'' She held out her left hand, and he slipped the ring on her third finger. ''And, actually, I thought I'd never say yes, not in a million years. But you learn something new every day, I guess.''

He stood, folding her into an embrace. ''Can I just say, I'm glad you finally got a clue?''

She laughed, then kissed him tenderly. ''And I'll echo that right back to you. No regrets?''

"No regrets,'' he repeated.

The puppy barked sharply, and as they laughed together, Erica knew she'd finally come home.

Epilogue

*F*rom New Mexico Today Magazine*'s "Tell All" society
column—*

Las Vegas, NM—Record crowds turned out Saturday
night for the culminating event of New Mexico's in-
augural Cultural Arts Festival, a spectacularly successful event planned by the firm of Dawson, Montoya and
Goldberg, which is headquartered in Santa Fe. What
drew 35,000 spectators? Not paintings, nor sculptures,
nor any of the other displays that had lured visitors to
the event center all week. No, what drew 35,000 out
of their homes on a Saturday evening was a wedding.
That's right. A wedding.

But these weren't your average nuptials. Event planner Erica Gonçalves, formerly with Dawson, Montoya
and Goldberg, married *piñatero* Tomás Garza, one of
the artisans participating in the festival, in an epic ceremony that included customs from at least seven dif-

ferent cultures—and possibly a few fairy tales? Garza and Gonçalves wanted their wedding to represent the rich cultural diversity of the state they call home, and they reached their goal with panache.

Gonçalves has recently launched her own planning firm, headquartered in Las Vegas, which specializes in weddings and other events with a cultural flair. If the turnout at her own wedding was any indication, Gonçalves's firm has a bright business future.

The wedding attendees were a veritable who's who of New Mexico society, but despite the crowds, it was clear to everyone that the bride and groom had eyes only for each other.

The priest who presided read the ceremony in English, Spanish and Apache. Musicians and dancers from the surrounding area participated, brooms were jumped, glasses smashed beneath shoes, and the bride and groom were encircled in white cording, to symbolize their new life together. A few more mainstream traditions, however, did remain.

The bride said, ''I do.'' The groom said, ''I do, too.''

But, as if to remind all 35,000 guests that this wasn't your average hitching, the groom's fifteen-year-old daughter, Hope, chimed in on the vows with a resounding, ''Finally!''

The crowd erupted into laughter, then into applause, and that launched the largest, most lavish reception New Mexico has ever seen, sponsored by Gonçalves's former employers.

Our prediction?

The first of many perfect nights to come for these destined-for-forever newlyweds.

*   *   *   *   *